THERE IS
NO RETURN

THERE IS NO RETURN

THE ADELAIDE ADAMS MYSTERIES

ANITA BLACKMON

COACHWHIP PUBLICATIONS

Greenville, Ohio

There is No Return, by Anita Blackmon
© 2013 Coachwhip Publications
Introduction © 2013 Curtis Evans
No claim made on public domain material.

Anita Blackmon (1893-1943), also published books and stories as
    Mrs. Harry Pugh Smith.
There is No Return first published 1938.

ISBN 1-61646-223-X
ISBN-13 978-1-61646-223-9

Cover Image: Cat © Cobalt Moon Design

CoachwhipBooks.com

CONTENTS

ANITA BLACKMON, CRIME QUEEN OF ARKANSAS
CURTIS EVANS

IN *MURDER FOR PLEASURE*, the classic 1941 study of the detective story as a literary form, Howard Haycraft listed ten women authors who constituted what he termed the "better element" of the so-called HIBK, or Had I But Known, school of mystery fiction, which was effectively founded by Mary Roberts Rinehart (1876-1958) over three decades earlier with the publication of her hugely popular novel *The Circular Staircase* (1908).

The Had I But Known school of mystery fiction—as it was so dubbed by (mostly male) mystery critics after the term was used by Ogden Nash in a satirical 1940 poem, "Don't Guess, Let Me Tell You" ("Personally I don't care whether a detective story writer was educated in night school or day school/So long as they don't belong to the H.I.B.K. school")—was composed of mysteries by women writers with women narrators given to lengthily expressing digressive regrets over the horrible consequences (usually multiple murders) of their various actions or inactions over the course of the novel. Though critics of like minds to Nash enjoyed mocking these books, they were in fact quite popular among mystery readers, both female and male.

Howard Haycraft's list of the ten premier Rinehart followers includes several names still fairly well-known to genre fans today, namely Mignon Eberhart, Leslie Ford, and Dorothy Cameron Disney (he gives Mabel Seeley her own sub-section, classifying her, in contrast with the rest, as an equal of Rinehart), but also some much more obscure names as well, including Anita Blackmon.

Anita Blackmon (1892-1943) published two mystery novels, *Murder á la Richelieu* (1937) and *There Is No Return* (1938). In the United States, both of Blackmon's mysteries were published by Doubleday Doran's Crime Club, one of the most prominent mystery publishers in the country. *Murder á la Richelieu* was published as well in England (as *The Hotel Richelieu Murders*), France (as *On assassine au Richelieu*), and Germany (as *Adelaide lasst nicht locker*), while *There Is No Return* was also published in England, under the rather lurid title *The Riddle of the Dead Cats*.

In classic HIBK fashion Blackmon employed a series character in both novels: a peppery middle-aged southern spinster named Adelaide Adams (and nicknamed "the old battle-ax"). In the opening pages of Adelaide Adams' debut appearance, *Murder á la Richelieu*, Blackmon signals her readers that she is humorously aware of the grand old, much-mocked but much-read HIBK tradition that she is mining when she has Adelaide declare: "Had I suspected the orgy of bloodshed upon which we were about to embark, I should then and there, in spite of my bulk and an arthritic knee, have taken shrieking to my heels."

Unfortunately, Adelaide confides: "There was nothing on this particular morning to indicate the reign of terror into which we were about to be precipitated. Coming events are supposed to cast their shadows before, yet I had no presentiment about the green spectacle case which was to play such a fateful part in the murders, and not until it was forever too late did I recognize the tragic significance back of Polly Lawson's pink jabot and the Anthony woman's false eyelashes."

Well! What reader can stop there? Adelaide goes on with much gusto and foreboding to relate the murderous events at the Hotel Richelieu, an establishment in an unnamed southern city (clearly Little Rock, Arkansas). Adelaide is a wonderful character: tough on the outside but rather a sentimentalist within, given to the heavy use of clichés yet actually quite acute.

The life in and inhabitants of the old hotel are well-conveyed, the pace and events lively and the mystery complicated yet clear (and at the same time fair with the readers). Perhaps most enjoyable of all is the author's strong sense of humor, ably conveyed through Adelaide's memorable narration. Blackmon clearly appreciated that HIBK tales can be a tad implausible in their incredible convolutions (as can the classical Golden Age mystery in general) and she has a lot of fun with genre conventions. Her readers should have a lot of fun too.

In Blackmon's follow-up from the next year, *There Is No Return*, Adelaide comes to the rescue of a friend from the Hotel Richelieu, Ella Trotter, who is embroiled in mysterious goings-on involving spiritual possession at a backwoods Ozarks hotel, the Lebeau Inn (the novel could well have been called, admittedly less originally, *Murder á la Lebeau*).

Return opens with yet another splendid HIBK declaration in the part of Adelaide: "As I pointed out, to no avail, when the body of the third disemboweled cat was discovered in my bed, had I foreseen the train of horrible events which settled over that isolated mountain inn like a miasma of death upon the afternoon of my arrival, I should have left Ella to lay her own ghosts."

The isolated setting in *Return* (Adelaide and the other guests are trapped with a multiple murderer at the Lebeau Inn after the bridge washes out) is memorably evoked by the author, though the tone of the book is grimmer, with more chills than chuckles (at times one is even reminded of Stephen King's *The Shining*). Yet *There Is No Return* is a worthy sequel to *Murder á la Richelieu* and it is very pleasing to encounter the old battle-ax in all her sleuthing finery one last time.

When Howard Haycraft published *Murder for Pleasure* in 1941, he clearly classed Blackmon as a major figure in the HIBK school, though she in fact had not published a mystery novel in three years. Two years later Blackmon passed away at the age of fifty, her fiction largely forgotten. So who was Anita Blackmon?

Anita Blackmon was born in 1893 in Augusta, a small city in northeastern Arkansas, located about eighty miles from Memphis, Tennessee. The daughter of Augusta postmaster and mayor Edwin E. Blackmon and his wife, Augusta Public High School principal Eva Hutchison Blackmon, both originally from Washburn, Illinois,

Anita Blackmon revealed a literary bent from a young age, penning her first short story at the age of seven.

By local accounts, Blackmon grew up into a vivacious, attractive, outgoing young woman (later in life, in 1938, she was described by Scribner's Magazine as "a physically strong, robust woman with tremendous vitality and enthusiasm"). The future novelist graduated from high school at the age of fourteen and attended classes at Ouachita College and the University of Chicago. Returning home from Chicago, she taught languages in Augusta for five years before moving to Little Rock, where she continued to teach school.

In 1920, Blackmon left teaching and married railroad man Harry Pugh Smith in Little Rock. The couple moved to St. Louis, where Blackmon had an uncle who served as a St. Louis and San Francisco Railroad vice president, and in 1922 Blackmon published the first of what would be over a thousand short stories. Blackmon's short stories appeared in a diverse collection of pulps, including *Love Story Magazine, Love Fiction Monthly, All-Story Love Stories, Cupid's Diary*—love stories were her specialty—*Detective Tales*, and *Weird Tales*.

Blackmon began publishing novels in 1934 with a book entitled *Her Private Devil*, which provoked scandalized talk back in Augusta. *Devil* was published by William Godwin, a press that specialized in titillating novels that pushed the sexual envelope of the day. Godwin titles by other authors in the writing stable such as *Delinquent, Unmoral, Illegitimate, Indecent, Strange Marriage*, and *Infamous Woman* give an idea of the nature of most Godwin fiction.

Blackmon's novel, which detailed the unhappy life of a southern small-town girl who gives in to her own overmastering sexual desires, is fairly bold for its time, but by no means a "dirty" book. In actuality it is a serious study of a troubled young woman handled with sensitivity and it is certainly not explicit by today's standards. Still, the book raised something of a stir in conservative Augusta, with locals expressing disapproval.

Over the next few years Blackmon published traditional, mainstream novels under the name Mrs. Harry Pugh Smith, some of which had been previously serialized, before concluding her run with her two mystery novels, published, like *Her Private Devil*, under her maiden name.

The best known of the Mrs. Harry Pugh Smith novels was *Hand-made Rainbows*, a tale of middle class Depression-era life in small southern city very like Augusta. Part of the enjoyment one gets from Blackmon's better novels stems from the author's effective depiction of unique southern local color. Blackmon's *Murder á la Richelieu* clearly is set in Little Rock, where there once was in fact a Richelieu Hotel, while *There Is No Return* is set far in the Ozarks.

Why Anita Blackmon produced no more Adelaide Adams mysteries during her last five years of life is unknown. However after a lengthy illness Blackmon died in 1943 in a nursing home in Little Rock, where she moved after the death of her husband. Probably under the circumstances she was not up to plotting and writing another full-length mystery novel, though she is said to have continued writing until shortly before her death.

The two mysteries that Anita Blackmon gave us before her untimely demise are examples of the twentieth-century HIBK tale at its best. Surely had modern mystery fans but known of this fine pair of detective tales they would have clamored for their reprinting. Happily, they are now back in print, courtesy of Coachwhip Publications, giving readers the chance to go on the hunt for murdering fiends with that indomitable and splendid old battle-ax, Miss Adelaide Adams.

NOTE: Information in this essay on Anita Blackmon's life was drawn from Woodruff County Historical Society, *Rivers and Roads and Points in Between* 3 (Fall 1975): 21-22, and interviews with Rebecca Boyles and Virginia Boyles. The author gives special thanks for his generous help to Kip Davis, Augusta City Planner.

THERE IS
NO RETURN

1

IT WAS NOT, as my foster son Stephen Lansing likes to intimate, that I had developed a taste for wild adventure which drew me into that macabre and sinister tangle at Mount Lebeau. Nor is it true, as Ella Trotter insists, that I rushed in where even angels feared to tread because I could not bear for her to steal my thunder. As I pointed out, to no avail, when the body of the third disemboweled cat was discovered in my bed, had I foreseen the train of horrible events which settled over that isolated mountain inn like a miasma of death upon the afternoon of my arrival, I should have left Ella to lay her own ghosts.

As a matter of fact, but for Ella Trotter's fantastic letter I should never have gone near the place at all. Ella has been my close friend for years, although we long ago agreed to disagree on practically everything. We are both, to put it mildly, what is commonly alluded to as strong-minded women. That is why the moment I had Ella's letter I knew something was up, in spite of the pains which she took to put me off the scent.

Ella likes to be in the center of any excitement and she has never forgiven me for having, as she said, deliberately shoved her off the stage at every opportunity during that sequence of tragedies which the police referred to as the Hotel Richelieu Murders. Heaven knows why she should have envied me my role in the affair, seeing that I was all but throttled in my bed upon one occasion and next door to murdered in a couple of other unseemly places. Nevertheless Ella did resent what she described as the persistent manner in which I had hogged the spotlight at that time.

She was distinctly cool to me for the next three months and for the first time in years she did not suggest that we take our summer trip together. Instead she barged off without a word, to me at least. July and August are torrid months in our little Southern city and well-nigh unbearable cooped up in the small residential hotel where I live. Moreover, with my adopted children, Stephen and Kathleen, indulging in a belated honeymoon to the West Indies, I was left stranded and decidedly lonely, as Ella knew perfectly well.

Nevertheless, although we had been in the habit of picking a convenient resort every summer, not, I admit, without considerable wrangling, and escaping to it till cooler weather, upon the last day of June Ella put her nose in the air and departed. Under the circumstances I did not expect to hear from her, except the customary "Wish you were here" postcard which, as Ella is aware, always infuriates me. However, after exactly two weeks I had the letter which was responsible for everything.

There was nothing extraordinary about the body of the letter, and that alone excited my suspicions. It is unlike Ella Trotter to be noncommittal, but she had taken a great deal of trouble to give me a completely colorless account of herself and Mount Lebeau Inn, where she was staying. There were no crossed-out words, such as usually clutter up her communications, Ella being the kind to blurt out whatever pops into her head and think it over afterward. The letter was painstakingly neat, if not prim, and more legible than anything which I had ever seen her write. I was positive she had recopied it, perhaps several times, and that in itself was enough to put me on my guard. Why should Ella Trotter, of all people, have gone to so much pains to give me an expurgated account of her activities, I asked myself with, I am afraid, a snort.

I did not at once notice the postscript. It was on the reverse side of the inner page. Ella had made an effort to treat it as an afterthought, but as soon as I read it I knew it was the motive for the entire letter. I have not played bridge with Ella for years for nothing, and she should have realized that I am not the sort of person who can be utilized to pull other people's chestnuts out of the fire without my knowledge. If she had surrounded the postscript with huge exclamation points in red ink I could not have been more certain that Ella was up to something and determined to keep me out of it.

"By the way, Adelaide," she wrote, "I wish you would send me that book on spiritualism or séances or swamis or whatever it is that you have on your book shelf. I want to prove to a woman that it is all tommyrot, just as you always said, about the dead coming back to consort with the living, and the like of that."

Now Ella will argue with the Angel Gabriel when her turn comes, so there was nothing unusual in her wishing to prove somebody wrong. Nor was there anything particularly startling about the book for which she asked. I had bought it some years before—immediately after the war, I think—when a wave of pseudo-spiritualism swept the country. I do not believe in tampering with matters which do not concern this world, granting it is possible to do so, which I had never granted until I stubbed my toe and literally nearly broke my neck over those weird and incredible manifestations at Mount Lebeau Inn.

The book in question was an obscure but clever exposé of the tricks and wiles of the gentry who prey on a gullible public with fake messages from the dead. It went into detail about the manner in which such hoaxes are staged, including everything from automatic writing to spirit voices and ectoplasms. I was surprised that Ella even recalled the book. I had been quite worked up over the subject at one time, but Ella had pooh-poohed the whole business, her argument being that only a fool would bother to expose what only a fool would be taken in by. Nevertheless she wanted the book enough to forget her pique and write for it and she spoiled her elaborate pretense of its being of no special importance by adding a sentence to the postscript.

"Send it by air mail, special delivery, Adelaide," she wrote and here for the first time she crossed out a line. In fact she blacked it out with conspicuous thoroughness, but I was able after some time to make out the words "before it is too late."

Like many well-to-do women, Ella Trotter has a phobia about being unduly careless with money. Nevertheless, although the time

saved could not be great, she had enclosed more than enough post-
age to send the book by air mail and special delivery, and where
she had blacked out the last line there was a large blot, as if her
hand had trembled. I cannot explain how I knew that Ella was terribly excited when she wrote that postscript, but I did know it, just
as I knew she would rather have died than have me suspect it.

I anticipated her reaction when I wired her that I was bringing
the book by hand, arriving late the following day. I was prepared
for her telegram in reply which insisted that there was no need for
my doing any such thing. I simply paid no attention to the telegram. As Stephen says—and I am in no position to deny it—I had
no one except myself to blame for walking into that dreadful business, myself and my hunch that Ella was trying to put something
over on me.

My only defense is that my hunch did not go far enough. But I
have never pretended to be clairvoyant and I still maintain that
there was no way on earth in which I could have foreseen that
malignant spirit which had apparently returned from the grave to
take up its abode in another's body; nor do I yet understand how I
could have been expected to know anything about Dora Canby's
horror of can openers or the chipped place in Judy Oliver's ear.

Lebeau Inn is in the extreme northwest and most inaccessible
corner of our state, located on Mount Lebeau, the highest spot
between the Cumberlands and the Rockies, or so the prospectus
reads. About twenty years ago the place had considerable reputation as a summer resort. I myself went there once with my father,
who was an invalid. The cool mountain air was highly recommended for elderly people and teething babies. The inn was new
then, a huge rambling place with enormous porches and large,
high-ceilinged rooms. As I remember, the place was filled that year,
although it never made any pretense at being fashionable.

From what I had heard, it had gone steadily to seed of recent
years. For one thing it was inconvenient to get to. For another a
newer and more modern hotel had been put up, closer to the railroad and blessed with the same salubrious air. I had been surprised
when I heard that Ella had gone to Lebeau for July and August.

Then I learned from somebody or other that the bank in which she is a major stockholder had been forced to take over the place and was making a mordant effort to turn the old white elephant into something resembling a paying proposition.

It was exactly like Ella to further her pocketbook, even at the cost of some inconvenience to herself. I did not doubt that she had demanded and received a special rate because of her bank stock, any more than I doubted that she was doing everything in her power to drum up business for the inn. But I did not delude myself into believing that she would receive me with any enthusiasm. To tell the truth, the nearer I came to my destination the more I regretted the impulse which had taken me there.

It was an unseasonably hot day, one of those days which people call weather breeders. It did not matter so much until I was compelled to leave the air-cooled parlor car at Egger's Junction in favor of a small, dirty, local train which stopped at every wide place in the road as it worked its tortuous way up into the mountains. I have said that Mount Lebeau is in the most inaccessible corner of the state. It not only is not on the main line of the railroad; it is off the principal paved highways.

"And in this machine age one might as well be dead," I remember thinking crossly, perspiring and covered with cinders, as I stared morosely out the window at the rutted dirt road beside the tracks.

Carrolton, where one leaves the train for Lebeau, is a sleepy country town located at the foot of the mountain and separated from it by a short tricky river. The town, so far as I could judge, had changed for the worse in the twenty years since I last saw it. It did not improve my temper to observe the vehicle by which I was to make the last lap of my journey. It was a disreputable-looking bus with a homemade body composed of four long narrow seats mounted upon what had once been the chassis of a Ford sedan. The driver was a snub-nosed, gangling mountaineer in blue jeans, distinguished by a huge cud of chewing tobacco in one leathery cheek.

"Is one expected to risk one's bones in this outlandish contraption in order to reach Lebeau Inn?" I asked him indignantly.

He shifted the cud to the other cheek before he condescended to answer. "Well, lady," he drawled, "it'd be quite a climb for your build."

Somebody chuckled, and for the first time I realized that I was not the only passenger bound for Mount Lebeau. Standing just behind me was a rangy, broad-shouldered young man with extraordinarily blue eyes. It was the impudence in Chet Keith's eyes which prejudiced me against him in the beginning, that and the too natty cut of his light gray suit. He was wearing a lavender tie which exactly matched his equally expensive shirt, and his dark hair looked as if it had been applied to his jaunty head with a brush. The glance I gave him should have withered him, only, as I was to learn, he was not the withering kind.

"My build," I remarked tartly, ostensibly addressing the driver but making certain that my voice carried, "may be a source of cheap levity to others, but it is my own concern, or rather it has ceased to be any concern to me for a number of years."

The young man with the lacquered hair grinned. "Don't look daggers at me," he said. "I can't help it if we're headed for the jumping-off place in the lineal descendant of the famous one-hoss shay."

I made no reply. It is not my habit to scrape acquaintance with strangers, especially slangy young upstarts who act as well pleased with themselves as this one did. My manner was intended to put him in his place once for all as I turned away with no inconsiderable hauteur to enter the bus. Unfortunately the desired effect was marred by the fact that, the space between the seats being extremely narrow, I had to insinuate myself inside by degrees and, becoming slightly flustered in the process, succeeded in hanging the placket of my skirt upon the handle of the ramshackle door. As a result I found myself in the embarrassing position of being able to go neither forward nor backward without an ominous ripping sound.

"Hold everything!" exclaimed the young man behind me.

As it happened there was nothing else I could do until he had unhoisted me by the simple process of prodding me from the rear while he lifted up on the door. To do him justice he accomplished this feat with the minimum of effort, even with a certain éclat, for which I might have been grateful if he had not spoiled it by another chuckle in which the bus driver joined. I gave *him* a look that wiped the grin off his face in a hurry.

"Have we taken root here?" I demanded.

The bus promptly started up with a jerk that knocked my hat down over one eye. By the time I had restored it to its position, along with the row of false curls which it is my custom to wear across my forehead, we were leaving the town behind. The driver was carrying on a desultory conversation with the other passenger, but I was in no humor for talk. It was still extremely sultry and I have never seen a more lurid sunset. Toward the west an ominous bank of clouds was sluggishly gathering. I remember thinking to myself that I should hate to be caught on that lonely road in a storm.

Two miles out of Carrolton it is necessary to cross the Carol River. "So this is the famous pontoon bridge," murmured the young man beside the driver. "No wonder they advertise it as the longest pontoon bridge in the world." He glanced back at me with a chuckle. "I don't suppose they'd tolerate one anywhere outside this state."

I bristled. His accent, as well as his self-assurance, stamped him as an Easterner; from New York, I thought. It has always nettled me, the way New Yorkers have of looking down their noses at everything west of the Hudson. The pontoon bridge over the Carol River is a ridiculous piece of work and maddeningly inadequate, as I was to realize, heaven knows, before we were through with that ghastly affair at Lebeau Inn, but I had no intention of admitting as much at this stage.

"If you are pointing your remark at me," I said icily, "I am not responsible for this bridge or any other, but I believe it has served for a number of years and will probably continue to do so, no matter what you may think on the subject."

"Pleasant old girl," he murmured sotto voce to the driver, "if one likes snapping turtles."

The driver shook his head. "This here pontoon is all right," he said cautiously, "provided it don't get beside itself."

"Beside itself?" I repeated with some sharpness.

"Course a pontoon bridge is just a floating raft tied to each bank," he explained, "and the Carol's like all mountain streams. If it goes on a rampage, can't nothing hold it. Three-four times it's done up and scattered this here pontoon bridge high, wide and handsome."

"Isn't that something to look forward to!" exclaimed Chet Keith with a sardonic smile. "I can think of several thousand places where I'd prefer to be marooned."

I studied him with some curiosity and I thought he changed color when he met my eye. It occurred to me that he was an odd type to be going to Lebeau. It had never attracted bright young people, and I was increasingly of the opinion that he was more at home in Times Square than anywhere else. I should have expected to find his prototype at Atlantic City or Jones Beach, entirely surrounded by pretty girls in very brief bathing suits, but not at a down-at-the-heel summer resort which catered to elderly invalids and teething babies.

It seemed to me that he changed the subject with suspicious haste. "What did they lay this road out with? A corkscrew?" he asked, wincing a little as the ancient bus jounced alarmingly on a hairpin curve.

"You would think that, with a gasoline tax of seven cents on the gallon, we might at least have decent roads," I muttered, holding on to the sides of the vehicle for dear life while we wheezed up the incline.

At this moment, with a warning blast upon its twin sirens, a long sleek machine passed us, throwing a flurry of fine pebbles and stifling dust into our faces.

"Let somebody run that can run, eh?" murmured Chet Keith.

The driver shook his head. "We'll overtake him," he said with what I considered unjustifiable confidence.

However, on the second hairpin turn we did indeed overtake the other car. It was having difficulty negotiating the narrow curve. The chauffeur was backing and filling, close enough to the edge of the precipice to make me shiver. I caught a glimpse of a tall thin man in the rear seat. He was fuming over the delay and he gave us a black glance as we went by. I heard Chet Keith whistle softly.

"Thomas Canby!" he exclaimed.

I don't say I should have recognized the power magnate if I had not heard the name, although I had met both Thomas Canby and his wife twenty years before, met them by a coincidence at Lebeau Inn the summer I was there with my father. Naturally that was before Canby developed into the millionaire he was to become. He was, in fact, at that time merely a lineman for the local light company, one of the companies which he later organized into his tremendous utility group.

As I have had occasion to recall, he and his wife had a very difficult time finding the money to keep her and their baby at Lebeau that summer. The child was quite ill and the doctors had prescribed mountain air. I had not thought of it in years, but I distinctly remembered now how terrified little Mrs. Canby had been and how she had hung over the baby day and night until it was better. She was a pathetic, colorless little woman, one of the timidest women I ever knew. I had not thought of it before, but I wondered what effect her husband's tremendous fortune and national reputation had had upon her.

"It's queer for Canby to be going to Lebeau," I remarked without realizing that I was speaking aloud. "I thought they were supposed to have a summer home at Southampton."

"They have a duplex on Park Avenue, a lodge at Asheville and a tepee of forty rooms down on Long Island. So what?" demanded Chet Keith.

I knitted my brows at him. "The daughter must be about twenty-two now," I murmured, still thinking aloud.

He gave me an odd glance. "Didn't you know that Gloria Canby died last fall?" he asked.

I got the feeling that he was watching me closely.

"Died!" I exclaimed. "And so young. What a pity!"

"Perhaps," he said with an ugly twist to his voice.

I gave him a scathing glance. "Are you one of those bolshevists who envy a capitalist everything, even his innocent children?" I demanded.

He shrugged his shoulders. "Thank God I've outgrown that rash," he said, "and God knows nobody envied Thomas Canby his daughter."

At this moment the power magnate's long maroon car passed us again with another indignant flirt of loose gravel. "Apparently Mr. Thomas Canby is in a hurry," I remarked dryly.

Chet Keith nodded, then smothered a sharp exclamation. The machine ahead had stopped so abruptly, it was all our driver could do not to pitch directly into it. For a moment both cars hung sickeningly on the edge of the bluff, and I felt as if my stomach had turned a somersault.

"What the hell!" exclaimed Chet Keith. "Sorry," he muttered with a perfunctory glance at me as he swung out of the bus.

The Canby chauffeur, a wiry, muscular-looking man in livery, had also leaped to the ground. They were joined by the bus driver. All seemed to be staring intently at something just around the short curve in front of us. I could see Thomas Canby craning his long thin neck from the back seat of the limousine. I suppose they expected me to have no natural curiosity. At any rate Chet Keith gave me an impatient glance when I crawled out of the bus and walked toward them.

"You might as well go back," he said curtly. "It's just a rock in the road."

"I can see that for myself," I retorted in a tart voice.

There was a large boulder lying on the inside of the curve. It seemed to have fallen from the side of the mountain just above, where there was a gaping hole of loosened earth and gravel.

"We'll have it out of the way in a jiffy," murmured the chauffeur, "if you'll lend me a hand, brother."

He glanced at the bus driver, who was scratching his head. "Funny what made that rock fall," he muttered.

Chet Keith again shrugged his shoulders. "Wouldn't have been so funny if either of us had hit it going round that curve," he said.

I shuddered and glanced away from the sheer drop at the edge of the precipice to our left.

"You'd think on such a road they'd take precautions against things like this," I remarked.

The bus driver was still scratching his head. "That's what makes it funny," he said. "They do."

The utility magnate spoke for the first time. "Can't you clear that rock away, Jay?" he asked in a testy voice.

The chauffeur touched his cap. "Watch me," he said.

He and the driver fell to and with considerable heaving and panting shifted the boulder off to the side of the road. Chet Keith did not lend a hand. Instead he climbed up the side of the mountain and stood looking down with a frown at the hole from which the rock had fallen. He was still there when the maroon car went on its way. The bus driver had gone back to his own machine, where he tooted his horn several times to attract our attention. I had not returned to the bus either. I was watching Chet Keith. He gave a start when he saw me staring up at him.

"Wind must have blown it over," he said, giving me what I regarded as a distinctly shifty glance.

"Except that there has been no wind all afternoon," I replied.

He frowned and tried to slip something into his pocket which he had picked up from a clump of withered grass at his feet.

"Accidents will happen," he murmured.

"I wouldn't call it an accident if a cold chisel had been employed to dig a rock loose," I said with a sniff.

He looked at me as if he would have enjoyed wringing my neck, but he produced the object which he had attempted to secrete in his pocket without my seeing it. It was a cold chisel. Bits of gravel and clay still clung to its side.

"It's probably been lying here for weeks," he observed in a defiant manner.

"That's why it's all rusty," I commented with elaborate sarcasm.

The cold chisel was not rusted. It looked bright and new.

"You don't miss much, do you?" inquired Chet Keith.

This time it was I who reached up and plucked something from a clump of withered grass clinging to the side of the mountain.

"Not a great deal," I said and would have pocketed my discovery without another word, but he caught my wrist and held it.

"A woman!" he exclaimed.

I nodded. "Looks as if."

The object which I was holding was a hairpin, an amber-colored hairpin made of cheap celluloid.

"Jees," he said softly and then grinned. "Any reason why somebody at Lebeau Inn should crave to see you reach a sudden end?"

I thought of Ella and shook my head. "If I should have been taken down with a mild case of poison ivy it might not have been unwelcome, but"—I took another shuddering glance at the bluff on our other side—"nothing like this."

"I wasn't expecting to be met with a brass band either," he admitted with his cocksure grin. "However, as you say, murder is a cat of another odor."

I caught my breath. "Murder!"

He gave me a sharp glance. "The real question before the house is: Who tried to send Thomas Canby to kingdom come?"

I gasped, but he was already walking toward the bus and, feeling suddenly infirm in the region of my knees, I followed.

2

I SHALL NEVER FORGET my first glimpse of Lebeau Inn that afternoon. The storm which was slowly gathering made a sullen background for the rambling frame structure with which twenty years of neglect had wrought havoc. An effort had been made to repair the sagging columns along the wide veranda at the front. The grounds closest to the building had been cleared, but there was still something frowzy and unkempt about the shrubs which grew up so high as to obscure the lower panes of the tall windows on the first floor. There were too many scraggly pines hugging the house. No wonder the place had a musty smell, I thought, it needed a good sunning. I remembered that, being so high above sea level, the clouds had a habit of meandering in and out of the inn at the least excuse.

"I don't know why everybody in the place doesn't come down with rheumatism," I grumbled as I was untangling myself from my cramped position in the bus.

Chet Keith grinned. "It does look a little on the dreary side," he remarked, then added in what he evidently intended for a facetious tone, "A swell setting for a murder."

I had succeeded in hanging my skirt again and, hearing a slight rip as I jerked myself loose, was not in the sweetest temper. "What are you going to do about that cold chisel?" I demanded.

"Do?"

"I suppose there is such a thing as police protection in this benighted spot."

He changed color. "I dare say you're right," he said slowly. "What we saw will have to be reported—at least to Thomas Canby."

"Well, I should think so," I snapped and stared with a slight shiver at that angry black sky behind us.

"We're probably making a great to-do about nothing," he said.

I glanced at him sharply but he turned away, following the bus driver, who, laden with our joint baggage, was leading the way into the inn. The lobby, or lounge as they call it at Lebeau Inn, is a huge, barn-like room with high ceilings and distempered green walls in which the oak armchairs and leather-seated settees look lost. At the right as you enter is the desk, a tall walnut contraption with pigeonholes behind the counter for room keys and the mail. At one end of the desk is a combination cigar and news stand. At the other is the door to the dining room. Opposite the desk is the entrance into twin parlors. At the rear of the lounge a single door leads into a long corridor from which opens a series of guest rooms, extending clear across the back of the building, there being only two stories to the inn.

A blond young woman was presiding over the old-fashioned register which she pushed toward us with an ennuied gesture. In spite of her bored manner she took a lively interest in the young man who gallantly permitted me to register first. I saw her watching him from under her eyelashes. I thought Mr. Chet Keith was aware of the fact. He struck me as a young man who was accustomed to exciting a ripple in feminine breasts. He was just a shade too nonchalant about the way he lit a cigarette and allowed his gaze to stray over the young woman's rather blatant curves.

"Lady-killer," I remarked to myself, having lived long enough about hotels to recognize the type which I abominate.

I did not miss the caressing gesture with which he accepted the pen from the girl behind the desk after I laid it down. However, upon reading the name which I had written the young woman transferred her attention to me.

"Oh, Miss Adams, Mrs. Trotter left word for me to let her know the moment you arrived," she said brightly. "I'll give her a ring while Jake takes you upstairs. I'm sure you'll both be pleased to know that we have been able to give you adjacent rooms."

I had my doubts on that score as I followed the elderly colored porter to the stairs at the rear of the lobby. Lebeau Inn does not boast elevators. It was a stiff climb to the second floor. My arthritis being what it is, I did not look forward to manipulating those steps several times a day.

"I should think I could have a room on the ground floor," I observed.

Jake shook his grizzled head. "First floor all reserved, ma'am."

"Reserved?" I protested. "I had no idea the place was crowded."

"No'm, 'tain't crowded, that's a fact," he admitted. "Ain't hardly nobody here, but the first floor is reserved for—for . . ." He gave me an odd look. "For Mrs. Canby and her doings."

"Doings!" I repeated sharply. "What on earth do you mean?"

But, like most darkies, Jake could keep a still tongue when he liked.

"Here you is, ma'am," he said, exactly as if he had not heard me, and conducted me into a large, bilious-looking room at the back of the second floor.

He hastily deposited my traveling bags beside me and made off so hurriedly I followed a sudden impulse and pursued him as far as the head of the stairs. It was my intention to insist upon an explanation, but as I reached the steps I glanced downward and was just in time to see Mr. Chet Keith chuck the young woman at the desk under the chin, at the same time managing to steal a kiss.

"I thought he was a fast worker," I said to myself. "The disgusting young whippersnapper!"

At that moment he glanced up and caught my eye, but instead of appearing in the least abashed by his conduct he had the audacity to wink, a piece of flippancy which I accepted with a disdainful snort. However, almost instantly the smile died upon his lips and he glanced past me, his handsome, insolent young face flushing darkly.

I turned to look over my shoulder. A girl was standing at my very elbow, though I had not heard her approach, a slim, rather frail-looking girl with pale gold hair knotted in a coil on her neck, and a slender, oval face, dominated by a wistful mouth and two enormous gray eyes. There were dark circles beneath the eyes, and one hand was clenched at her side as she stared past me at the young man in the lounge.

The next minute she was gone, and down the hall a door opened and I heard Ella Trotter's voice call out. "Adelaide! Thank God you have come!"

Before I could recover from my astonishment Ella bustled into the hall and seized me by the arm. You would have thought from the feverish manner in which she clutched at me and drew me into her room after her that I had arrived in direct answer to prayer. I was so overcome by her unexpected reception, I am afraid I merely gawked at her, and she had the grace to blush.

"I was never so glad to see anyone," she said.

I drew myself up to my full height, which is not inconsiderable.

"Seeing that you took every possible means to keep me away," I began haughtily.

"That was yesterday," interrupted Ella and then she clutched my arm again and glanced over her shoulder. "What was that?" she whispered.

"It sounded to me like a cat squalling," I snapped, beginning to wonder if Ella had gone into her dotage.

She turned so white, I thought she was going to faint. "A cat! Oh, Adelaide!" she cried and sank down into a chair as if her knees would no longer support her.

"For heaven's sake!" I exclaimed crossly. "What on earth has put you into such a stew? You've heard alley cats squall before."

Ella was trembling and I saw a little row of sweat beads on her upper lip. "They've found two cats in two days," she said in a breathless voice. "Dead!"

"And what of it?" I demanded impatiently.

"You don't understand, Adelaide," quavered Ella. "They were— were—their stomachs were ripped to pieces."

At that moment there came the first roll of thunder. I found myself clutching Ella's arm quite as tightly as she had clutched mine the moment before.

"Well," I said, striving to throw off the eerie chill which persisted in playing up and down my spine, "cats have clawed each other to pieces before this and will again, I dare say."

Ella was whispering, and there was something about the way she kept glancing over her shoulder which made me nervous.

"There was no sign of claws," she said. "They—they'd been cut, Adelaide, cut all to pieces with a sharp knife and left to die like that in *agony*."

Her voice cracked on the last word, and for the second time I thought she was going to faint. I went over to the door and closed and locked it. Then I got myself a chair and sat down across from Ella.

"You'd better tell me all about it," I said.

Nothing could better illustrate the state to which Ella had been reduced than the docility with which she accepted my suggestion. As a rule one has only to offer Ella Trotter advice to have her fly off in the other direction.

"How much do you know about Thomas Canby and his wife?" she asked, still sounding very tremulous.

"I know what everybody knows," I said curtly. "Thomas Canby started with nothing and built up a fortune."

"You knew their only child died last year?"

"I heard so this afternoon. She was very young to die."

Ella shivered. "She didn't just die, Adelaide."

I glanced at her sharply. "It isn't like you to beat about the bushes, Ella," I said. "For goodness' sake, what's wrong?"

"I wish I knew," said Ella with a gulp like a sob. "Anyway, Gloria Canby killed herself, Adelaide."

"Killed herself!" I ejaculated. "A young girl like that, with everything to live for!"

"She opened her wrists with a razor blade."

"Good heavens!"

"She was quite dead when they found her."

"It must have been terrible for the mother," I murmured. "I recall how devoted she was to the child when they stayed here at Lebeau Inn twenty years ago."

Ella gave me a look that startled me. "They say Dora Canby's devotion to her daughter was almost an obsession," she whispered, again glancing over her shoulder, although the door was locked.

"What ails you, Ella?" I demanded.

Ella's lips were actually quivering. "The dead can't come back, can they, Adelaide?"

"Are you crazy!" I exclaimed.

"I'm beginning to think so," said Ella wearily and then she got to her feet and, going over to the dresser, took a folded newspaper, out of a drawer and handed it tome.

"I ordered this from an old news dealer," she explained. "It came out at the time of Gloria Canby's death."

The headlines marched clear across the page. GLORIA CANBY, THE POWER MAGNATE'S DAUGHTER, COMMITS SUICIDE, they announced. There was a picture, blurred like most newspaper cuts, but I could make out the features well enough.

"I saw that girl not five minutes ago on the stair!" I cried, feeling grateful for the chair under me.

Ella shook her head. "You saw Sheila Kelly."

"Sheila Kelly?"

"The resemblance is marked," said Ella, "but that isn't what makes it so uncanny."

"Do stop talking in riddles, Ella," I said as severely as possible.

"The thing that is so awful," whispered Ella, "is that Sheila Kelly looks more like that—that terrible girl than she did a week ago, than she did even this morning."

"What terrible girl?"

Ella drew a long breath. "Gloria Canby was a very unpleasant person, Adelaide. She was never quite normal, I think." She shuddered. "They say even when she was a child she used to pull wings off butterflies and stick pins into puppies just—just to see them suffer, and once—once when she was only ten she—she cut a kitten's stomach all to pieces."

There was another rumble of thunder, so close I flinched. Ella leaned nearer to me and again she lowered her voice. I had to bend down to hear.

"Gloria Canby killed herself because her father was about to have her committed to an institution, or so she believed," she whispered.

"An institution!"

"She—she tried to kill him."

"Her own father!"

"Made an attempt to poison him, or so they say, although every effort was made to hush it up."

"The girl was mad!"

"Of course," said Ella, "that's why her father was having her put away."

"Only she killed herself first?"

I found myself glancing over my shoulder, as if it were contagious.

"Poor Dora Canby!" I sighed.

"But that's just the trouble," said Ella. "Dora Canby never realized that the girl wasn't—wasn't right. She seems to have been able to close her eyes to every bit of the evidence. You know how stubbornly blind foolishly doting mothers of problem children can be."

"I know," I admitted grimly, thinking of more than one such phenomenon which I had witnessed.

"I suppose her husband shielded her as much as possible from the truth," Ella went on, "which is what makes the present situation so dreadful."

"What is the present situation, Ella?" I demanded with asperity. "Do you realize how you are hemming and hawing?"

"It must have been sheer accident that Dora Canby came across Sheila Kelly and the professor," muttered Ella, paying no attention to me, "or was it an accident?"

"What professor and who is Sheila Kelly?" I asked crossly.

"Professor Thaddeus Matthews is a fraud of the cheapest rank, of that one thing I am convinced, explain the rest of it as you will," snapped Ella. "He pretends to be a spiritualist—messages from the other world and that sort of thing. You've only to look at the man to know that the only spirit he ever contacted intimately was liquor. That is what makes it all so inexplicable."

"All what, Ella?" I asked, praying for patience, a commodity of which I have never possessed an over abundance.

"I told you," said Ella wearily, although she hadn't. "The professor has been conducting séances for Dora Canby. The girl Sheila Kelly is his stooge or medium or what have you. The idea has been to get in touch with Dora Canby's dead daughter, as you might guess."

I made a grimace. "As I remember Mrs. Canby, she is exactly the material to be victimized by that kind of drivel."

Ella looked relieved. "It *is* all drivel. It couldn't be anything else," she said as if she were trying to convince herself.

"The dead don't return," I said harshly.

There was a flash of lightning, so bright as almost to blind me, and the light in the chandelier above our heads flickered wildly. Ella clutched my arm again.

"Even a perverse mad spirit like Gloria Canby cannot come back to carry out its evil designs," she whispered. "I can't, I won't believe it!"

I stared at her incredulously. "What sort of tommyrot is this? Of course there isn't any return!"

"You haven't attended the séances, Adelaide. I tell you there is something. The way that girl looks, the way she's changed, even in the week I've known her, and you can't—can't get away from the cats!"

"Are you trying to make out that—"

Ella interrupted me. "The girl herself is terrified. She had hysterics yesterday afternoon when she found the canary in her room."

"Canary?"

"Dora Canby's pet canary; it had been strangled."

"Strangled!" I gasped, beginning to feel like a well-trained parrot myself.

"During Gloria Canby's lifetime," said Ella in a shaky voice, "Mrs. Canby never dared have a bird. You see, her—her daughter had a mania for wringing their necks."

I took a firm grasp upon my sanity and Ella's left wrist. "Just exactly what are you trying to intimate, Ella?" I demanded in my sternest voice. "That this charlatan of a professor and his stooge, as you call her, have succeeded in raising Gloria Canby's unhappy spirit from the grave?"

My manner had a salutary effect upon Ella. She drew a long breath and looked more like herself than she had since I arrived.

"It's preposterous," she said.

"Of course!"

"It is so perfectly apparent that it's all a cheap trick to get money out of Dora Canby."

"I should think so," I remarked indignantly.

"She's practically keeping the professor and the girl."

"The woman must be a fool!"

"Oh, she is," assented Ella, then she frowned. "But still . . ." She was glancing over her shoulder again, and outside it had begun to rain in torrents accompanied by a wailing wind. "I was prepared to laugh at the whole business, Adelaide." She shivered. "Well, I'm not laughing."

"No?"

She clutched my arm. "I tell you the girl is terrified and so, I sometimes think, is the professor. I believe they started out with their customary bag of tricks and then—and then . . ." She paused and regarded me intently. "Did you ever hear, Adelaide, that suicides cannot rest in their graves?" she whispered.

"You'll be telling me that you believe in vampires next!" I scoffed.

Ella turned white. "I killed a bat in this very room yesterday," she announced in a sepulchral voice.

I simply stared at her and she winced.

"I know I'm talking like an idiot," she confessed, "but—but supposing, Adelaide, that—that the professor and this girl started out to work upon Dora Canby's credulity and—and something—something over which they have no control took advantage of their pretense at bringing Gloria Canby's spirit back to earth and now—now they can't control the force which they have let loose?"

"If I supposed anything of the kind I'd be a greater fool than Dora Canby," I said, getting briskly to my feet. "The dead don't come back, Ella. Make up your mind to that. Whatever may be going on in this mildewed house, it is not the work of the undead, rest assured of that."

I was thinking of the cold chisel which Chet Keith had found
on the side of the mountain that afternoon, and of the amber-
colored hairpin which had been lying beside it.

Ella patted my arm. "I can't tell you how glad I am you're here,"
she said in a husky voice.

I was touched and, never having been very eloquent at putting
my softer emotions into words, was at a loss what to do about it,
when somebody began to pound upon the door.

"Mrs. Trotter! Mrs. Trotter!" cried an excited voice. "Do let me in!"

"It's Judy Oliver, Dora Canby's niece," murmured Ella and
opened the door.

The young woman who entered was too perturbed to recognize
my presence. She was a slight young thing with short black hair,
cut in a fringe along her forehead, and brown eyes that were now
enormous.

"Uncle Thomas was nearly killed this afternoon!" she cried in
a choked voice. "But for the fact that Jay had to slow down to pass
the bus, the car would have gone over the side of the bluff. Oh,
Mrs. Trotter, what does it mean? What can it mean?"

The girl's teeth were positively chattering, and for the second
time Ella tottered to a chair and sat down. I stared from one to the
other, and Ella made a feeble gesture in my direction.

"This is my friend Adelaide Adams, Judy," she said, and the
girl turned sharply and caught her breath. "The one who's bringing the book?" she faltered.

I nodded and Judy Oliver made an effort to recover herself.

"There must be some sane explanation," she stammered.

She sounded as if she badly needed reassurance. "Of course
there is an explanation," I said, though by no means certain of what.

Ella drew a long breath. "You see, Adelaide, last night when
Sheila Kelly was in her trance she—she said . . ."

Her voice trailed off and Judy Oliver took up the thread.

"It was horrible!" she whispered. "She looked like Gloria, she
talked like her. I could have sworn it was Gloria, and she—she said
that she couldn't rest because Uncle Thomas was still alive. She
said that she never would rest in her grave while he is alive."

"I suppose Gloria Canby had long hair and wore amber-colored hairpins," I remarked sarcastically.

Judy Oliver stared at me with startled eyes. "Yes," she said, "she did. How did you know?"

I tried to answer but my breath had deserted me, and to my relief somebody outside the door called Judy's name.

"It's Jeff," she said, blushing delightfully. "We always play a game of Russian bank before dinner."

She ran on out, and I looked at Ella and shrugged my shoulders.

"A woman can never mention her beloved's name without giving herself away," I said.

Ella gave me an odd look. "Jeff Wayne is Gloria Canby's fiancé, not Judy's."

"You mean he was her fiancé. The girl is dead."

"You think so?" murmured Ella in a voice I did not like.

I got impatiently to my feet. "I'm going to my room," I said. "I have just remembered that the door has been unlocked and open all this time. That's what comes of taking this sort of rubbish seriously. At your age you should know better, Ella."

Ella tossed her head. "Far be it from me to expect you to take an interest in any theory of mine," she said tartly. "You always have to be the belled cow or nothing, Adelaide."

I felt better. I was much more accustomed to being snapped at by Ella than to having her weep upon my shoulder.

"I'll see you at dinner," I said curtly.

"Don't trouble yourself on my account," remarked Ella and, picking up her knitting bag which she is seldom without, though I never knew her to finish an article, began to knit with elaborate unconcern.

The door to my room was ajar, just as I had left it, my traveling bags piled up where Jake had deposited them in the center of the floor. I remember grumbling to myself that he might have left the dressing case right side up, although nothing was spilled except my handkerchief case, which had got a little mussed. I was annoyed. I had placed the spiritualism book on top of the case to hold it solid. It was then I realized that the book was not there. It was not

in any of the other bags either. For the first time it occurred to me
to wonder if, after all, that boulder on the road had been intended
for Thomas Canby.

"Don't be a fool," I scolded myself angrily. "You're worse than
Ella."

I still contend that I was not frightened when I saw the bat
clinging to the side of the wall, just above my shoulder. I simply
do not like bats. They are nasty, slimy things. I did not, as Ella
Trotter, persists in claiming to this day, lose my head and try to
brain myself. I merely struck at the horrid creature with my
clothesbrush. It was pure accident that it flew right at my eyes, so
that I had to duck and succeeded in winging myself on one temple.
Naturally I screamed. Somebody jerked the door open behind me
and the bat darted out.

"For Pete's sake, Miss Adams," muttered a sarcastic voice, "are
you doing a war dance or what?"

I did not realize until that moment that I was jumping up and
down, flourishing the clothesbrush wildly in all directions, with
my skirts clutched tightly about me.

"Young man," I informed Chet Keith coldly, "there was a bat in
the room."

"A bat?" he murmured softly and picked up something from
the floor at my feet.

It was an amber-colored hairpin.

3

THE DINING ROOM at Mount Lebeau Inn was inadequately lighted and much too large for the handful of people which drifted in to dinner that stormy July night. There seemed to be an endless procession of vacant tables stretching into the shadowy recesses of the room, away from the one at which Ella and I were seated. It may have been the effect of the huge central chandelier, which had a green shade, but it seemed to me that everybody, including Ella, had a strained look about the eyes. At any rate none of our fellow diners were in a convivial mood, that is certain. Glancing around me, I thought I had never seen quite such a haggard gathering.

As the colored porter had admitted, the inn was not crowded and, thanks to Ella, I was able to identify the guests at the next table. The girl Judy I had met already, but not Jeff Wayne, who had been engaged to her cousin. He was a clean-cut young chap with fair hair and ingenuous blue eyes, I thought, only he had a worn expression about his mouth, as if he suffered from nerves, which seemed to me absurd at his age. I noticed that he ate practically nothing and kept his gaze upon his plate. Once when Judy addressed him he started violently and sloshed the coffee in his cup.

Ella gave me what I feel sure she intended for a significant glance. "The boy's haunted," she whispered.

"Don't be silly," I snapped.

Ella compressed her lips. "Judy is always trying to call him back—from somewhere."

"'Men have died . . . . but not for love,'" I quoted rather sourly. "I dare say the young fool is young enough to think the bereft lover is a romantic role."

"But that's just it," said Ella. "It seems he wasn't in love with Gloria Canby, not toward the last, anyway. He was afraid of her. If you ask me he still is."

"Tommyrot!" I exclaimed, and then something occurred which gave me a turn.

Judy Oliver was speaking and she leaned slightly nearer and put her hand over Jeff Wayne's where it was lying on the edge of the table. I saw his fingers tighten on hers, then he seemed to shiver and looked over his shoulder. Instantly he released Judy's hand, as if it had stung him, and his face suddenly appeared quite ghastly in the dim glow of the green chandelier.

"You see," murmured Ella at my elbow.

The boy was afraid all right, I could not deny that. In that unguarded moment before he remembered to lower his gaze I had read terror and something else, very like horror, in his eyes.

"And that, I suppose," I said, following his glance, "is the professor and his assistant."

Ella nodded. Under pretense of observing the rain which was streaming down the windowpanes, I studied Professor Thaddeus Matthews. He looked exactly what he was—a charlatan of the first water. You have seen him or his like on cheap vaudeville stages all over the country before vaudeville went out, a tall, portly old man with sagging jowls and a large nose veined in red and protuberant black eyes beneath a shock of greasy black hair, patently dyed. He was wearing a rusty black suit, a high stock collar and a limp black string tie. He looked pompous and a little apoplectic and distinctly shifty, but on his left hand he wore a handsome cabochon ruby in a massive, old-fashioned gold setting.

Ella saw me staring at it. "The gift of Mrs. Canby," she explained with a shrug.

"The pickings seem to have been remarkably good," I said, staring at the string of green beads which Sheila Kelly was wearing around her neck.

Like the professor, she was shabbily dressed. I felt sure her white chiffon evening gown had been part of her stage act. It looked wilted, as if it had cost too little in the first place and been packed into too many theatrical trunks in the second place, but the string of jade about her throat was genuine, I'd have staked my life on that.

Ella nodded. "No wonder Thomas Canby thought he'd better come and look into things."

"Is that why he came?" I asked, still watching the Kelly girl.

Like Jeff Wayne, she was merely toying with her food, and her face, too, was drawn.

"Of course that's why he came," snapped Ella. "That's why they are all here."

"All?"

She made an impatient gesture toward the others who were sitting at the table with Judy Oliver and young Wayne. "They're Dora Canby's natural heirs, her nieces and nephews. They wouldn't like to see her divert all those millions to a cheap trickster and his stooge."

"The woman may be a fool, but hardly such a fool as that," I said, "even if the professor has convinced Mrs. Canby that they can bring her messages from the dead."

"You don't understand," said Ella. "Dora Canby doesn't think they bring her messages from the dead. She thinks that Gloria Canby has come to life again in the body of Sheila Kelly."

I made a grimace, but the protest into which I was about to plunge was forestalled by an exclamation from the handsome young woman sitting beside Jeff Wayne.

"Hogan!" she cried with, it seemed to me, genuine astonishment.

A man had come into the dining room, a good-looking, debonair young man with a desiccated face and extremely sophisticated eyes.

"Hallo, everybody," he murmured, making straight for Lila Atwood.

Even then I noticed what a striking couple they made, sleek dark Hogan Brewster and Lila Atwood with her shingled, blue-black hair and brilliant dark eyes above a restrained though sensitive red mouth.

"Darling," she murmured, "how ever did you find us?"

He grinned. "I put the bloodhounds on the trail," he said. "How are you, Allan?"

For a moment I thought Allan Atwood was going to strike the other man, then he seemed to make a terrific effort to pull himself together.

"I'm all right," he muttered. "Have you had dinner? Will you join us?"

"Will I?" exclaimed the other, laughing as he pulled out a chair. "If you don't think it was a nightmare driving up that mountain in this storm, you're loopy. A dozen times I thought I was a goner."

"Yes?" murmured Lila Atwood's husband. He did not add, "No such luck," but he looked as if he wanted to, and I raised my eyes at Ella, who nodded. "The old, old triangle," she said. "The affair has been an open scandal for months."

She went into some detail on the subject while I covertly watched Allan trying with poor success to act as if he were unaware of Hogan's bold flirtation with Lila under her husband's very nose. According to Ella, Dora Canby had had two sisters, both now dead. Judy Oliver and her brother Patrick were the children of the younger sister, Allan Atwood the only child of the elder. Thomas Canby had had his wife's niece and nephews about his neck for a number of years or so I gathered. At any rate he had given them a home and educated them and taken both the boys into his business in a minor capacity.

"One of those fifth or sixth vice-president affairs with which rich men take care of their ineffectual hangers-on," explained Ella.

There was something ineffectual about Allan Atwood's face, I thought to myself, although he was rather attractive in a vague way. He had regular features and thick, slightly curly brown hair, and a cleft chin, but he gave the impression of being too loosely knit, as if he might ravel under strain. Even the movements of his well-kept hands were uncertain, and his gray eyes were slightly bloodshot.

There was nothing vague about his wife. She had been a famous beauty, so Ella said, and she had all the poise of a woman accustomed to being singled out for her looks. She belonged to a blue-blooded Maryland family, one of those aristocratic branches which, while run to seed financially, manage to cling to a place in the social register. Ella said she was supposed to be a superb horse-woman, and I could easily imagine Lila Atwood with her long limbs and straight back putting a thoroughbred at a five-foot fence without batting an eye.

"I suppose the only horse the husband can ride is a wooden one in a merry-go-round," I murmured, staring at Allan, who had managed to upset his water glass in his lap and who colored darkly when everybody, especially Hogan Brewster, laughed at the mishap.

Ella nodded. "He has a perfect genius for tripping over his own feet. It's painful to watch him. Judy says he was always like that, awkward and self-conscious, only it's been worse since his marriage. He's hopeless at all the things at which his wife excels—she and Hogan Brewster."

"Nowadays they call it poor co-ordination," I murmured. "It's supposed to be a nervous complex, like stuttering."

"Judy told me that Allan stepped on his bride's train at the altar and, metaphorically speaking, has been stepping on it ever since, poor devil."

"I suppose she married him for his money?" I hazarded.

"For Thomas Canby's money," Ella corrected me. She frowned. "Only why doesn't she divorce him, now she's got Brewster on the string? That's what nobody can understand. He is a millionaire in his own right, one of the Long Island polo-playing crowd, though they say he's artistic too. Paints as well as skis, and flies his own plane. You'd think he and Lila were made to order for each other."

I lifted my eyebrows. "Maybe he is not the marrying kind," I said. "Not all dashing young men who run after a handsome married woman are anxious for her to rush off to Reno on their account."

"I suspect you're right," said Ella, "though Judy thinks Mr. Hogan Brewster has what she calls 'a genuine pash' on Lila."

I stared at Allan Atwood's wife. She was gently brushing off his coat where the glass had overturned, using her napkin and smiling at him.

"There," she murmured softly, "it'll never show, darling."

Her tone reminded me of young mothers who kiss their babies' bruises and coo, "Never mind, Muvver 'll make it well." I thought he recognized the accent, for again he flushed darkly and pushed her hand away with an angry gesture.

"Don't!" he cried almost savagely.

Ella compressed her lips. "She's always very nice to her husband," she said, "you have to give her credit for that, but it seems to get on his nerves."

I was again looking at Allan Atwood's wife. Hogan Brewster had leaned over and murmured something in her ear, something flattering, I felt sure from the glint in his black eyes. I saw her flush and look up at him and her gaze was definitely hostile. He seemed slightly taken aback, although he recovered himself at once.

"At least she doesn't treat Brewster as if he were a child, a clumsy inept child whom she is impelled to mother," I muttered.

Ella flung me a startled glance. "Lila does act a little as if she felt called upon to pick her husband up out of the dirt a dozen times a day and wipe his nose."

"How long have they been married?" I asked.

"A little over a year and, again quoting Judy, Brewster has been a fixture in the family group almost from the first."

"No wonder Allan looks a little wild," I said. "Why on earth doesn't he do something—kick the fellow out or forbid him the house or take a horsewhip to him?"

"Perhaps that's why subconsciously his wife thinks of him as a dimwit. He more or less asks for it."

"Then why doesn't she leave him?" I demanded impatiently.

"I told you that is what neither I nor anyone else can understand," said Ella.

At this moment a young man waltzed into the room and, calling out a helter-skelter greeting to everyone at the table, seated himself between Judy Oliver and Allan Atwood. He was about twenty-four, I judged, and reminded me of a Dachshund pup that was not yet housebroken. He had shaggy chestnut hair and wriggly brown eyes and an overexuberant smile. I thought of the proverbial bull in the china shop as he clapped Allan on the back and at the same time hailed Hogan with every evidence of delight.

"Fancy finding you in this moth-eaten dump, Hoge!" he sang out. "Lord, Lila, you've cost me five dollars. I bet Judy even your beeyooteous countenance wouldn't be enough to drag the boy friend this far from night clubs and what have you."

His sister Judy must have kicked his shin, for he winced and uttered a loud "Ouch!" but Lila did not turn a hair.

"I don't suppose you dropped Hogan a wire that we were here, did you, darling?" she murmured.

Apparently, like so many of the younger generation, she called everyone "darling," but I thought the glance she gave Patrick Oliver had a knife in it, and it seemed to me he looked disconcerted for a moment before he summoned up his exuberant grin.

"Who, me?" he asked. "Can't anything happen around here without my being blamed for it?"

Lila shrugged her shoulder. "I wouldn't know, darling, and I must remind you that you haven't answered my question."

Brewster leaned a little forward and gazed rather intently at the circle of faces around the table. "As a matter of fact," he said, "I did get a telegram telling me where you people had fled to."

Lila frowned. "A telegram?"

Patrick Oliver laughed, not very pleasantly. "That was a good guess you made, Lila, about its being a telegram, if it was a guess."

Allan was staring at his wife and biting his lips.

"I didn't wire Hogan, Pat, if that is what you mean," said Lila, speaking in a very level voice. "I thought we agreed it was best to keep this—this business as much in the family as possible."

"My God, yes!" breathed Allan Atwood in a stifled voice.

Brewster gave him a slightly contemptuous glance. "So something funny is going on," he said.

"Funny!" muttered Judy, drawing closer to Jeff Wayne.

Lila turned sharply upon Brewster. "Why should you think anything funny is going on?"

He grinned, but his black eyes narrowed and I saw that he was watching them all. "You see," he said very quietly, "the telegram was signed 'Gloria.'"

"Oh no," whispered Jeff Wayne.

Judy laid her hand over his, and again I saw him jerk away.

"It's somebody's idea of a joke, Hogan," she faltered. "Sending you a telegram and signing Gloria's name."

Patrick, her brother, laughed loudly, and I thought of a small boy whistling as he marched off to the dentist.

"Sure, somebody did it to be funny," he said.

"Funny!" breathed Judy again in a despairing voice.

Brewster was looking at Atwood. "Only," he said softly, "I'd have sworn that nobody on earth except me knew that Gloria used to call me Shot, for Hot Shot."

It seemed to me that everybody around the table was holding his breath, and at that moment Sheila Kelly rose from her seat and came slowly across the room, her heart-shaped face as pale as death, her hands before her as if she were feeling her way through a fog.

"Still looking for trouble, Shot?" she whispered in a voice that shocked me, a mocking, defiant voice which seemed to have nothing to do with that pale tragic face and drooping, wistful mouth.

Hogan Brewster stared at her as if he were transfixed, then suddenly Professor Thaddeus Matthews was there, clutching the girl's arm.

"Sheila!" he cried sharply. "Sheila!"

She gave a start, flung up her hands, looked wildly around and then ran out of the room, pursued by the professor, who stumbled and nearly fell over the doorsill.

"Who in heaven's name is that?" demanded Hogan Brewster.

"That," said Patrick Oliver with a twisted grin, "is the vaudeville stunt which I introduced our aunt Dora to in a moment of aberration."

4

It was Allan Atwood who suddenly took exception to the fact that every word they said was audible at our table, the others seeming to be quite indifferent to the matter.

"Is it necessary to let the whole world into our confidence?" he demanded with a scowl in our direction.

After that Lila pointedly changed the subject and the others followed her lead, although none of them bothered to lower their voices. Neither Thomas Canby nor his wife was in the dining room that night. Ella explained that Mrs. Canby usually took her meals in the small sitting room attached to her suite. It seemed that, although her health was quite good, Dora Canby lived a very retiring life.

"She is the most shrinking person I ever knew," declared Ella. "It amounts to a phobia."

I nodded. "I remember how extraordinarily timid she was even as a young woman."

That was how Thomas Canby's wife happened to be at Lebeau Inn, or so Ella explained. It seemed that, if humanly possible, Mrs. Canby avoided all contacts with society and she had balked at spending the summer at her Long Island home. She disliked the bright young people with whom Patrick Oliver ran around. She had even less liking for the smart young married set to which Allan Atwood and his wife belonged. She particularly objected to Hogan Brewster, although Ella said that, curiously enough, Mrs. Canby's resentment in that case was directed, not at Lila, as one might expect, but at Allan.

"Mrs. Canby seems to blame her nephew for doing nothing about the situation," said Ella.

At any rate Dora Canby, accompanied by her niece Judy Oliver, had turned her back upon Southampton and beaten a retreat to Lebeau Inn.

"That must have been rather hard on Judy," I murmured, glancing about the big, almost empty dining room with its vast shadowy corners.

As I had anticipated, with the exception of the Canby party and ourselves, the only guests were elderly invalids and anxious mothers of ailing babies.

Ella compressed her lips. "From what I can gather, Judy more than earns her keep in the Canby ménage."

"Poor relations usually do," I said.

"They never let Mrs. Canby go anywhere alone. She's one of those helpless individuals who would be sure to get on the wrong train."

So Mrs. Canby and her niece had settled down for a very dull time on Mount Lebeau. Then Patrick Oliver had stopped off on his way to Mexico or some such place to spend a few days with his aunt. It was Patrick who discovered the small movie theater in Carrolton and decided it would do both his aunt and Judy good to drive down for a performance.

"That was two weeks ago," said Ella, looking grim. "The professor was putting on a psychic act. From what I have been able to gather, he's been touring the tank towns for years with some moth-eaten gag, but this time, as you say, he struck pay dirt. That first afternoon a message came through for Dora Canby."

"From her daughter Gloria?"

"To be sure. She insisted on going back the next day and the next. Then she moved the professor and the girl up here. She is paying all their expenses. They stage a séance every night in the parlor."

"For Mrs. Canby?"

"The public is invited," said Ella, "but you'd be surprised how few of the guests have gone back a second time."

"I wouldn't be surprised at all," I said sharply. "In the first place anybody with a grain of common sense would be bored to tears with an exhibition like that, and in the second place all these people look the type to be in bed by nine o'clock."

Ella gave me a wry look. "Whatever else you may be, Adelaide, I guarantee you won't be bored by the performance tonight."

"I don't suppose there will be a performance," I snapped. "I am sure you are right. Thomas Canby came down here to put a stop to this business."

"If he can," murmured Ella.

I did not remember a great deal about the multimillionaire, except that he had been as difficult to talk to as his wife. However, even twenty years before, I had known that it was not timidity with him. He was simply a person with one idea. According to everything I had read about him, he had hewed a deadly straight line, allowing nothing to swerve him.

"I can't imagine his permitting himself to be turned aside from anything to which he had set his hand," I said, "much less by a palpable fraud like this humbug of a professor."

Apparently Ella did not agree with me. "The others thought they could stop it too, but they didn't."

She was referring to Lila Atwood and her husband and Jeff Wayne, who, Ella said, had abandoned Long Island in a hurry when they got wind of what was going on.

"I suppose young Wayne came along for the ride and to see Judy Oliver," I murmured sarcastically.

Ella shook her head. "Oh no. Like all the rest, he is interested in the pie."

"The pie being Thomas Canby's fortune?"

"Mrs. Canby looks upon Jeff as one of the family, precisely as if he had married her daughter Gloria, so he also has a sixth or seventh vice-presidency in Thomas Canby's company."

There is something demoralizing about the expectancy of inheriting a great deal of money or even a modest sum, as I have had occasion to note. Waiting around to step into dead men's shoes does something to people. I suffered a revulsion of feeling about the whole affair.

"If poor Dora Canby gets any pleasure out of the professor and his spirit messages, why don't they let her be?" I demanded. "From what I've heard, it's precious little else her husband's money has been able to do for her. Suppose she is wasting a few dollars on a cheap vaudeville team, there will be plenty left for her precious nephews and nieces. Too much, in fact! It might do them all good to have to get out and root for themselves for a change."

"Undoubtedly!" agreed Ella with emphasis. "But people don't give up their claim to several millions without a struggle."

"Without disputing that point," I remarked tartly, "the fact remains that it isn't Mrs. Canby's money. It's her husband's, and I don't suppose anybody believes that he could be victimized by a fraudulent spiritualistic act."

"All the money goes to his wife at his death."

"Even so, the odds are that he'll outlive her."

"But don't you see?" exclaimed Ella. "That's why they are so upset. That girl said last night that Thomas Canby would not live out the week."

I should have told Ella then and there about the chisel which Chet Keith had found that afternoon. I don't know why I didn't, unless it was because I had set out to make little of the whole affair and I hated to crawl down off my high horse. At any rate I merely looked scornful and muttering "Rubbish!" rose to my feet and stalked out of the dining room.

Ella did not immediately follow me. She was detained by a wisp of an old man who wanted to ask her advice about his tendency to break into a cold sweat after eating. Knowing how nothing so delights Ella as the chance to prescribe for somebody, I walked through the lounge to the front door and stood for a moment staring out at the rain which the wind was hurling against the windowpanes.

"You might be interested to know," murmured a voice over my shoulder, "that Mr. Thomas Canby considers me a snooping newspaperman who'd damn well better stop nosing into his business or words to that effect."

I turned sharply. Chet Keith was standing right behind me, grinning like a Siamese cat. I recall thinking again that he was much too good looking and entirely too well pleased with himself.

"You told him, then?" I asked.

He gave me a wry glance. "Didn't we agree it was my duty to put the gentleman on his guard? As for receiving a figurative kick in the seat of the pants for my trouble, let me assure you that is neither the first nor likely to be the last time."

"Are you a newspaperman?" I demanded.

He grinned. "If I'm not, I'm drawing a salary under false pretenses."

I frowned. "What are you doing away off down here?"

He laughed. "That is exactly what Mr. Thomas Canby wished to know. I'll give you the same answer. Believe it or not, I didn't come for my health nor yet for the scenery."

"Which isn't saying why you did come."

"Not easily put off, are you?" he inquired, and when I sniffed he went on with a good-natured smile. "'Mine not to reason why, mine but to do or die,'" he quoted. "In other words the city editor got a tip that something was doing in this outlandish spot, and here I am."

"Something doing?"

"Thomas Canby is always news, and have you seen the professor?"

"I've seen the professor," I admitted shortly, "and also the girl."

I looked at him sharply and I thought he winced. "They'll both be sent packing in the morning. I have Thomas Canby's word for it," he said.

"Good riddance of bad rubbish," I muttered.

He shrugged his shoulders. "Oh, I don't know," he said. "If Mrs. Canby gets a kick out of the old charlatan's bag of tricks, where's the harm? From all I've been able to hear, it's little else she gets out of life."

He was merely voicing what I had said to Ella only a few moments before, but I had no intention of chiming in with his sentiments.

"They ought to be in jail, the two of them!" I cried indignantly. "Befuddling a poor grief-stricken creature! Deliberately preying upon her sorrow and credulity!"

Chet Keith looked at me curiously. "Maybe that is why Thomas Canby has sent for the sheriff."

"The sheriff!"

"I have it from the girl at the switchboard."

I remembered then that I had seen him chucking the pert young woman at the desk under the chin. He must have remembered that I had witnessed that encounter, for he grinned at me.

"In my trade it never pays to neglect any possible source of information," he said airily. "The lady's name is Maurine Smith. Wouldn't it be? And she tells me that not half an hour ago Thomas Canby got in touch with the forces of law and order, which in this godforsaken hole happen to be the lord high sheriff."

"He intends to have the professor and his assistant arrested!"

"On the other hand," said Chet Keith softly, "perhaps Mr. Thomas Canby was more impressed than he cared to let on with the cold chisel which I produced as Exhibit A."

I caught my breath. "He also believes it was an attempt upon his life!"

"He distinctly derided such a possibility," murmured Chet Keith, "but methought the gentleman didst protest too much."

Behind me the wind gave a prolonged and agonized shriek, and I shivered and glanced over my shoulder.

"I don't envy the sheriff his trip up the mountain in this storm," I said.

Chet Keith grinned mirthlessly. "According to my informant, the sheriff would have pled off, but Thomas Canby was obdurate. He seemed to think the matter was not one that would be the better for being slept upon."

"I don't like it," I muttered.

The flippant smile vanished from Chet Keith's sardonic face as if it had been sponged off. "Neither do I," he said gravely.

And then Ella descended upon us. She glanced curiously at my companion and plainly expected me to present him, but I moved away, and Ella, looking injured, trailed along.

"Who is that young man?" she inquired before we were entirely out of earshot. "He is handsome enough for a movie star."

"And conceited enough to imagine that every woman he sees thinks so," I remarked tartly.

In the rather wavy mirror behind the desk I saw Chet Keith grin as if he enjoyed my comment, which had not been my intention.

"The séance starts in ten minutes," murmured Ella. "We might as well go on into the parlor and pick out our seats."

I frowned. Ella has a genius for managing people, and there is nothing I dislike more than being pulled about like a puppet on a string. It was sheer perversity which made me refuse to yield to her suggestion.

"Go ahead, if you like, and pick out seats," I said coldly. "I'm going to run up to my room for a minute."

"Have it your own way as usual," said Ella and walked over to a small, fluffy-looking woman with iron-gray hair and small black eyes like a Pekingese's.

The rain had made my arthritis worse and as I toiled up those steep stairs I cursed myself for an obstinate old fool. The long corridor on the second floor was dimly lighted, and my footsteps echoed when I walked down it. Not half the rooms which opened off to either side were occupied at any time, and at this hour I seemed to have the upper story of the inn to myself except for the howl of the wind and the steady and melancholy swish of the rain.

I had the most unreasonable disinclination to close the door of my room behind me, but on turning on the light I found nothing to account for the state of nerves in which I seemed to be. There was no bat clinging to the wall and nothing had been disturbed during my absence. Nevertheless I had no desire to linger and, catching up my crocheted throw to put about my throat because the dampness was beginning to start that bronchial tickle which is so annoying, I turned to the door again. I had my hand upon the knob, in fact, when I heard the voice on the other side of the partition.

"I can't go through with it! I won't!" it cried.

It was a woman's voice and quite desperate. The man sounded desperate, too, and very tremulous.

"You've got to," he said.

"You don't know how awful it is!" she wailed.

"It's too late to think of that now," he insisted.

The next moment I heard the door next to mine open and I peeped out into the corridor. Patrick Oliver passed so close to me, he could have reached out and touched my hand if I had not turned out my light so that he failed to see me. I watched him hurrying down the stairs, stepping very softly as if he did not wish to be heard. I did not realize that I was not alone until Chet Keith spoke to me from the darkness of his own room directly across the hall.

"And what do you make of that, Miss Adams?" he asked, keeping his voice quite low.

I started. "Of what?" I asked crossly, not relishing being trapped in the active role of eavesdropper.

He crossed the hall to my side. "Who's your neighbor?"

I shook my head. "I don't know, though there's a connecting door between us, of all things. There! I'm going to sneeze. I knew I'd catch my death of cold in this drafty barn."

"Don't you dare sneeze," snapped Chet Keith and without a by-your-leave pushed me back into my room, closing the door behind us to a crack through which it was barely possible to see into the corridor outside.

"Young man, you presume entirely too much," I said haughtily. "Just because you have a great deal of what the present generation calls charm, do not think you can wind me around your finger. This is the second time you have unceremoniously walked into my room. I'll thank you to walk out at once and stay out."

"Oh, for Pete's sake, be still, you old fuss-budget!" exclaimed Mr. Chet Keith.

Sheer anger throttled my tongue and at that moment I realized that the door to the next room had again opened and somebody was coming slowly down the hall toward us. The corridor was dimly lighted, but we were in complete darkness and we both saw her distinctly, the pointed wan face, the shadowed gray eyes, the coil of pale gold hair knotted on the nape of her slender neck.

"Sheila Kelly!" I whispered. "The professor's stooge!"

"And young Oliver, Thomas Canby's nephew!" said Chet Keith.

"The girl told him she couldn't go through with it, only he said she had to. He said it was too late to back out."

Chet Keith stared at me and this time it was he who said, "I don't like it. I don't like it at all."

5

UNDER THE BEST of circumstances the parlors at Lebeau Inn are not cozy, consisting of two huge cavernous rooms separated by large folding doors which are seldom closed. A dreary green carpet runs the full length of both rooms, dotted at stated intervals with clumsy sofas and stiff upright chairs upholstered in faded red plush. On this night, with the rain beating a wild tattoo against the tall windows and the wind howling around the top of the mountain like a frustrated hyena, the people gathered in the near corner betrayed a tendency to huddle together like frightened sheep. Even the fire burning dispiritedly in the open fireplace did not mitigate the gloom, and it seemed to me that everybody there had acquired Ella's habit of glancing uneasily over her shoulder.

Ella herself was sitting with the small woman with the fuzzy iron-gray hair and shoe-button eyes which had already reminded me of a Pekingese dog. Her name, it appeared, was Parrish, Mrs. Frances Parrish, although Ella persisted in calling her Fannie, much to the lady's annoyance. I thought she resented the fact that Ella had saved me a place on her other side. At any rate she continued right on with her conversation as if my arrival had been no interruption. Later I was to learn that nothing short of an earthquake or some other cataclysm of nature could check the flow of Fannie Parrish's small talk.

"Nothing, positively nothing, except that I have always wanted to see Thomas Canby in the flesh, would have persuaded me to attend another of these awful sessions," she said with emphasis.

She was the sort of woman who is unable to state anything without emphasis. "But I consider it my duty, absolutely my duty to my poor dear Theo, to forget myself. Nobody can say that I *ever* neglected my duty to my husband."

"Fannie is a widow, Adelaide," interpolated Ella.

"Frances," amended Mrs. Parrish and went right on. "Theo always said I had no head for business but he said he liked me that way. So many men do prefer little butterfly women, don't you think, Miss Adams?"

I made no reply. I was watching Professor Matthews, who was arranging a circle of chairs radiating from a small round table upon which he had placed a large parlor lamp with a dingy red silk shade. He, too, kept glancing over his shoulder, and I received the distinct impression that he was merely fidgeting to kill time while awaiting the arrival of Dora Canby and her husband. Sheila Kelly was sitting listlessly in a corner of the room, her gaze fixed upon her thin white hands which were locked in her lap. Lila Atwood and Hogan Brewster were whispering together over the head of her husband, who stared at the floor. Behind him Judy and her brother were engaged in some sort of argument. Jeff Wayne stood a little apart, his brows drawn. At the edge of the room I saw Chet Keith, frowning over a cigarette and watching Sheila Kelly, I would have said, although he took care to seem intent upon his own thoughts. Near us a nervous young mother conversed in low tones with a dyspeptic-looking old gentleman. Apparently no other guests in the hotel intended to attend the séance.

I realized that Fannie Parrish was prattling on. "Theo would want me to be here," she announced dogmatically, "if only to show Thomas Canby that in spite of his efforts to ruin my husband Theo left me well provided for."

Again Ella undertook to enlighten me. "Theo Parrish was one of the many Thomas Canby took for a ride on his way up in the world."

I suppose no man ever accumulated a great fortune without making enemies. It takes a certain amount of ruthlessness and, from what I had heard, Thomas Canby had never hesitated to wrest the advantage for himself from weaker men.

"No, I'm not the only one who has good reason to feel bitter toward Dora Canby's husband," said Fannie Parrish. "Only, as Theo used to say, I can never hold a grudge. After all, if Theo never got to be a great financial power like Thomas Canby, he did have red blood in his veins."

This somewhat cryptic utterance Ella interpreted for my benefit.

"Fannie contends that Mr. Canby isn't a flesh-and-blood man at all," she explained. "She says he's just a money-making machine."

"No wonder his poor wife walks around in a fog!" exclaimed Mrs. Parrish indignantly. "The man's inhuman!"

There was something extremely cold and calculating about the man who at that moment entered the room. Although Fannie Parrish exasperated me I felt inclined to agree with her that Thomas Canby looked as if he might have ticker tape running through his veins. He had been tall and thin even as a young man. He was almost emaciated now, and the sparse wiry hair which clung to his concave skull was gray. I have never seen a grimmer mouth or more penetrating eyes.

To my surprise Dora Canby had changed very little in twenty years. She still had mousy brown hair, unbecomingly fluffed with a curling iron, and peering, near-sighted blue eyes and a drooping mouth. I have no doubt her clothes were expensive but she looked just as dowdy as she had looked that summer when it was all her husband could do to find the money to keep her and their sick child at the inn. I recall thinking then that the woman looked crushed, as if life was too much for her. Apparently this had grown upon her with the years. Her niece Judy hurried forward to place a chair for her. Her nephew Patrick produced a small footstool for her feet. Both the professor and Lila Atwood attempted to be useful in getting Dora Canby settled. Only her husband made no fuss over her. He simply stood there, expressionless, until the to-do subsided.

"You see," murmured Fannie Parrish, "he has no sympathy to waste upon that poor soul or anybody else."

"Watch the professor," Ella whispered to me.

Under Canby's unwinking gaze Professor Thaddeus Matthews was attempting to do the honors of the occasion and making a clumsy job of it. There was sweat upon his long upper lip and his naturally booming voice betrayed him occasionally by going off into the most disconcerting squeak.

"Did you know the professor tried to call the meeting off?" asked Fannie Parrish.

Considering that she never stopped talking to listen, that woman, as I was to discover, was able to gather an astonishing amount of information.

"But Thomas Canby wouldn't let him off," she said. "I don't imagine he ever let anybody off in his life, do you?"

"Of course he knows it's a fake," I muttered, "but I dare say he realizes he will never convince his wife unless he catches the tricksters in the act."

"You can't mean you don't believe in the phenomenon, Miss Adams!" protested Fannie Parrish.

"I am unable to imagine anybody with brains being taken in by such folderol," I said severely.

Ella shrugged her shoulders. "You will feel different when this is over, Adelaide."

"Don't be absurd!" I protested irritably. "As you know perfectly well, Ella Trotter, I investigated this spiritualist racket years ago, when it swept the country. I am familiar with every one of the dodges, from ectoplasm to automatic writing. I venture to say right now I could call out the professor's paces step by step with out ever having seen him in action."

"You don't say!" breathed Fannie Parrish, staring at me with round eyes. "It must be wonderful to be so strong-minded, though as my poor dear Theo used to say, it rather puts men off, don't you think?"

This last with that complacent condescension with which even the most unhappily married women are accustomed to look upon the spinster. Nothing irritates me more and my voice has a trick of rising along with my temper.

"I have conscientiously resisted the belief that it takes a congenital idiot to rope in a man," I said, "but after scrutinizing various wives I meet I wonder if they can be accounted for on any other basis."

"Attagirl, Miss Adams. Don't let them get you down," murmured a voice behind me.

Chet Keith had pulled up a chair at my back. He leaned forward as if he intended to say something else, but Miss Maurine Smith, seeming a bit breathless, slid into the place beside him.

"I didn't think I could get off," she said, "but at the last minute old man French offered to take over the desk."

I had not known till then that Captain Bill French was still managing the inn. It gave me a turn to hear him referred to as an old man. That one summer I had spent on Mount Lebeau, Captain French had been a very dashing and gallant figure, especially among the lady guests. He had acquired his title in the Spanish-American War, and wore it and a handsome black mustache like a pair of decorations. I sighed. I supposed to a young person of Miss Smith's age anybody over forty had one foot in the grave. There was no way to escape the almost lyrical glance she bestowed upon Mr. Chet Keith, a little to his dismay, I thought.

"All's well that ends well," he murmured, leaning slightly away.

She beamed at him. "Thank goodness you're here to hold my hand if I get scared," she said naïvely. "The only time I came to one of these sittings I was paralyzed, simply paralyzed."

"Not really!" murmured Mr. Keith, squirming in his seat.

It occurred to me that, like most ladies' men, he probably had a great deal of trouble ending the flirtation which he started for one reason or another. I did not miss the glance he shot from under his eyelashes at that thin, dejected figure sitting across the room with downcast golden head and locked white hands, but if Sheila Kelly was aware of him or of anyone else in the room she gave no sign.

"If you'll close the doors," murmured Professor Matthews to Patrick Oliver, "we will begin."

With a grimace young Oliver swaggered across the room and shut the doors into the lounge and the corridor. He also, to my surprise, bolted them from the inside.

"It is absolutely necessary," intoned the professor, "that we have the strictest privacy in an experiment of this nature. Those who have passed on are extremely sensitive to the presence of un-friendly elements."

"I never knew spooks required so much coddling," remarked Patrick Oliver in a tone which he intended to sound facetious, al-though it seemed to me that, like the professor, he was inclined to quaver.

"Remarks like that," said Professor Matthews in a tone of pomp-ous dignity, "are especially hostile to the forces which we are endeavoring to invoke."

"Phooey!" exclaimed Patrick Oliver inelegantly.

"For God's sake," muttered Jeff Wayne in a tortured voice, "cut out the comedy. Can't you see nobody's in the humor for your eter-nal horseplay?"

It was, however—or so I thought—a reproachful glance from his aunt which caused Patrick Oliver to subside, that and the hand which his sister placed peremptorily upon his shoulder.

"You must understand," continued the professor with a wary glance at Thomas Canby's rigid face, "that it is impossible in an experiment of this nature to guarantee results. One can only put oneself in the way of a demonstration and hope for the best."

He again glanced, almost pleadingly it seemed to me, at Tho-mas Canby.

"How the old crook would like to be out of this business," mur-mured Chet Keith at my elbow, "but he hasn't a Chinaman's chance. Canby would crucify his own mother before he yielded a point."

I rather thought so myself, studying the millionaire's impas-sive face with the rat-trap mouth and fixed basilisk eyes.

The tremor in the professor's voice was more pronounced as he went on. "The fact that during the past two weeks we have been remarkably successful in—er—our endeavors to cross the Great Divide which separates things terrestrial from—er—the spiritual does not necessarily mean that we shall with equal success tonight rend the thin curtain between the visible and the intangible."

"The man is appallingly third rate," I muttered. "Even his pat-ter is antiquated."

"Isn't it?" murmured Chet Keith behind me.

"One would think he might have thought up something newer, if not cleverer," I remarked.

"That's what makes it so impressive," said Ella sharply. "The professor is not clever at all."

She was right. There was nothing novel about Professor Matthews. As he explained in his hoarse, faltering voice, he was by no means certain of what to expect, if anything.

"I do not claim, I never have claimed," he insisted with another abject glance at Thomas Canby, "to possess psychic powers. I have—er—only the gift of releasing those powers in another, providing that person is amenable to my—er—influence."

He then went ahead to explain in deprecating accents that Sheila Kelly did possess authentic psychic powers which she was, however, unable to free of her own volition. To liberate her psyche it was necessary, said the professor, to put her into a hypnotic trance.

"It's worse than I thought," I muttered. "How could even Dora Canby be taken in by such charlatanism? Hypnotism indeed!"

"Wait," whispered Ella.

The professor, moistening his thick lips, was saying something about Little Blue Eyes which, it seemed, was Sheila Kelly's control. At least it appeared that until recently Little Blue Eyes had been the voice through which Sheila Kelly effected communication with the spirit world.

"If that—that other will come through tonight," said the professor, his words suddenly running together so that I had some trouble understanding them, "or if it will refuse to manifest itself, I cannot say, nobody can say." He drew a long breath and ended in a tremulous quotation: "'There are more things in heaven and earth, Horatio, than are dreamt of in your philosophy.'"

"Every fake spiritualist on record takes refuge in that statement," I said scornfully.

"Only," murmured Chet Keith, "I think for the first time in his checkered career the professor has quoted Shakespeare with conviction."

I nodded, noting how Professor Matthews' liverish hand trembled as he clicked off the chandelier in the center of the room, leaving no illumination except the parlor lamp with its red silk shade, which threw a lurid and rather ghastly shadow upon the small round table where it sat. Nothing else was needed to add to the eerie atmosphere, I thought, stirring uneasily in my place. We were all now seated in the circle which was broken at one point by the table. The professor motioned the girl to a chair directly in front of it while he took up his position before her.

"Are you ready?" he asked in a hollow voice.

The girl's lips parted, but no sound came. Finally after a painful silence she nodded. There was something almost convulsive in her movement. The professor drew a long breath and then he began to wave his hands before her eyes, murmuring softly in a sonorous voice.

"Sleep. You are going to sleep. Do not fight off sleep. Sleep," he repeated over and over.

I got the impression that the girl was struggling against the monotonous spell of his voice. Her hands were clenched on the arm of the chair. In the ghastly glow of the red lamp her, face was all acute angles, as if she might also be clenching her teeth, but her eyes were already beginning to dull.

"Sleep," chanted the professor. "You must let go and sleep."

Skeptical as I was about the whole performance, there was something horrible about that unctuous voice beating down upon the girl's tense figure. The wind and the hypnotic swish of the rain seemed to be in conjunction with him, as if even the elements were conspiring to rob her of her self-mastery. I found that I, too, was clenching my hands on the arms of my chair and when, almost at once, Sheila Kelly's slim body went limp and her eyes glazed, I shuddered.

"She's under," whispered Ella.

I had not been prepared to believe that the professor possessed genuine hypnotic powers or anything else genuine. I had been convinced that he was a fake in every sense of the word, but I had not expected anything so realistic as the way that girl sagged in her chair.

"Can you speak to us?" inquired the professor. "Is the presence here?"

Sheila Kelly was moaning softly and wringing her hands. Presently she began to speak in a high piping voice, a child's voice.

"I have a message, I have a message," she said in a shrill sing-song.

"It is Little Blue Eyes," murmured the professor, looking relieved, or so it seemed to me.

"Theo sends his love," piped Sheila Kelly. "Theo says you are not to grieve. Theo does not want his Little Butterfly to be sad."

"Is there anyone here to whom this message means something?" inquired Professor Matthews with unmistakable complacence.

"Yes, oh yes!" cried Fannie Parrish breathlessly. She threw me a reproachful glance. "Isn't it marvelous? Theo always called me Little Butterfly. You can't doubt now, Miss Adams, that the phenomenon is authentic!"

I shrugged my shoulders. The message was precisely such as I had expected. I began to shake off the feeling of horror which had enveloped me. To be called Little Butterfly might convince Fannie Parrish that the message came from the other world, but I did not doubt that five minutes after her arrival at Lebeau Inn everybody in the place knew poor dear Theo's favorite name for her.

"Can Little Blue Eyes tell us anything else?" intoned the professor.

Sheila Kelly moaned again. "Somebody named Catherine has a word for Margaret," announced the childish voice.

The professor again glanced around the circle. "Is there anybody named Margaret who has a loved one Catherine in the spirit world?"

The anxious young mother leaned forward, looking very white and shaky. "I am named Margaret and Catherine, my mother, has passed on."

"You are not to worry, Margaret," chanted Little Blue Eyes. "The baby will get well."

"Isn't it wonderful!" breathed Fannie Parrish.

I raised my eyebrows at Ella. "The same old stuff!" I said.

Ella nodded. "Wait," she said again.

Little Blue Eyes had a message for somebody named James. The dyspeptic-looking old gentleman admitted that his name was James and that he had a deceased brother Peter, but did not seem impressed when warned by Little Blue Eyes that Peter advised against his taking a trip to the West Indies in his present state of health.

"I have told several people here, including Mrs. Parrish, that my brother Peter died last spring," he said dryly, "and I suppose anybody with eyes could observe that my health is unequal to an extended trip."

To my relief I discovered that I had completely retrieved my cynical attitude toward the whole business. I had attended enough séances to recognize the messages for the stereotyped forms which they were. I felt sure they originated in the brain of Professor Matthews. How far the girl was involved I was not prepared to say. That she was actually in some sort of hypnotic trance I was reluctantly inclined to concede.

The professor was speaking again. "Has Little Blue Eyes anything else to give us?" he asked, fumbling nervously at his tie.

Sheila Kelly sat up suddenly in her chair. "To hell with Little Blue Eyes," she said distinctly.

Dora Canby uttered a stifled wail. "Gloria! Gloria!"

Sheila Kelly looked at her. "Don't be more of a damned fool than usual, Mother," she said.

The voice was brazen and defiant, with a mocking, perverse harshness that was indescribably shocking. I saw Thomas Canby whiten. I saw him shrink as Sheila Kelly turned upon him.

"You killed me," she said. "You think you are God because you have made a god of money and can buy and sell people's souls. So you killed me, but I can't rest in my grave. I never will rest in my grave while you are alive."

She had started to her feet. She stood there swaying as she confronted Thomas Canby, a thin slight girl in a crumpled white evening gown, clutching a large chiffon handkerchief to her breast. Even in that dim room, lighted only by the red lamp and the dying fire, I could see her blazing cheeks and the dreadful look in her eyes as they traveled slowly around that circle of blanched faces.

"You all hate him," she said, "just as you hated me. But not one of you has the guts to stand up against him. Even you, Mother, would have let him put me away. Only he couldn't put me away far enough. Not even six feet under the ground was deep enough or wide enough."

She laughed horribly, and the blood in my veins crawled as something slid across my instep. I thought for one awful minute that it was a worm which she had brought with her out of the tomb. Then I saw it was merely the extension cord to the red lamp which was attached to a floor socket half the width of the room from the table upon which it sat.

Sheila Kelly had turned again to Thomas Canby, who cowered in his seat. "You destroyed my soul!" she cried. "Doomed me to wander forever without peace, but I will no longer wander alone!"

Her voice had risen to a screech, the hair stirred upon my scalp. Behind me I heard Chet Keith smother a cry. Ella clutched my hand, and then the lights went out, followed almost at once by that horrible groan which at times still echoes in my ears. For a moment I think we were all frozen in our seats. I know I was still sitting there, petrified with horror, when Chet Keith snapped on the central chandelier. Even then I could not move. I do not think anybody moved or even breathed. The girl, Sheila Kelly, was lying in a huddle in the center of the room, and in his chair Thomas Canby was weaving slowly from side to side with a hideous gash in his throat from which the blood gushed in a ghastly fountain.

6

IT IS DIFFICULT even now, in spite of how often it has been threshed over, for me to say exactly what happened in those dreadful ten minutes after the lights came on again and we saw Thomas Canby gasping in his death agony, unable to speak because his throat was cut from ear to ear, but with the most terrible urgency in his sunken eyes as his thin, bloodless hands clawed the air.

I have a confused recollection of Judy Oliver burying her head against Jeff Wayne's shoulder, of his arms tightening about her; of Dora Canby sitting there in a state of suspended animation, staring not at the dying man beside her but at that limp figure huddled on the floor at her feet; of Lila Atwood catching her husband's sleeve and turning him away so he could not see his uncle; of Hogan Brewster for once in his life confronting something which he could not meet with flippancy; of Patrick Oliver holding onto the back of his chair and crying "Oh, God!" over and over in a thin whisper; of Professor Matthews, looking suddenly old and stricken, covering his face with an agued hand.

At my side Fannie Parrish, being completely without inhibitions, was indulging in a fit of hysterics. Ella had gone quite rigid. Back of me Miss Maurine Smith was uttering a series of sharp bleating cries, not unlike a stuck sheep. The young mother was trying to tell the dyspeptic old gentleman that he must not look while he was assuring her that he had no intention of doing so, although he did not once remove his eyes from that crimson gap in Thomas

Canby's throat which widened as life went out of the body and the head fell back against the top of the chair.

Over by the door Chet Keith still stood with his hand on the light switch. I have never seen anything sharper than his blue eyes as he looked us all over.

"Don't touch him!" he said sharply when Patrick Oliver took a tentative step toward the dead man.

"But oughtn't we to do something?" demanded Lila Atwood, only the slightest tremor marring her lovely voice. "He—maybe he isn't dead."

Chet Keith's blue eyes raked hers. "He's dead all right," he said. "No doubt of that."

I glanced at that ashen face lying back against the headrest of the chair. No, there was nothing anybody could do for Thomas Canby.

"The authorities will want everything left exactly as it is," Chet Keith went on. His voice grated, "After all, this is murder."

"Murder!" whispered Sheila Kelly.

She had dragged herself to her feet. She stood there trembling. Nobody went to her assistance. Everyone stared at her with unconcealed horror. She flung up her hand as if to ward off our hostile gaze or possibly to shut out the sight of that sagging form in the chair.

"I didn't kill him," she whispered.

Her eyes traveled piteously around the circle. "I didn't kill him," she repeated in a lifeless voice and began to tear the handkerchief in her hands to pieces, as if she had to do something. It appeared to me that her gaze rested longest upon Professor Matthews, but he did not look at her. He was shivering. He could not seem to stop.

Fannie Parrish started up from her chair. "I'm going to my room!" she wailed.

Chet Keith shook his head. "Nobody can leave until the officers arrive."

"I can't, I won't stay in this horrible place!" cried Fannie.

"I think so," murmured Mr. Chet Keith, standing with his back four-square against the door.

"I'm going to be sick!" shrieked Fannie, turning quite green.

"Nonsense!" I exclaimed crossly. "You can't. There aren't any facilities for your being sick in this room."

Fannie gulped, but she went back to her seat, and Chet Keith gave me a grateful glance. Apparently, like myself, he knew enough feminine psychology to realize that Fannie Parrish was the last woman in the world to be messy in public, and when Miss Maurine Smith attempted to throw a faint in his arms he disposed of her very neatly upon one of the hard red sofas where she immediately came to, looking remarkably chagrined.

Somebody was pounding on the door. "What's the trouble in here?" demanded a voice. "What's happened?"

Chet Keith frowned as he slid the bolt back. I thought he wished he could postpone the interruption, but there was no help for it. Captain Bill French was not a man who could be put off when he saw his duty and he was the manager of Mount Lebeau Inn. The fact that he was also a veteran of the war of '98 did not prevent his turning as green as Fannie when he saw that ghastly figure across the room.

"For God's sake, what's happened?" he cried again.

Chet Keith shrugged his shoulders. "I should think it is self-evident," he said coolly. "One of your guests has been murdered."

"Murdered!" quavered Captain French, and I realized that Miss Smith was right. The dashing widower of twenty years before had become an old man with a paunch and a toupee.

For the first time Dora Canby spoke. "It's my scissors," she said, looking like the etching of a woman which had blurred. "He was killed with half of my scissors."

I had until that moment been too rattled to identify the object, the hilt of which still protruded from Thomas Canby's throat, but it undoubtedly was half a pair of scissors. The handle was gold-washed and represented some sort of bird, a swan probably, only half of it was missing.

"It is Aunt Dora's scissors," whispered Judy Oliver. She stepped forward, but Chet Keith was too quick for her.

"Don't touch it," he said sharply. "I've warned you, nothing must be touched."

Jeff Wayne glanced bitterly at Sheila Kelly's bowed head.

"What's the difference?" he demanded. "The case is open and shut. *She*—into the words he put almost savage hatred—"she killed him. We all saw it."

I frowned at him. "Are you able to see in the dark, Mr. Wayne?" I inquired sharply.

"In the dark? No, of course not, but we all heard her. We all know she killed him."

"I didn't," whispered Sheila Kelly.

Chet Keith looked at her. "You're on the spot," he said curtly. "If you'll take my advice you'll say nothing until the authorities arrive."

She gave him a wondering glance as if she could not make him out, but she took his advice.

It was Allan Atwood's nerves, characteristically enough, which first frazzled under the strain. "You've no right to keep us cooped up here with a murderess!" he cried. "Wait for the sheriff if you like. I'm getting out."

"No," said Chet Keith and then asked, "So you knew your uncle had sent for the sheriff?"

Allan Atwood turned very white. "You—you said the sheriff was coming," he stammered.

Chet Keith shook his head. "I haven't mentioned the sheriff."

"Allan means," interposed Lila Atwood quickly, "that we all knew Uncle Thomas had sent for the sheriff."

Chet Keith eyed her steadily but she had a gaze as level as his own.

"Did you know your uncle had summoned an officer?" he asked Judy Oliver suddenly.

She shook her head, and with a smile Lila Atwood amended her previous statement. "I should have said that any of us could have heard him telephoning. It was just before dinner, and we were all in Aunt Dora's sitting room."

"I see," murmured Chet Keith.

Captain French abruptly realized that he was cutting no sort of figure in the proceedings. "Mr. Keith is right," he said. "You must all remain here until the authorities arrive." He twisted the ends of his mustache nervously. "Though heaven knows, the thing is clear enough."

Dora Canby roused herself from the apathy in which she seemed to have sunk. "He tried to put her away," she said. "If Gloria had lived her father would have put her in an institution." She stretched out her hands to Sheila Kelly in a gesture of passionate tenderness. "He ruined your life, my darling, just as he ruined mine. You had to kill him, didn't you? Mother knows you had to kill him."

"Don't! Oh, please don't!" cried Sheila Kelly, in an agonized voice.

Judy Oliver sobbed once. "It's too awful! I can't bear it!"

She turned blindly and again would have buried her face upon Jeff Wayne's shoulder, but he moved aside and glared at Sheila Kelly.

"What I want to know is," he demanded in a smothered voice, "where is the other half of those scissors?"

Allan Atwood flung out his hands in a wild gesture. "I suppose she is saving it for the rest of us!" he cried. "She hated us all! As much as she hated him!"

Hogan Brewster smiled. "It was you, wasn't it, Allan, who told Thomas Canby that his daughter put arsenic in his soup?"

"I didn't!" cried Allan Atwood furiously. "I merely told him that I saw Gloria take some of the weed killer from the shelf in the gardener's room."

"Gloria only took the weed killer to kill a mouse in the attic. It was annoying her," murmured Dora Canby. "You told me so, didn't you, darling?" she asked Sheila Kelly.

The girl flung her a despairing glance. "Please, Mrs. Canby," she said brokenly.

The professor suddenly came to life. "It's all your fault!" he cried, shaking his fist at the girl. "You couldn't let well enough alone. Do you realize that we'll both go to the electric chair for this night's work?"

"I don't get it," whispered young Patrick Oliver. The professor gave him a malevolent glance. "At that we may have company," he said.

Allan Atwood laughed unpleasantly. "Take care, Pat, that you don't get the other half of those scissors in your throat. If I remember rightly our cousin Gloria had it in for you too; something about Judy's ear, I think."

"Gloria did not intend to chip Judy's ear with the can opener," said Dora Canby with a shudder. "It was an accident, wasn't it, darling?" she asked Sheila Kelly.

The girl quivered all over, though this time she did not protest, and Patrick Oliver flung her a bitter glance. "Sure it was an accident," he said, "but if I hadn't jogged her elbow she would have gouged Judy's eye out."

Dora Canby glanced at him reproachfully. "Gloria believed that Judy had stolen Jeff's heart away from her."

Jeff Wayne's hands clenched. "Gloria was mistaken," he said, staring steadily at Sheila Kelly. "Gloria is the only woman I ever loved or can love."

Judy Oliver caught her breath as if he had struck her, but Dora Canby smiled at her and then at Jeff.

"I know, I know, my boy," she said softly. "You belong to Gloria, doesn't he, darling?" she asked Sheila Kelly.

The girl flung out her arms in a gesture of despair. "Make her stop!" she cried. "Can't you make her stop?"

She addressed Chet Keith, but I found myself unable to keep still.

"You are laboring under a delusion, Mrs. Canby," I said. "Whatever else she may be, this girl is not the reincarnation of your daughter Gloria. You have been the victim of a cruel trick. The dead do not come back."

"Precisely," said Chet Keith.

"I think you are the newspaperman whom my husband threatened to kick off the mountain," murmured Dora Canby. "Poor Thomas, he was always threatening to kick somebody out; first Patrick because he is always in debt, then Judy because she tried to steal Gloria's lover, then Allan because he will not stop his wife from dragging us all into a scandal, and finally you, Mr. Keith, isn't it? But Thomas will never threaten anybody else. Gloria has revenged herself, haven't you, darling?"

"Oh, God!" whispered Sheila Kelly.

I cannot explain why I was possessed to defend the girl, unless it was because she was so utterly alone.

"If she killed Thomas Canby she was merely acting under suggestion!" I exclaimed and pointed my finger dramatically at Professor Matthews. "Under his suggestion!"

To my horror the professor began to weep. "See what you've done!" he cried, again shaking his fist in Sheila Kelly's face. "I tell you we'll both go to the electric chair!"

He was a horrible, sniveling object, one that unmanned me, but Hogan Brewster seemed amused at the spectacle.

"That amounts practically to a confession," he said.

"You think so?" drawled Chet Keith. "Why did they do it?"

"It's apparent on the face of it," said Allan Atwood quickly. "They have Aunt Dora wound about their finger. She is capable of spending a fortune on them, but Uncle Thomas was going to send them packing, so they killed him."

"And what good will a fortune do them in the electric chair?" demanded Chet Keith.

"Oh, but they'll never send my Gloria to the chair," murmured Dora Canby. "You can't electrocute somebody who is already dead."

"Anyway," I put in quickly, "the girl was hypnotized. She was not responsible for her actions. We can all swear to that."

Hogan Brewster gave Chet Keith a triumphant glance. "Turn a good lawyer loose with that defense and plenty of the Canby money and see how far the prosecuting attorney will get with a conviction," he said.

The professor was sniveling again. "They'll say I did it. They'll say I put her up to it."

"Of course you did," snapped Chet Keith.

And then the sheriff arrived, accompanied by two deputies.

I was informed later that Sheriff Tom Latham was serving his third term, and when it came to locating stills in the mountains and breaking up a fight at a country dance he was probably a highly efficient weapon of the law, as were Butch Newby and Mart Butler, his assistants and only slightly less burly versions of the grizzled sheriff. I could picture the three of them wading lustily into a free-for-all and cracking heads and otherwise enforcing the peace in a rural community, but in the complicated and sinister tangle which awaited them at Mount Lebeau Inn on that stormy July night they were hopelessly inadequate without the saving grace of realizing as much.

It was Chet Keith who again assumed the initiative and gave Sheriff Latham in a curt and succinct manner an account of what had happened. The sheriff interrupted him only once and then to send one of his henchmen to telephone for the coroner. It appeared that the rain was assuming the proportions of a cloudburst, and the sheriff had some uneasiness about the bridge over the Carol River.

"All we need to make this disaster complete," I muttered to Ella, "is to have that pontoon bridge wash out."

Sheriff Latham gave me a severe glance from under his beetling brows. "We'll have no whispering," he said.

I tossed my head and Chet Keith grinned as he went on with his recital. It was his newspaper training, I suppose, which enabled him to present the facts in the fewest possible words without omitting any of the essential details.

"Anybody else anything to add?" inquired Sheriff Latham at the end, treating us all to one of his heavy scowls.

Nobody said anything and Sheriff Latham, chewing his thick underlip, studied Sheila Kelly in silence for a moment.

"What's your name?" he asked. "Your real name, not your stage moniker."

She flushed. "Kelly is my real name, Sheila Kelly." The sheriff frowned and jerked a splayed thumb in the direction of Professor Thaddeus Matthews. "How long you been teamed up with the old codger?"

"Six months, maybe a little more," she said in a low voice.

"What were you doing before you joined his act?"

"Starving."

"Eh?"

"I'd been out of work for almost a year," she said wearily.

"And before that?"

"Ask him," she said, shrugging her shoulder at Chet Keith.

I thought he flinched as the sheriff whirled upon him. "You knew this girl before?"

"Yes."

"How come you didn't say so?" demanded the sheriff.

Mr. Chet Keith's usual nonchalance was badly cracked, but he made an attempt at his customary insouciance.

"I was waiting for the proper moment," he said airily.

"This is it," snapped the sheriff. "Where did you know this dame before and what do you know about her?"

Chet Keith hesitated, but Sheila Kelly made a small gesture as if relieving him of responsibility. "You may as well tell," she said. "I'm already in so bad nothing can make it worse."

"She was a fan dancer in a night club in Chicago. The joint was raided. I covered the story for my paper."

"So you were a fan dancer," remarked the sheriff in a scathing tone.

"I had to eat," said Sheila Kelly.

"So she said at the time," commented Chet Keith. "That's why the judge let her off with a warning."

The sheriff's florid face darkened. "And then you tied up with this fake spiritualist?"

The girl's haggard eyes turned to the professor. "It was just— just an act until—I mean, there was no harm in the—the messages, or so he said," she faltered. "Lots of people were comforted by them."

"It was getting money under false pretenses, to say the best."

She flushed painfully. "Nobody ever gave us money until . . ."

She paused and again glanced at the professor.

"You are trying to say," I interposed, "that until you made this connection with Dora Canby it was just a vaudeville turn."

"Yes."

The sheriff glared at me. "I ain't asked for your assistance, lady," he said, then turned back to the girl, his small muddy eyes narrowing. "Vaudeville turns don't end in murder," he snapped.

Her drooping lips twitched convulsively. "No," she whispered.

Once more, in spite of the sheriff's glare, I took a hand in the deal. "You say the professor told you the messages were harmless. Don't you know?"

Her thin white hands turned and twisted in her lap. "No."

The sheriff wriggled his heavy shoulders. "Are you trying to make out that you was really hypnotized?" he demanded.

"Yes."

"So that's your story?" he demanded with impressive sarcasm. "You was hypnotized and don't know what you was doing when you killed this man."

She started to her feet, her eyes quite wild. "I didn't kill him! I didn't!"

"Thought you was hypnotized?" sneered the sheriff. "Thought you didn't know what happened while you was in this trance?"

She was trembling from head to foot. "You don't remember what you do in a hypnotic trance unless you are ordered to remember, but I—I didn't kill him! I couldn't have!"

"Oh yeah?" murmured Sheriff Latham, exchanging a knowing grin with the younger of his henchmen, the one called Butch, for obvious reasons, or so it seemed to me.

The girl's defiant pose faltered and broke. "I didn't kill him," she repeated dully.

"Yep," said Sheriff Latham, "you killed him, sister. You two saw a chance to feather your nest for life with that poor woman you've imposed upon, but her husband was going to show you up for a fraud, so you killed him."

It would have been better had I kept my mouth shut, but I didn't.

"It is a scientific fact, Sheriff Latham," I said, "that hypnotic subjects are not amenable to suggestions which are averse to their moral code."

The sheriff glared at me again and I do not take kindly to such treatment, so I went on with considerable heat. "I have a book which explains all about hypnosis," I said and then paused abruptly. "At least I have mislaid the book for the moment, but it leaves no doubt upon this point. A hypnotic subject cannot be made to perform an act which violates his inherent sense of right and wrong."

I saw Chet Keith frown, and Ella stared at me curiously. In the excitement of my arrival she had chosen for reasons of her, own to ignore the book which was my excuse for being there at all, but by her expression I knew that she was thinking it extremely unlike me to mislay something and say nothing about it.

The sheriff continued to regard me with pronounced disfavor.

"I haven't asked your advice, lady," he repeated, "but since you seem determined to butt into this business I'd like to inform you that we may live in the backwoods, so to speak, but we wasn't born yesterday, eh, Butch, and we ain't having no wool pulled over our eyes."

There is on use denying that the man stirred all my hackles.

"I take it," I said coldly, "that you put no faith in my theory that it would be impossible for the professor to suggest murder or any other crime to the young lady after he had placed her in a hypnotic trance?"

Behind me Chet Keith groaned. "Good Lord," he whispered, "must you provide the professor with an out?"

The sheriff gave me an acrimonious glance. "I not only don't take no stock in your theory," he announced, "I don't take no stock in hypnotism or any of the rest of this twaddle."

"You tell 'em, Lathe," murmured Butch.

"Nevertheless," said Chet Keith quietly, "hypnotism is a scientific fact and the girl was hypnotized, whether you believe it or not."

Sheriff Latham permitted himself a skeptical grimace. "Dress it up as fancy as you please," he said, "She killed a man with the professor's help, and I'm taking both of 'em in for murder."

I glanced involuntarily at Professor Thaddeus Matthews. To my surprise he had recovered his composure. He was even smiling. I saw Chet Keith studying him with a frown.

"You're arresting Sheila Kelly and the professor without further investigation?" demanded the newspaperman.

The sheriff nodded. "Don't need to investigate what happened. It's as plain as the nose on my face"—which was very plain indeed.

Sheila Kelly's face was ashen. I thought she was about to faint, but Dora Canby went over to her and laid her hand on her arm.

"Nothing is going to happen to you, Gloria," said Mrs. Canby.

The girl shrank away and covered her eyes with her hand.

Sheriff Latham motioned to Butch. "Bring them on," he said. "I want to git down off this mountain while we can."

But he was already too late. At that moment Captain French bustled into the room, his mustache bristling with excitement.

"The bridge is out!" he exclaimed. "The coroner just called up from a filling station down the road. It went out just after he crossed."

I distinctly heard Chet Keith mutter, "Thank God!"

7

SO THERE WE WERE, isolated on the top of a mountain with a dead man and two people accused of his murder and no chance to get away until they recovered the pontoon bridge which Captain French assured us was careening at breakneck speed down the Carol River.

"However, the highway department is on the job," he said.

Ella sniffed. "Whatever that may mean."

"It means more of the brand of efficiency which we have already seen demonstrated by Sheriff Latham and his yokels," I said bitterly.

The sheriff had taken things over with a vengeance. I think he enjoyed the thought of spending a day or two in enforced idleness as a guest of the inn. At any rate he commandeered two of the best rooms in the house for himself and his men, rooms directly across the hall from those occupied by Sheila Kelly and the professor.

"Got to keep an eye on the prisoners," explained the sheriff.

Chet Keith cocked an eyebrow at me. "That puts you right in the front row, Miss Adams."

I nodded, but to tell the truth I was not so averse as I might have seemed to occupying quarters in such close proximity to those three burly protectors of the law. While I had no respect for Sheriff Latham's acumen, and even less for the type of brains exhibited by his sinewy assistants, I did think they possessed a great deal of unimaginative courage and muscular initiative and there was something reassuring about knowing that they were just across the hall when I went up to my room shortly before midnight that night.

It was still raining furiously, and I have never heard a place so full of odd creakings and rattlings as that old frame building. As Ella said, coming in with me as if she hated the thought of being left alone, you were always thinking you heard something behind you but when you looked there was nothing there. I suppose each of us was painfully conscious, though neither of us admitted it, of that sheeted form which had been locked in the rear parlor after the coroner had arrived and executed what I can describe only as the gesture of an examination.

The coroner was staying on, so I gathered, there being nothing else for him to do. They were, I understood, planning to hold an inquest the next morning. A mere formality, insisted Sheriff Latham, since in his opinion the case was cut and dried. In the meanwhile Thomas Canby's body was left to rest in peace upon one of those dreary red sofas in that depressing parlor downstairs from which everybody was to be excluded until further orders.

"As if anybody would want to look at the horrible place again!" I cried with a shudder.

Ella nodded. "Do you know, Adelaide, I think that good-looking young newspaperman is in love with Sheila Kelly."

I had had somewhat the same idea, but it is second nature with me to take the opposite tack from Ella.

"Don't be absurd!" I protested. "He's the kind that chucks every woman he sees under the chin if he can get by with it."

"I think he's rather sweet," murmured Ella.

"Sweet!" I exclaimed. "You might call him a conceited young upstart who has too much sex appeal for his own good, but never sweet."

"Just the same," pursued Ella, whom nothing ever throws off the track, "he means to get her out of it."

I frowned. "I'm afraid that will take some doing."

Ella stared at me. "Are you on their side?"

"I'm on nobody's side," I declared irritably.

Ella did not seem greatly impressed by my vehemence. She has always exasperated me by pretending to believe that my bark is more formidable than my bite.

"Of course she will have all of Dora Canby's money working for her," she said and gave me a significant glance. "I suppose you realize that it is her money now, Adelaide."

Ella has a penchant for picking up what she calls wisecracks, but I have as a rule avoided her example, only in this instance nothing else seemed quite apropos.

"So what?" I demanded.

"You can't get away from the strangled canary, Adelaide, and those two mutilated cats."

"Are you still trying to tell me that Gloria Canby's spirit has managed in some way to take possession of Sheila Kelly's body?" I demanded impatiently.

"You weren't at the other séances," said Ella in a stubborn voice. "They started out to be the usual thing. You heard Little Blue Eyes tonight. All the messages were like that at first, as innocuous as new milk. Little Blue Eyes had a message for Gloria's dear mother. Gloria's mother was not to grieve. Gloria was very, very happy in the spirit world—that sort of thing. If they had continued in that vein I should never have got the wind up. Please credit me with that much intelligence, Adelaide, difficult as you may find it to do so."

I was listening to the muffled sound which was a girl weeping forlornly and very softly on the other side of the partition, and merely shrugged my shoulders by way of reply.

"I still say," insisted Ella, "that the first time this new personality shoved Little Blue Eyes off the scene Professor Matthews was flabbergasted. It was exactly as if Charlie MacCarthy had suddenly come to life and started kicking Eddie Bergen around."

"The girl was in some sort of trance," I declared. "I said I'd swear to it and I will."

Ella paid no attention. "The professor is as crooked as a pretzel. I think he'd stoop to anything to turn a dishonest penny for himself; anything except murder. I don't believe he has either the intestinal fortitude or the ingenuity to concoct so elaborate a plot as this."

"That rounds out the circle," I commented sourly. "You don't think the professor put Sheila Kelly up to murder, but you do think she killed Thomas Canby while temporarily under the spell of his dead daughter, and you base your preposterous theory upon two disemboweled cats and a strangled canary."

Ella tossed her head. "You can make it sound as ridiculous as you please, Adelaide, but something gets into that girl and it's something devilish."

"Poppycock!"

"You saw her tonight in the dining room. Do you think she knew what she was doing when she spoke to Hogan Brewster? Do you think she remembers a word of that tirade against Thomas Canby? Any more than she was able to recall what had happened when she came to in her room yesterday afternoon with the dead canary clutched in her hands."

"So it must have been a phantom," I said with appreciable disdain.

Ella got angrily to her feet. "I should know better by this time than to argue with you. Thank heaven I, at least, have always had an open mind."

"Too open," I retorted, "considering the rubbish you put into it."

Upon this she flounced out of the room and a few minutes later I heard her door slam. I was conscious of being bitterly tired, yet as I began my preparations for bed I realized that I had never been more wide awake in my life nor less anxious to be left alone with my thoughts and the sound of that forlorn weeping in the next room. When I heard the rap at the door I was positive it was Ella, returning as usual for the last word. I did not replace the row of false curls which I wear across my forehead, Ella not harboring any more illusions about my physical shortcomings than I do about hers. However, when I opened the door it was not Ella.

"You've got to help me, Miss Adams," said Chet Keith, brushing past me into the room.

"Young man," I began in my most intimidating manner, which as a rule is no laughing matter, but he was neither intimidated nor abashed.

"I know I called you a snapping turtle and an old fuss-budget," he interrupted with a grin which was definitely meant to be disarming, "but I'm at my wit's end and I need somebody whose head is screwed on tight." For the second time I admired his grasp of feminine psychology.

"I recognize this as a sample of your skill in getting around the female of the genus," I remarked rather weakly. "Nevertheless I am prepared to listen to your request, though I can promise nothing else."

So far from being disheartened by my lukewarm reception of his dramatic appeal, he had the impudence to place me upon the defensive.

"For heaven's sake," he exclaimed, "stop trying to shove that switch or whatever it is out of sight! Do you think I've been a newspaperman for ten years without knowing that most women keep their beauty secrets in the dresser drawer at night?"

I was for one of the few times in my life at a complete loss for words, but I assume that my gaze was eloquent enough as I thrust my false hair out of view.

"Sorry," he said, looking like an embarrassed small boy.

"I imagine your mother believed in sparing the rod and spoiling the child," I said loftily.

Again his grin was disarming. "I do not remember my mother, Miss Adams. I came up like a weed, selling newspapers in New York, then office boy for a big daily, promoted, if you care to call it that, to leg man for one of the tabloids, later taken on as feature writer on a Chicago paper. Not much of a career perhaps—a poor thing, but my own. What I'm trying to get over is that I've never had a leg up from anybody. I've never asked one till now."

His face was quite red. I imagined, as no doubt I was meant to, that Mr. Chet Keith had been a lone wolf all his life and that it went decidedly against his grain to be anything else. I was also aware that I was succumbing to his charm and that he knew it.

"What precisely do you want me to do?" I inquired.

"Help me engineer an interview with that girl next door," he said promptly.

For the second time his audacity reduced me to speechlessness, but he pretended not to notice. "They're having the inquest in the morning," he said. "I've got to talk to her first."

"If I heard correctly the sheriff left orders that she and her accomplice were to be held strictly incommunicado," I said, eying him severely, "and unless my eyes deceive me a deputy is stationed in the hall outside for that express purpose."

"I don't imagine your eyes deceive you very often," he said with his flippant though ingratiating smile.

"Are you suggesting that I help you compound a felony?" I demanded.

He grinned. "What's a little felony between friends?"

"Aside from the fact that we are not friends," I said haughtily, "I happen to be a law-abiding citizen. And anyway, the door between my room and that unfortunate girl's is locked. I've tried it."

"I bet you have," chuckled Mr. Chet Keith.

He then proceeded to produce a slender, sinister-looking object which I instinctively recognized as a skeleton key, though I had never seen one before.

"You never know when one of these is going to come in handy in my business," he murmured and strolled over to the door which connected my room with Sheila Kelly's.

"You actually propose with my connivance to talk to that girl against the sheriff's orders?"

He grinned. "And how!" he said and placed the key in the lock.

"Of course you realize," I said sternly, "that it is my duty to report you to Sheriff Latham before this goes any farther."

"Sure, only you won't. Come on."

"Come on?" I stammered.

"I told you I had to have help," he said. "She wouldn't see me alone."

I stared at him and he smiled ruefully. "Miss Sheila Kelly unfortunately formed the opinion, when I met her some months ago, that no woman was quite safe in my presence from more or less dishonorable proposals."

"So you propositioned her that time she was arrested?" I suggested.

"If you must know," he said, "I did and got the worst turning down in my experience."

"I suppose you thought a fan dancer who had been arrested in a raided night club was easy game," I remarked scornfully.

"At that time," said Chet Keith with a grimace, "I thought all women were easy."

He again laid his hand upon the door, but once more I stopped him.

"Just how do you propose to account to the deputy in the hall outside for your prolonged presence in my room?" I inquired.

He grinned. "Didn't I tell you? I'm supposed to be interviewing you for a feature article on 'How to Live Alone and Like It,'" he said impudently and took advantage of my outraged stare to open the door into Sheila Kelly's room.

She was lying face downward across her bed, still wearing that bedraggled white evening gown, and her eyes were red with weeping, but she sprang to her feet when I entered and stood staring at me, her gaze quite frantic. To my relief there was no connecting door between her room and the professor's. That was the first thing of which I made certain. The available space was taken up by two bathrooms, as in the case of the wall between my room and Ella's.

Somewhat to my surprise Chet Keith had not followed me, seeming at the last minute to be overcome by the first sign of shyness which I had seen him betray. "If she isn't dressed tell her to put on something in a hurry," he called out.

The girl flushed. "What do you want?" she demanded.

"To talk to you of course." He sounded cross. "Come in here where the deputy can't hear our voices."

"There's nothing to say," she protested bitterly. "I'm done for."

"You've always been too hardheaded for your own good," he snapped.

"Because I didn't fall for your line?" she said.

"Do we have to go into that again?" he asked. "I thought we agreed the day you walked out on me that I was a heel. Can't we let it go at that?"

"I saw you tonight," she said, "kissing that girl at the desk before you hardly set foot in the house."

"Sure," he admitted with a scowl, "I said I was a heel."

I glanced nervously at the door. "Don't you think we had better transfer this discussion to my room?"

I had no desire to be caught by Sheriff Latham's man in the act of talking to his prisoner behind his back. Sheila Kelly looked at me.

"You are Mrs. Trotter's friend?" she asked. "The one who was bringing the book?"

"So you knew about that," I murmured, eying her sharply. "Apparently everybody knew about it."

"Mrs. Trotter told Mrs. Parrish," said the girl, as if that were sufficient explanation. Which it was, so far as I was concerned.

"Fortunately, although the book is missing, I have all the information in my head," I said.

Not until later did I realize what a dangerous admission that was and how close it came to signing my death warrant. It might have been different if Chet Keith had not been too busy herding us into the other room to listen to that brief byplay between Sheila Kelly and me. On the other hand, probably nothing could have stopped the malignant spirit which was at work in Lebeau Inn, not until it had played out its tragic hand.

"Well," murmured the girl, "you've had your way. Where do we go from here?"

It seemed to me that young Mr. Keith was rather put to it to answer that question, though it may have been the truculent manner in which she stared at him that threw him momentarily off his stride.

"What on earth possessed you to walk into a racket like this?" he demanded.

"I told you. I was starving. I had to have work and—and the professor isn't a bad old duck."

"Letting him hypnotize you! You must have been crazy!"

"No, just hungry and desperate. You'd be surprised at what even you might do if you hadn't eaten in three days."

"I've been hungry and desperate too," he said grimly.

"And at first hypnotism didn't enter into the contract," she went on. He stared at her. "No?"

"When I signed on the hypnotism stuff was supposed to be all fake, part of the racket, you know. I was just—just to pretend to be in a trance. I don't know when—when it ceased to be like that. I don't even know when I realized that I wasn't pretending any more."

"The old bastard!" growled Chet Keith.

I nodded. "In the beginning they often make the subject think he is faking a hypnosis, in order to break down his resistance to mental suggestion," I said, "or so I've been told."

Her eyes were curiously dull. "At first I was horrified. I think"— she drew her hand confusedly across her brow—"I think I threatened to quit but—but I didn't, did I? Lately I—I don't seem to have worried about it. You can get used to anything. I think I decided it was—was easier than trying to fake a trance. It's just like going to sleep, you know, and waking up tired and limp but without any responsibility for how good or how rotten you were in the act."

Chet Keith glanced at me. We both had the same thought, I feel sure. The girl had played into the professor's hand. She had permitted him to gain control of her will power and now she could not throw off his influence if she tried. Worse still, or so it appeared to me, she had been robbed of the desire to try.

"And then," said Chet Keith in a tight voice, "our friend Dora Canby entered the picture."

She turned very white. "Yes."

"Did you know she was in the audience that first afternoon?"

She shook her head. "I never heard her name until the professor told me we were coming up here to give private readings for her."

He was watching her intently. "Nevertheless Little Blue Eyes delivered a message from Gloria to her mother that first day."

She flushed. "The professor was Little Blue Eyes," she said with a trace of defiance. "I never remember what I say in a trance."

"Or do?"

She flung him an agonized glance. "But I didn't kill Thomas Canby! I couldn't have!"

"Whatever you said or did in a trance the professor suggested to you?" I put in quickly.

She hesitated. "It was like that until—until . . ."

"Go on, until what?" asked Chet Keith in a sharp voice.

She glanced over her shoulder. "I'm sure the professor didn't know about the canary," she whispered.

He frowned. "What canary?"

"Dora Canby's pet canary," said the girl in a stifled voice. "The professor would never have suggested anything like that to me. He may be crooked but he isn't vicious. He's been square with me. I mean, kind and considerate, almost fatherly. And he—he likes birds."

Chet Keith scowled. "What happened to Mrs. Canby's canary?"

She shuddered. "It was strangled."

"Strangled!"

"I came to in my room. I felt tired and limp, just as I do after I've been in a trance, only I was not supposed to have been in one. I—I had the canary in my hands and it had been—it was dead!"

Her voice rose to a wail and I shivered.

Chet Keith leaned forward and laid his hand over her trembling fingers. "Take it easy," he said more gently than I would have believed possible. "So you weren't supposed to be in a trance?"

"No."

"Has it happened before or since? Your going off like that out of office hours?" he asked.

"Never until—until lately."

"But it *has* happened before?"

"Yes," she said, her face stark with fear.

"You've come to yourself unable to account for your actions during a period of time?"

"Yes."

She stared at him and her eyes were dreadful. "That's what makes it so horrible!" she cried. "I just come to and I don't know—I don't know how I got where I am or what—what I've been doing."

"This afternoon, for instance?" I inquired.

She looked at me and I saw the panic in her eyes. "Yes," she said.

"Where were you when you woke up?" I demanded.

"Down on the road," she whispered. "On the road where Thomas Canby was nearly killed and my—my hands were covered with dirt as if—as if I had been digging in the ground."

I am certain she heard me gasp, but not a muscle in Chet Keith's face moved.

"Then later tonight in the dining room," she went on hysterically, "I was quietly eating my dinner. Only all at once, I don't know how, I found myself clear across the room and the professor was shaking me."

"Yes?" said Chet Keith softly.

"There was a man there I had never seen before, but the professor said I called him by name."

"The man was Hogan Brewster," I explained. "You called him Shot. It seems Gloria Canby was in the habit of calling him that."

"How did I know?" she cried, wringing her hands. "How could I have known?"

"I imagine the professor collected that piece of information, as he collected all the rest, to add verisimilitude to the act," murmured Chet Keith, his lip curling.

"But the professor was furious with me," protested Sheila Kelly.

"And Hogan Brewster was under the impression that no one except himself knew Gloria Canby's nickname for him," I volunteered and bitterly regretted it, for the girl went all to pieces at my remark.

"I told you I was done for!" she cried. "Nothing can save me."

"Stop it," said Chet Keith brusquely. "We haven't time for hysterics."

"But don't you see?" she asked with a sob. "It's true, what Dora Canby thinks. It's true!"

He grasped her wrists. "Hush!"

She was past listening. "I killed him," she announced in a voice that horrified me. "Or rather Gloria Canby killed him with my hands, just as she strangled the canary. She has taken possession of me, body and soul. Oh, God!"

"You've got to get hold of yourself," said Chet Keith sternly. "You mustn't fall for that stuff."

"I speak with her voice," she whispered. "They all say so. When I first came they showed me her picture. There was some resemblance. She was a blonde and very thin. But I look more like her today than I did a week ago, or even—even yesterday."

"Listen," said Chet Keith. "Get this and hang onto it for dear life. The dead don't come back. Not even anybody as devilish as Gloria Canby can return from the grave to torture the living."

She seemed oblivious of everything except her tortured thoughts.

"This morning very early I woke up," she whispered. "I don't know how I came to be there, but I was in Dora Canby's sitting room, and I had something in my hands."

"Yes?"

"It was—was her scissors, the scissors with a handle like a swan in flight."

Again I gasped, but Chet Keith's voice was perfectly even.

"You had the scissors," he said quietly. "What did you do with them?"

"I don't know."

He was watching her intently.

"You don't know?" he asked.

"After a while I was back upstairs in bed," she whispered. "I never thought of the scissors again until—until Thomas Canby was dead."

She drew a long breath and got to her feet. "It's useless," she said. "Don't you see how useless it is?"

"Not by a damned sight!" cried Chet Keith, but she walked past us without looking at either of us and into her own room and a minute later I heard her shoot the thumb bolt on her side of the door.

8

IT HAS BEEN my experience that a stout offensive is the best defense, so when I went to the door with Chet Keith on his way out that night I fastened my most forbidding glance upon Butch, the deputy, as he sat propped back against the wall in a straight chair, his hat tilted over one eye.

"If that was you I heard snoring a minute ago," I said severely, "I shan't find it necessary to report it this time, but don't let it happen again."

It was purely a shot in the dark, as I am sure Chet Keith recognized, for he uttered a choked sound which he tried to cover by clearing his throat. However, I appeared to have scored a bull's eye, for the deputy turned very red and the cynical amusement with which he had been staring from me to my companion altered abruptly.

"The sheriff never said I couldn't catch a wink or two of sleep," he said sulkily, "long as nobody can get in or out of these here rooms without my knowing."

He indicated the door to Sheila Kelly's room and the one to the professor's on the other side. The deputy's chair was about midway between and he seemed to consider that he had every approach under guard. Needless to say I did not disillusion him, nor did Chet Keith, although he gave me an odd look.

"Why don't you bunk in with your friend Mrs. Trotter for the rest of the night?" he asked suddenly.

I stared at him. "Don't be silly," I snapped. "Why should I?"

He said nothing and it was not until I was back in my own room that it dawned upon me that the deputy's presence in the corridor was little if any protection to me. I had heard Sheila Kelly shoot the thumb bolt on her side of our connecting door, but while there were screw holes, indicating that there had once been a bolt on my side, there was none there now. I tried to recall if Chet Keith had relocked the inside door after the girl left us. To the best of my recollection he had not. For a moment I believed it would be impossible for me to stay in that room with nothing between me and Sheila Kelly except the bolt on her side of the wall. I even took a rapid step on my way to remedying the matter, then my common sense reasserted itself.

"People can't be hypnotized into doing things contrary to their moral principles and the dead don't come back to life," I said to myself, a litany to which I was to cling with both hands during those dreadful twenty-four hours which followed.

I had denied to Ella that I was on Sheila Kelly's side and I do not know even now why, with all the evidence against her, I could not bear to think of her as a murderess. It may have been partly because the sheriff had aroused all my antagonism. As Ella insists, I do like to be the belled cow or nothing, and everybody except Chet Keith seemed determined to hang the crime upon Sheila Kelly. Partly, I think, it was because the girl herself was so pitiful that I shrank from believing her guilty. It seemed to me much more probable that Professor Thaddeus Matthews had used his unholy influence over her mind to put her on the spot, while he himself committed the actual murder.

"She's the victim of an unscrupulous scoundrel!" I muttered.

Having argued myself into that state of mind, it behooved me to have the courage of my convictions, so I did not send for Chet Keith to return with his skeleton key. Instead I went soberly to bed and lay for a long time wide awake, listening to the stealthy creakings of the old frame building, unable to close my eyes without seeing that hideous gash in Thomas Canby's throat and recalling that the other half of those sharp gold scissors had not been found.

I could have sworn I had not slept at all. Apparently I was mistaken, for I woke up the next morning at eight by my traveling clock on the bedside table. The rain had stopped but there was no sign of the sun. It was one of those depressing days which I recalled from my former stay at Lebeau Inn, when the clouds hang low over the mountain and wander in and out of the windows in a cold gray mist like fog, only wetter and more dismal.

Even my shoes felt damp when I slid into them, and the white linen collar on my black knitted dress was as limp as the cheap towels in the bathroom which was cut off one corner of my room. There was a similar bathroom in Ella's room, which is why there was no connecting door between us, as I have said. I heard her grumbling about there being no hot water as usual, while I was brushing my teeth. Except in the bathroom it was impossible to hear any movement on her side of the partition, but I distinctly heard Sheila Kelly when the deputy knocked and asked what she would like for breakfast.

"Nothing," she said in a low, spiritless voice. "I'm not hungry."

"Suit yourself, lady," was the reply.

I put my head out into the hall. "Of course she wants some breakfast," I said crossly. "Have them bring her plenty of hot coffee and buttered toast and an egg."

The deputy Butch looked at me as if he wanted to tell me to mind my own business, but he thought better of it when I frowned him down.

"You heard the order, George," he said to the elderly colored porter who had conducted me to my room the night before.

According to my recollection, the porter's name was Jake but he appeared willing to answer to anything. In fact he scuttled off as if only too glad to get away.

Butch grinned. "He's scared the hant will get him."

"Hant?" I asked.

He motioned with his shoulder toward Sheila Kelly's door. "Darkies are strong for ghosts. You can't make George believe that that girl ain't possessed of a vampire. He claims he has seen her more than once, wandering around up here in the shape of a big black bat."

"Tommyrot!"

"Sure, but Jake swears he caught her, or maybe it was the bat, hovering over a cat which had been cut all to pieces, and he says she was the only person on this floor the next day when another cat come tearing down the stairs with his insides hanging out."

I felt sick but I tried to tell myself it was because I had had no breakfast. "You don't believe such drivel?" I demanded sharply.

Butch hoisted one shoulder in a bored manner. "Nope," he said, "when you bury 'em they stay buried. The gal's a killer all right, but she ain't doing her killing for nobody except herself."

"How about the professor?" I asked indignantly.

"I and the sheriff figure he's just her tool."

"I should say it was definitely the other way around," I announced haughtily.

Butch regarded me with cynical amusement. "You mean you think there is such a thing as hypnotism?" he inquired.

"Certainly there is such a thing."

Butch tittered. "'Sfunny how education makes it easy for folks to swallow a lot of fool notions," he said comfortably. "Now I and the sheriff and Mart Butler and Coroner Timmons, we don't pretend to be no college graduates, but we ain't took in very easily. In fact we ain't took in at all. We know that gal killed Canby and we know she knew what she was doing when she done it, and Sheriff Latham ain't the man to be throwed off the track by a lot of crazy talk about mental suggestion and a dead woman's vengeance."

I had the impression that one might as well butt one's head against a brick wall as attempt to make any impression upon the deputy's fixed idea. I felt depressed as I walked slowly down the hall and I thought Chet Keith looked much the same when I met him in the lounge downstairs, although he gave me a bright smile and his voice sounded positively blithe.

"Nice morning, isn't it, if you don't mind a cloud roosting on your chin," he said.

I nodded. "Any news of the bridge?" I inquired.

"I understand they've corralled it somewhere down the river. Getting it upstream against the current is now the problem."

Fannie Parrish, looking more than ever like a shaggy, beady-eyed lap dog, joined in the conversation. "It's terrible, positively terrible, for us to have to stay in this horrible place!" She glanced nervously over her shoulder. "I heard people creeping about all night. I simply never closed my eyes. I had the most awful feeling that if I did I'd wake up with my throat cut from ear to ear."

Captain Bill French, who was behind the desk, gave her a worried look. "There is positively no danger, Mrs. Parrish," he said. I suppose he was thinking of what a blow to his business all this was. "With the murderers under lock and key and the authorities on guard, nothing can happen to the guests in the house."

"With the authorities on guard indeed!" cried Fannie. "As if that means anything! I ask you, what good are bolts and keys against a man like the professor? If he can raise the dead he can walk right through doors and everything."

"Nonsense!" I exclaimed angrily. "The professor can't raise the dead!"

Fannie did not pay me the slightest attention. "Isn't there any way a person can get down off this awful mountain without crossing the river?"

Captain French sighed. "I assure you there is no need for the guests at the inn to feel uneasy," he said feebly.

Ella touched my arm. "If you ask me, Captain French isn't so easy in his own mind as he lets on."

"Naturally he hates to think of the place being deserted in midseason and he realizes there will be a general exodus the moment the road is open," I said, "thanks as much as anything else to the alarms of your friend Mrs. Parrish."

Ella stared at me intently. "Fannie Parrish *is* a silly woman, but she's right about one thing," she said in a low voice. "The sheriff's precautions did not keep the prisoners from mingling around last night."

I gave a guilty start, believing for a minute that Ella knew about Sheila Kelly's visit to my room the night before.

"What do you mean?" I stammered.

"I don't for a minute believe that Professor Matthews has super-natural powers," said Ella. "I never, have believed so, Adelaide, whatever you choose to think. But somebody or something visited the professor, last night in spite of locked doors and the sheriff."

"Someone visited the professor!"

"I couldn't sleep either," explained Ella. "It seemed to me I could hear a mumble of voices." She eyed me suspiciously. "Were you talking to somebody in your room after I left last night, Adelaide?"

I did not tell a falsehood; I merely evaded the question.

"What if anything are you driving at, Ella?" I demanded with considerable hauteur.

"It seemed to me," repeated Ella with a frown, "that people were talking. I looked out into the hall. That deputy was fast asleep—so much for the protection of the officers. I intended to wake the man up and tell him what I thought of such negligence. After all, we pay taxes to be protected. But just as I opened my mouth I saw a shadow down the hall. At least I thought for a moment that it was a shadow." She paused.

"Go on," I exclaimed impatiently.

"It was standing just outside the professor's door."

"Yes?"

"I couldn't swear it came *through* that locked door, Adelaide."

"I should hope not!"

"But I am sure it did," finished Ella.

"Ridiculous!"

"It's all very well for you to scoff at everything and everybody," said Ella wearily, "but you can't deny that some very queer things have happened and are continuing to happen in this place."

"Such as a shadow you saw in the hall!" I jeered. "As if that upstairs corridor isn't alive with shadows with only one dim light bulb to illuminate it."

"But you see, the shadow moved away toward the stairs."

"Just a trick of your imagination," I said crossly.

"And it looked"—Ella's voice trembled—"it looked exactly like an enormous bat."

"Are you spoofing me or what?" I demanded.

"No," said Ella meekly, and curiously enough I was more impressed by that than by anything she had said. It is very unlike Ella Trotter to be meek. "I'm not spoofing you, Adelaide. The thing was like a bat, all black and shapeless, like a huge bat with its wings folded, and it moved away toward the stairs without making a sound."

I was convinced that Ella's imagination had deceived her, although it did occur to me to wonder if Chet Keith had a monopoly on all the skeleton keys in the house.

"I suppose you woke the deputy up and had him investigate," I said to Ella.

She gave me a defiant glance. "Not being a born meddler, like some people I could name, I did nothing of the sort. Instead I locked my door and went back to bed and, if it is any satisfaction to you, I put my head under the covers and kept it there."

I must have eyed her severely, for she bridled. "I suppose you would have dashed off after that thing and chased it to its lair," she said in what she evidently intended for cutting accents.

"If people are hobnobbing with the prisoners behind the sheriff's back he has the right to be told of it," I announced weakly.

Ella shook her head. "I have changed my mind," she said. "When I sent for that book, Adelaide, I intended, as I told Fannie Parrish, to expose the professor. In other words I meant to take a hand in whatever is going on in this wretched place. But"—she shivered and stared at me fixedly—"that was before the devilish thing got into Sheila Kelly which mutilates stray cats and strangles pet canaries and cuts people's throats."

"I may as well tell you, Ella," I said with a frown, "that I don't seem to have arrived with the book. At any rate it is not in my luggage anywhere."

"Thank heaven!" cried Ella and then she regarded me sternly. "I know your penchant, Adelaide, for dabbling into things which do not concern you, but here is one piece of advice I urge you to take. Let this fiendish business alone, just as I intend to do from here on."

So saying, she led the way into the dining room, the doors to
which Captain French had at that moment thrown open. Because
of the general dreariness of the day and the murky effect of the
clouds, which had settled down upon the mountain like a coverlet
of wet gray down, the room was again lighted by the big chandelier with the green shade, and the guests who straggled in by ones
and twos to breakfast looked even more haggard and drawn than
on the night before. Nobody appeared to want to be alone. I saw
Fannie Parrish beckon to her table the young mother who had been
at the séance, and shortly afterward they were joined by the dyspeptic-looking old gentleman who had received the message from
his brother Peter.

Ella made a grimace at me and said, "They are going to have the
inquest the first thing this morning, and Fannie is all of a twitter."

I was spared the effort of a reply by Judy Oliver, who at that
moment came into the dining room and hurried over to us. "Do
you mind if I sit with you?" she asked a little breathlessly.

I raised my eyebrows. None of the Canby party had put in an
appearance at that time except Jeff Wayne, who was sitting by himself, pretending to be absorbed in a paper, although there were no
morning papers of course, and I was positive he was merely using the
crumpled sheet in his hand for a shield behind which to hide his face.

"I don't feel as if I could bear my own company this morning,"
said Judy.

She did not look at Jeff Wayne, and the only sign he gave of
being aware of her presence was an involuntary twitch of the hand
which held the newspaper.

"Sit down by all means," said Ella cordially and gave me a mu-
tinous glance.

Ella and I rarely like the same people, but I merely raised my
eyebrows again, and to my surprise Judy Oliver colored painfully.

"Jeff and I haven't fallen out or anything," she declared in a
tone of false levity, or so it seemed to me. "It's just that—that . . ."
She caught her breath and started all over again. "You see, we never
were—I mean, it was all a mistake thinking that we—that we were
in love with each other."

I stared at her curiously. She could not even speak the boy's name without tripping over it. She could not meet my eyes, either, and her hand strayed without her volition to that tiny piece which had been clipped out of her ear.

"Jeff was in love with Gloria," she said sharply. "He still is."

"So I heard him say last night," I remarked in a dry voice.

She glared at me. "It's true!"

"Only you didn't believe it until last night," I said, "and your cousin Gloria died not believing it."

Her small pointed face crinkled as if she were about to burst into tears. "You have no right to judge people by what Gloria Canby thought or said!" she burst out. "She was a horrible person." Her lips quivered. "I know you aren't supposed to say things against the dead, but Gloria—she was three years older than I. She was sixteen when our father died and Patrick and I came to live with Aunt Dora. We hadn't a penny to bless ourselves with and nowhere else to go and—and Gloria never let any of us forget for a minute that we were living off charity."

I felt myself weakening and Ella must have seen it, for she gazed at me triumphantly. I realized that she had heard all this before.

"I had to wear Gloria's old clothes," went on Judy in a bitter voice. "Aunt Dora would have bought me new ones and Uncle Thomas was not stingy, so long as he had the say-so, but Gloria begrudged me everything, even—even friends. She threw a tantrum every time I had a new hair ribbon, and if people acted as if they liked me it made her furious. She told them all sorts of terrible tales to put them off. She said I was a little sneak. She said I couldn't be trusted not to steal your purse or—or your sweetheart behind your back."

"People usually aren't greatly deceived by slander like that," I said. "Generally if they know a person they form their own conclusions."

"But you see, nobody knew me very well," said Judy. "I've always had to be—to be kind of a companion to Aunt Dora. Unless you were around the house a lot you never knew me well at all."

"Jeff Wayne was around a lot after he got engaged to your cousin?" I suggested with what I considered perfect suavity.

Judy winced. "Yes," she said, "Jeff was around a lot."

"Maybe he took your part against Gloria?"

She flushed. "Yes, he did," she said, then added quickly, "But it wasn't because he had fallen in love with me, as Gloria thought. It wasn't that at all. He just—just . . . She really was rotten to me!" she finished passionately. "Jeff knows it; so do Allan and Lila. Anybody in the family can tell you how Gloria loved to torment things, animals and—and people, anything she could make suffer."

"You all hated her?" I ventured.

"Yes!" she cried. "How could we help it? We were her poor relations and she loved to humiliate us. She liked nothing better than to goad us into a fury. It amused her because we were so helpless."

"Helpless?" I repeated. "It seems to me there were numbers of things you might have done."

She shook her head. "No," she said, "we were quite helpless."

"You might have appealed to your aunt," I suggested.

"Gloria could always make Aunt Dora think that black was white."

"Or your uncle?" I persisted.

She shook her head again. "It was no use going to Uncle Thomas with your troubles. You might as well have tried to get sympathy or understanding out of an adding machine."

"You could always have left the house," I said shortly.

"But I told you," she protested. "We hadn't any money, except what Uncle Thomas chose to give us."

"You might have got a job. Other people with rich relatives have," I pointed out with some irritation.

"Don't you think we tried?" she cried. "Every one of us tried. Patrick loathes being an auditor in Uncle Thomas' company. Patrick has no head for figures. He wanted to go in for aviation, and I think he'd have been quite good at it, but Uncle Thomas was determined to make an accountant of him. That was the only kind of schooling he'd pay for, so Patrick flunked and flunked before he finally got through college and he's gone on flunking ever since, although he's a vice-president. He says he isn't worth a grain of salt in the office and he has quit several times, but you know how hard it's been to get jobs since the depression and, after all, Uncle

Thomas was a rich man. When Patrick tried to get on somewhere else people told him his uncle ought to give him a job. They told Allan that too." She smiled crookedly. "Did you know you couldn't even get on relief nowadays if somebody in your family has money enough to feed you?"

"I seem to have heard something to that effect," I admitted.

"Allan hates being a figurehead in Uncle's office; he hates it as much as Patrick does, maybe more," said Judy. "Allan wanted to write. He even ran off once and started a novel, but he blundered into an epidemic of scarlet fever. Allan has always been unlucky. He was very ill and they notified Uncle, and of course he had Allan brought home and Gloria found the novel and burned it, but not before she had memorized parts of it. She used to recite them to people and die laughing. They were pretty amateurish, or she made them sound so. Anyway it finished Allan's attempt to be a writer, and then of course he met Lila and she married him for Uncle's money and after that he had to stick."

I stared over her head. Allan Atwood and his wife were just coming into the dining room. He was very pale and there were dark circles under his eyes, but the beautiful Lila was the freshest-looking person I had seen that morning.

I frowned. "It seems to me a little farfetched for Lila Atwood to have married your cousin for his uncle's money. As near as I can make out, the money goes to your aunt. There is no certainty that Allan will get a lot of it. At the time of the marriage, with Gloria Canby still alive, there must have been even less chance of Allan Atwood's coming into his uncle's fortune."

"Oh, but didn't you know?" asked Judy as if it were common knowledge, as no doubt it was in their circle. "Lila's family was quite dreadfully hard up. Her father had signed a note or something and couldn't pay. He was in very serious trouble. I think he might even have gone to jail. Uncle Thomas paid the note."

I stared at her aghast. "You mean he practically bought Lila for his nephew."

"That—that girl told the truth last night," said Judy in a smothered voice. "Uncle Thomas did like to play the god, but he was

terribly poor when he was a boy. He told me once that he had nothing to eat one whole week except raw turnips. I suppose it was then
he got the idea that nothing matters except money. At any rate
that's why he paid the note for Lila's father. You see, with all
Uncle's millions we had never cut any figure in society. You know
what a dud Aunt Dora is at that sort of thing, and Gloria was ex-
pelled from three exclusive finishing schools. Once for lashing a
thoroughbred horse until he bled when they were trying to teach
her to ride. Once for doing something horrible, I never knew what,
to a poor little French teacher who tried to discipline her for sneaking obscene words into her translations. Anyway, although Uncle
spent a fortune on her debut party, Gloria didn't click with the best
social groups, so Lila was a godsend."

"You mean she had the proper social entree?"

"Yes," said Judy. "After she married Allan the best people called
on us and asked us places, so I suppose in a way Uncle Thomas
was right. It does seem that all things are possible if you have
enough money."

She smiled bitterly and I leaned a little forward in my chair.
"Sheila Kelly was right about something else last night, wasn't she?"
I asked.

Judy's small hand tightened on the edge of the table. "What do
you mean?"

"You all hated Thomas Canby," I said.

Every particle of color drained out of her face. "Yes," she said
at last, "we all hated him like sin."

9

IT WAS PERFECTLY apparent, when Sheriff Latham had herded us into that dreary parlor on the first floor at Lebeau Inn, that to him at least the inquest was a mere formality. The folding doors for the first time in my memory were closed, so that we were spared the sight of Thomas Canby's dead body stretched out on a red sofa in one corner of the second room, although the jury filed in and viewed the corpse at the opening of the proceedings and filed back to their seats, looking a little seasick. I think all of us drew a deeper breath when Butch, the deputy, pushed the folding doors to again.

The coroner, a withered little old man named Timmons, Dr. Riley Timmons, had been put to considerable trouble to collect a jury, what with the bridge being out. However, there was a gaunt old man who, it seemed, hunted and trapped on the mountain and lived the year around in a shack back of the inn, and a young fellow who ran a filling station in connection with the hotel, and a couple of guests of the house, elderly men who plainly wished themselves elsewhere, and Captain Bill French himself.

"'Tain't as if this was more than a matter of form," explained Sheriff Latham.

Coroner Timmons nodded, and Chet Keith and I exchanged a frown. It was obvious to both of us that the coroner was the sheriff's echo.

"All you got to do," Sheriff Latham informed the jury, "is decide to the best of your knowledge how this man come to his death and who in your opinion done it. Then it is up to the grand jury to indict."

Nobody on the jury looked any the happier for this admonition, especially after Sheila Kelly entered with Mart Butler. She must have been conscious of everybody staring at her, but she did not lift her head as the deputy led her to a chair beside the table at which the coroner sat with Sheriff Latham at his right hand. Despair was in every line of the girl's drooping figure. Not so the professor, who was escorted into the room by the deputy Butch. The night before I could have sworn that Professor Thaddeus Matthews was on the verge of collapse, but he appeared to have taken a new lease on life. He was positively chipper, and the glance he bent upon us all lacked no assurance. It was, in fact, next door to insolence.

"Why should *he* be so blooming?" I muttered to Chet Keith, who was sitting directly behind me.

"If we could guess that one we'd be a lot closer to the truth," he said.

Both of us leaned a little forward, the better to see Dora Canby, who at that moment entered the room upon Judy's arm. I do not know exactly what I expected, but it was startling how well Thomas Canby's widow looked that morning—almost as if she, too, had taken a new lease upon life. Although her nephew Patrick hurried after her with a pillow and a gray knitted shawl, and her other nephew Allan made as if to steady her arm, she walked quite firmly to her seat beside Lila Atwood, and if Mrs. Canby had shed any tears the night before for her husband the effects were not apparent.

"I had to be carried to poor Theo's funeral," said Fannie Parrish in a sibilant whisper, "but then, she couldn't have cared for Thomas Canby; nobody could."

Ella, sitting between Fannie and me, compressed her lips. "It's a pity shrouds don't have pockets, so he could carry all that money with him."

Although I agreed with her sentiment I said nothing. I was watching Dora Canby trying to smile at Sheila Kelly. I think Mrs. Canby would have gone over to the girl and spoken to her, but Lila Atwood laid her hand on the older woman's arm.

"I wouldn't, Aunt Dora," she said softly. "Can't you see she is at the breaking point?"

"Gloria could never be intimidated, Lila," protested Dora Canby.

Nevertheless she settled back into her chair, and behind her Jeff Wayne drew a shaking hand across his brow. I noticed how careful Judy was not to look at him and what pains he took never to meet her eyes, as much pains as Allan Atwood went to in order to avoid his wife's glance. Hogan Brewster, on the other hand, pulled his chair nearer to Lila's and whispered something to her, something flippant, I suppose, for he was smiling, but she did not answer.

The coroner rapped, rather indecisively, to signify that the meeting was about to open and, looking very nervous and ill at ease, called Sheriff Latham to the stand. The sheriff, more forcefully than grammatically, related the circumstances of his being summoned to Lebeau Inn by the dead man. He said that Thomas Canby had been most insistent upon seeing the officers that very night.

"He was all set to get rid of that shyster and the gal," explained Sheriff Latham with a dark glance which the professor met with complete aplomb.

"Just a moment," interposed Chet Keith. "Did Mr. Canby tell you that he required your presence for the purpose of arresting Professor Matthews and Miss Kelly?"

Sheriff Latham beetled his brows at the interrupter with, so far as I could see, no visible effect upon the young man.

"You ain't on the witness stand," he said, "and you ain't got no right butting in like that."

I sat up very straight in my chair. "I was under the impression, Sheriff Latham," I said in my most critical accents, "that this is strictly an informal hearing. If you are going to insist upon being technical there are several matters which I might call to your attention."

"Attagirl," whispered Chet Keith behind me.

Coroner Timmons cleared his throat nervously. "I reckon we ain't trying to enforce a lot of red tape."

"But you want the truth," I snapped, "or don't you?"

I looked sharply at Sheriff Latham, who rose to the fly.

"Certainly we want the truth," he declared belligerently.

"All right," murmured Chet Keith, "suppose you answer my question."

The sheriff's florid face wore a nettled expression. He did not relish the manner in which the situation was threatening to slide out of his hands, but he did not know quite how to prevent it. It was true, as I had pointed out to his annoyance, that if he chose to put the investigation upon a technical basis there were several points at which he had slipped up.

"I don't know that Mr. Canby said in so many words that he wanted me to come up here and arrest Professor Matthews and Miss Kelly," he admitted, "but it's sort of self-evident, in the light of what's happened."

"As a matter of fact," said Chet Keith, "isn't it true that Thomas Canby didn't tell you what he wanted with you?"

The sheriff squirmed uncomfortably. "Well, not in so many words."

I saw Miss Maurine Smith, who was sitting as close to Chet Keith as possible, draw a breath of relief. I suppose she had been afraid of being called upon to testify to the telephone conversation which she had overheard, if not eavesdropped upon, and, contrary to orders, repeated to Chet Keith.

"You have merely jumped to the conclusion, Sheriff Latham, in the light of what happened later, that Thomas Canby wanted you to remove the professor and Miss Kelly from the inn," I said severely.

The sheriff scowled at me. "If that wa'n't what he wanted, what was it?" he demanded, giving every evidence of exasperation.

Chet Keith grinned. I got the idea that he was not particularly interested in the question which he had raised. It struck me that he had wanted to badger the sheriff into a position where it would be possible to take a hand in the investigation. If that was the object, between us it had been successful. In the face of the sheriff's attitude I was delighted to pursue the advantage.

"Isn't it possible that Mr. Canby wanted to see you about the attempt which was made upon his life yesterday afternoon?" I asked. "Or have you heard about that attempt?"

"Sure, I heard about it," said the sheriff testily. "I ain't deaf, and I guess there ain't nothing happened up here in the past month I ain't heard about."

He glanced pointedly at Fannie Parrish, and I remembered that she had buttonholed him for quite a while the night before and again that morning.

"Then for all you know," I said, "your summons may not have had to do with Professor Matthews and Miss Kelly at all."

My tone was purposely argumentative but, although I could see that Sheriff Latham was tempted by it, he managed to recall with a visible effort that he was upon the witness stand in the middle, supposedly, of giving testimony.

"This ain't the place to argue this and that, lady," he said with a scowl. "As I was saying, Canby sent for me, and I and my two deputies came."

He then proceeded to give a somewhat verbose but accurate enough account of his arrival at the inn, with the discovery of the tragedy.

"It was plain enough what happened," he said with truculence. "The gal killed Canby. She had his wife wrapped around her finger and Canby was going to put a stop to it, so she cut his throat."

"If we *were* being technical, Sheriff Latham," I murmured in an urbane voice, "I'd be forced to remind you that it is not your duty to give the jury the benefit of your opinion in this matter but to produce evidence to substantiate it."

The sheriff looked at me as if I were a bee which he had suddenly discovered under his shirt. "I'll produce the evidence all right!" he growled, reseating himself beside the coroner and proceeding to manipulate the little man as if he were a marionette to which Sheriff Latham possessed the only strings.

Although it seemed unnecessary to me, everyone who had been present at the fatal séance was required to give his testimony as to what had occurred. The accounts were strikingly alike. None of them differed in salient points.

"A pure waste of time," I muttered.

"Certainly," admitted Chet Keith, "but the sheriff is no fool. He knows the value of cumulative evidence."

He glanced significantly at the jury and then at the girl in the cheap black dress, sitting there with bowed, dejected head, her hands locked in her lap. I sighed. There was no question but that each of us who took the stand made the picture darker for Sheila Kelly. After all, what could we do except say over and over that she had, allegedly in the character of his dead daughter, threatened Thomas Canby with violence before the light was extinguished and when it came on again he was done to death?

Although the coroner had not questioned him about it, it was Chet Keith, during his stay upon the stand, who brought up the matter of the parlor lamp. "I suppose the sheriff has checked up on how it came to go out at the strategic moment," he said.

The flush upon Sheriff Latham's swarthy face was ample proof that he had done nothing of the sort. "I don't see what difference it makes why the lamp went out," he protested.

"I should think it made a great deal of difference," I said promptly, being constitutionally unable to concur with any opinion expressed by that gentleman.

Chet Keith nodded. "The cord was jerked out of the socket, as of course you noticed when you examined it, Sheriff."

Sheriff Latham's expression showed that he had not noticed.

"The lamp was attached by a long extension cord to a socket clear across the room," continued the newspaperman. "The plug does not fit tightly. The slightest tug is sufficient to pull it away from the socket. I think you'll bear me out in this, Professor."

Professor Matthews started and plucked nervously at his black string tie. "What is that?" he inquired.

"I was saying," murmured Chet Keith, "that the lamp on the table, which you connected before the séance started, was attached to a floor socket clear across the room by a plug which fitted quite loosely."

The professor swallowed twice before answering. "To the best of my recollection, yes," he said.

"What's the difference?" demanded the sheriff again. "As I remember the setup, the cord was in easy reach of both the professor and the girl. Either of them could have kicked the cord loose with one foot."

"Either of them or anybody else on the right side of the circle," amended Chet Keith smoothly.

I gave a slight start. I remembered during Sheila Kelly's tirade the night before feeling something crawling across my ankle and looking down to perceive that it was only the light cord.

"On the right side of the circle?" repeated the sheriff with a frown.

"The cord stretched inside the circle from the right side of the table clear across the room," said Chet Keith.

"But we were all on that side!" exclaimed Judy Oliver, then closed her lips tightly, her eyes widening in her stricken face.

Chet Keith began to tick them off upon his fingers. "Yes, Miss Oliver," he said, "you and your aunt and your cousins and your friends, Mr. Wayne and Mr. Brewster, and Miss Adelaide Adams were in a position to have jerked the lamp cord out of its socket."

"Are you trying to make out that Judy and Allan and—and the rest of us had anything to do with this thing?" blustered Pat Oliver. "If so, let me warn you, we won't stand for it!"

Chet Keith smiled. "Let me see now," he mused. "It was you, wasn't it, who first introduced your aunt to Professor Matthews?"

The bluster faded out of the boy's carriage as if he were a tire which had suddenly encountered a tack.

"I took Aunt Dora to a picture show in Carrolton where the professor was putting on a stunt, if that is what you mean," he said sulkily. "I—I thought it might amuse her."

"Yes?"

"I didn't—I didn't know there was a fake spiritualist on the bill," muttered the boy.

I leaned forward and stared at him. "In your opinion, then, the professor is a fake?"

"Sure he's a fake!" cried Patrick Oliver defiantly.

I glanced at Professor Matthews; he was smiling complacently.

"You didn't know when you induced your sister and your aunt to take in the movie in Carrolton," pursued Chet Keith, "that the professor was part of the show?"

"They don't usually have vaudeville turns in small-town movies," said the boy sullenly.

"That wasn't my question," murmured Chet Keith. "I asked you if you knew the professor was on the bill."

"And I told you I didn't," declared the boy angrily.

"You are quite certain about that?"

"Certainly I'm certain," snapped Patrick Oliver.

I saw his sister move closer to him with terror in her eyes.

"You arrived at Lebeau Inn on the morning of the day on which you took your sister and aunt to the show in Carrolton, I believe," murmured Chet Keith.

"And what of it?" retorted Patrick Oliver.

"When did you arrive in Carrolton?"

"You just said it," muttered Oliver. "On the morning of the day I took Aunt Dora to that darned movie."

"You mean to say you came straight from the train to the inn?" asked Chet Keith. "Before you commit yourself, Mr. Oliver, perhaps I should warn you that, though we are temporarily cut off from town, the telephone is still working."

Not until later did I realize how much use Chet Keith made of the fact that, while we were physically marooned upon Mount Lebeau, the wires to town were not down. It was possible to get in touch with the outside world by telephone and consequently by telegraph, if necessary.

"For various reasons," the, newspaperman went on, "I considered it advisable to check up on you, Oliver, the principal reason being a clandestine visit which you paid to the second floor, last night."

The boy turned white. "I don't know what you are talking about," he said in a vain attempt at his usual bravado. "I wasn't on the second floor last night."

"It will do you no good to prevaricate, young man," I said with acidity. "I saw you with my own eyes."

Patrick Oliver bit his lip and scowled at me as if he would have liked to wring my neck. "Nosy old hen!" he muttered.

Chet Keith grinned. "Do you persist in your statement, Oliver, that you came straight to the inn when you arrived in Carrolton?"

"Look here," interrupted Jeff Wayne furiously, "who is conduct-ing this inquest?" He frowned at Sheriff Latham. "Are you going to sit there like a chump and let this smart-aleck reporter and that battle-ax of an old maid run things to suit themselves?"

I saw Judy Oliver give him a passionately grateful glance be-fore she remembered to turn her eyes away. I suppose I should have been abashed by the epithet bestowed upon me, but it was not the first time I have been alluded to in such a manner, so I did not allow it to ruffle me—on the contrary.

"Sheriff Latham is as anxious as I am to arrive at the truth, aren't you, Sheriff?" I murmured with an ironical smile.

The sheriff's large mouth gaped like a fish, fighting for air, but Chet Keith gave him no chance to speak.

"Maybe you'd rather explain to the coroner, Oliver, why you are unwilling to admit that you spent a night in Carrolton before you appeared at the inn," he said.

"You're crazy," protested Patrick Oliver.

"No," said Chet Keith quite genially, "like Miss Adams, I merely have a passion for the truth, and you're lying, Oliver, lying about this whole business."

"You're talking through your hat," muttered the boy, biting his lips.

"You arrived in Carrolton by a late train, as I have taken the trouble to find out," murmured Chet Keith. "The bus had made its last run of the day to the inn. You registered under your own name at the Carrolton House. Apparently at that time you had no inten-tion of denying your presence there. I have talked to the clerk at the hotel by telephone. He remembers you distinctly. You asked him what a feller could do in a one-horse burg like that after nine o'clock in the evening. The clerk recommended the local picture house."

"What if he did?" demanded Patrick Oliver furiously. "That's no proof I went to the damned show!"

"No," admitted Chet Keith, "and unfortunately the girl at the ticket window and likewise the ticket taker have been unable to identify you as being present."

"Because why?" almost snarled young Oliver. "Because I wasn't there."

"It wasn't you, then, who called Professor Matthews afterward at the cheap rooming house where he and Sheila Kelly were staying, and asked him to meet you at the town square?"

"I don't know what you are talking about!"

Chet Keith turned to the professor. "On the night before Dora Canby's first appearance in your audience you were called to the telephone shortly after your return from the theater, or so your landlady informed me by phone this morning. She heard you make an appointment to meet somebody in the town square in ten minutes. Right?"

The professor's sonorous voice was beautifully even.

"My landlady did call me to the phone on the evening in question," he said, "and I did agree to meet somebody in the specified time upon a—er—matter of business."

Patrick Oliver was frowning at him, but the professor seemed equal to it; he even smiled benevolently.

"As a matter of fact," he continued, "I met Mr. Patrick Oliver."

"You double-crossing old crook!" cried Patrick with a sob.

His sister clutched his arm and stared defiantly at Chet Keith, who, I thought, regarded her with pity.

"So," he murmured softly, "there was nothing accidental about your taking Dora Canby to that movie, Oliver."

Patrick Oliver seemed to go to pieces all at once. "All right, all right," he cried in a tormented voice. "I did see the professor beforehand and I did fix up a job on Aunt Dora. So what?"

"Patrick!" wailed Judy.

Jeff Wayne suddenly was there beside her. "Keep still, Patrick!" he cried harshly. "This fellow hasn't any right to ask you questions."

The sheriff glared at Chet Keith. "You're supposed to be on the witness stand, not putting innocent people through the third degree," he protested in his most vociferous manner.

This was more than I could stand. "How can you be sure all these people are innocent?" I demanded. "Every member of Thomas Canby's family, including his own wife, hated him. Ask them if you don't believe me. Every one of them stood to gain by his death and not one of them but had as good an opportunity to kill him last night as Sheila Kelly."

"The woman's crazy!" protested Jeff Wayne. "The girl killed Canby. We all saw it."

"In the dark?" murmured Chet Keith.

Allan Atwood had got to his feet, his face congested with anger.

"They're trying to lead you by the nose, Sheriff!" he cried unsteadily. "Maybe none of us had any love for Uncle Thomas, but we aren't killers. You can ask anybody who was here. The girl killed him!"

It was then I had one of my unfortunate brainstorms.

"It seems to me that if this affair had been properly conducted," I exclaimed indignantly, "there ought to be no question. If Sheila Kelly cut Thomas Canby's throat, her fingerprints should be on the handle of the scissors, though"—I gave Sheriff Latham a withering glance—"I don't suppose it occurred to you to look for them."

The sheriff returned my hostile gaze with accrued interest.

"In spite of not being a storybook detective," he said with top-heavy dignity, "I ain't such a back number as certain people would like to make out. We did examine the scissors for fingerprints. Butch here took a correspondence course in such things."

Determined as I was to believe in Sheila Kelly's innocence, I had a very bad moment. However, Chet Keith displayed a faith which made me ashamed of myself.

"You did not find Sheila Kelly's prints on the scissors, Sheriff," he said softly.

"No," admitted Sheriff Latham, "there wa'n't no prints on them."

"Doesn't that seem highly significant?" I demanded.

"Significant of what?" asked the sheriff bluntly.

"This whole affair was staged to leave the impression that in some sort of trance Sheila Kelly killed Thomas Canby," said Chet Keith. "If that were true her prints should be on the scissors, as Miss Adams pointed out."

For the first time the sheriff looked a little nonplused.

"She killed him all right," he muttered doggedly.

"Without leaving any marks upon the weapon?" I said caustically.

Fannie Parrish uttered a little moan. "A dead hand leaves no trace," she declared with traces of hysteria.

Dora Canby nodded. "No," she said in a bemused voice, "the dead have no fingerprints."

The sheriff reminded me of a baited bull. "I don't take no stock in that stuff," he said, "and I don't take no stock in this trance business. The girl knew what she was doing and she cut Canby's throat."

The professor smiled comfortably to himself.

"If Sheila Kelly killed Canby," I contended, "there are two facts you can't get around. Why did the room have to be dark and why aren't her prints on the scissors?"

And then Jeff Wayne for the second time injected himself into the discussion, his voice quite violent. "She had a handkerchief in her hand," he said. "She held the scissors inside the handkerchief."

I sighed. I had forgotten until he mentioned it, but I distinctly remembered the large chiffon handkerchief which Sheila Kelly had clutched and later torn to pieces between her fingers after Thomas Canby's death.

"She did have a handkerchief!" exclaimed Fannie Parrish. "One of those large expensive chiffon ones! I recall thinking that Mrs. Canby must have given it to her."

"I did give Gloria a pretty handkerchief, didn't I, darling?" murmured Dora Canby fondly.

The girl shivered but did not raise her head.

"She tore it up before the sheriff arrived," said Jeff Wayne. "I saw her tear it to shreds."

So had we all for that matter.

"That's it!" exclaimed the sheriff in fine fettle. "She used the handkerchief to hold the scissors, so as to leave no fingerprints, and then she tore it up to fool me. I dare say there were bloodstains on it."

"No!" cried Sheila Kelly in a stifled voice. "I swear there were no—no marks on it."

Sheriff Latham leaned over until his swart face was very close to hers. "Where is it now? What did you do with the pieces?" he demanded.

"I—I burned them," she whispered.

"Burned them?"

"I threw them into—into the fireplace over there before you took me upstairs."

Sheriff Latham fairly beamed at Chet Keith. "There you are!" he cried. "If she was innocent, why should she have destroyed evidence?"

"We have no proof that the handkerchief was evidence," said the newspaperman.

"Why did she destroy it then?" asked the sheriff almost with glee.

"I suppose if the handkerchief was ruined there was no point in keeping it," I said tartly.

"You suppose," repeated Sheriff Latham in sarcastic tones. He winked at the jury. "But to a sensible man, to plain sensible folks like us, it's pretty clear that the girl did away with the handkerchief because she didn't dare let it fall into the hands of the law."

Sheila Kelly glanced at Chet Keith. "I told you it was no use," she said in a despairing voice.

"Keep still," he said sharply. He seemed to give his shoulders a little shake, as if he were settling them to a burden, but his voice was perfectly self-possessed when he turned again to the coroner. "She didn't kill Canby," he said. "I can prove it."

Everybody present caught his breath, and I saw a flicker of hope in Sheila Kelly's eyes as he went on.

"You are a doctor, Coroner Timmons, and you and the jury have viewed the dead man. Thomas Canby died of a severed carotid artery. Right?"

"Sure you're right," said the sheriff testily, "though I don't guess me and the jury knows the name of it. Canby died of having his throat cut."

"The *left* carotid artery, Coroner Timmons," persisted Chet Keith.

Coroner Timmons gave him a startled glance. "It was the left carotid, yes," he admitted.

"Sheila Kelly is left-handed, Coroner Timmons," said Chet Keith.

"What of it?" demanded the sheriff in an irascible voice.

Chet Keith suddenly produced a fountain pen. "Take this, Sheriff Latham, take it in your *left* hand, face me and go through the motions of cutting my throat."

"What's the idea of all this tomfoolery?" protested the sheriff angrily.

Nevertheless he took the fountain pen and pretended to lunge at Chet Keith's throat. He lunged a couple of times and there was a very peculiar expression upon his face.

"Get it, Sheriff?" asked the reporter softly. "Thomas Canby's throat was cut from *left to right*. It would be impossible for a left-handed person to have dealt the wound."

The sheriff made a fumbling attempt to draw the fountain pen across Chet Keith's throat in the prescribed direction without changing the pen into his right hand.

"Can't be done, Sheriff," murmured the reporter, his eyes gleaming.

Sheila Kelly was trembling, but the flicker of hope which I had seen in her drawn face was now a flame.

"Could be if she was standing behind him," muttered Sheriff Latham, who was never one to abandon his position without a struggle.

"But we have the testimony of everybody in the room that Sheila Kelly was directly in front of Canby!" I said triumphantly.

"Anyway," muttered the sheriff, "we ain't got no proof the gal's left-handed."

"I am left-handed, Sheriff," said Sheila Kelly with a little sob. "Thank God!"

The radiance in her face brought a lump to my throat. I had not realized until that moment what a very pretty girl she might be if she were less haggard.

"I think we'll have no trouble proving that Sheila Kelly is left-handed," said Chet Keith and smiled at her. "Plenty of people must have seen her, since she's been at the inn, using her left hand."

Fannie Parrish could always be trusted to bob up with miscellaneous information. "She writes with the left hand, I've seen her!" she exclaimed excitedly.

"Of course," remarked Ella dubiously, "many left-handed people are ambidextrous." She frowned at the sheriff. "In case you don't know, that means they can use either hand if necessary."

The sheriff grasped at a straw. "That's it," he said and glared at Sheila Kelly. "She's ambi—ambi— She can use one hand as well as the other if she wants."

"Gloria was born left-handed like me," contributed Dora Canby archly, "but it always got on Thomas' nerves, my using the wrong hand. Nearly everything I did seemed awkward and irritating to him. So he insisted that Gloria be taught to write with her right hand, but she can use both hands equally well, can't you, darling?" she asked Sheila Kelly.

"Don't! Oh, please don't!" whispered the girl.

"It's Judy's left ear that's clipped," put in Jeff Wayne in a constrained voice.

"Those cats," said Allan Atwood loudly, "were cut from left to right. I examined them."

The radiance had drained from Sheila Kelly's face, leaving her so white I shivered.

"It's no use," she said again with a despairing glance at Chet Keith.

"Hush!" he cried brusquely and fixed his eyes upon the professor. "As a spiritualist, you're a fake and admit it," he said in an ominous voice.

The professor colored slightly, but his composure was not even threatened. "It's true that the—er—messages which I suggested to Sheila Kelly did not originate in the other world."

"Oh!" gasped Fannie Parrish. "The old fraud!"

The professor seemed amused. "As is the rule in such—er—demonstrations," he explained smoothly, "I collected the data in advance."

"How could you possibly have known that my poor dear Theo called me his Little Butterfly?" protested Fannie indignantly.

The professor ignored her interruption. "I am referring, naturally, to the Little Blue Eyes messages," he said. "As for that other tragic personality which manifested itself at the séance, I deny all responsibility."

Chet Keith scowled. "You do, do you?"

"Absolutely."

"That will be nice for you if you can get by with it," I snapped. "But you can't deny that you have been tampering with this girl's mind for months, subjecting her to daily hypnotic trances, breaking down her resistance to your domination. It is true, isn't it, Professor Matthews, that a constant regime of that sort breaks down the victim's ability to resist mental suggestion?"

The professor smiled with perfect good humor. "It's quite true, Miss Adams, that it is easier to exert a hypnosis the second or third time upon what we scientists prefer to call the subject, not the victim, of the experiment."

"Scientists!" exploded Chet Keith, looking like a furiously disgusted small boy. "You infernal quack!"

The professor smiled deprecatingly. "I fear you are allowing your emotional reactions to distort the known facts in this case, Mr. Keith," he murmured with repulsive benignity. "It is true, as I said, that once a subject has become habituated to hypnosis he offers little if any resistance to mental suggestion, so long as the suggestion is not contrary to his moral code. May I repeat that for emphasis? *So long as the suggestion is not contrary to his moral code?*"

"That's your defense, is it?" demanded Chet Keith.

The professor gave him a smug smile. "Undoubtedly."

"You are going to claim that you could not have prevailed upon Sheila Kelly in a hypnotic trance to kill Thomas Canby?" I demanded, feeling helpless.

"And science will bear me out in the statement."

Hogan Brewster uttered a mirthless laugh. "I tell you if they turn a good defense lawyer loose with that theory, he'll go to town."

Professor Matthews smiled upon him gently. "I'll never sit in the electric chair."

Chet Keith flushed darkly. "There are other ways to die," he said.

For the first time the professor looked disconcerted. "Are you threatening me?"

"I'm reminding you that half of those gold scissors is unaccounted for," said Chet Keith.

The professor smiled. "I assure you they will not be discovered in my body, Mr. Keith."

"For some reason you think you're sitting pretty," said Chet Keith, "but you know something and I'm going to get it out of you."

"You think so?" murmured the professor, his lips curling.

"I know it," said the younger man. "You're yellow, Professor, as yellow as butter, and you'll welsh when the heat's turned on."

"You can't bully me, Mr. Keith," snapped the professor, but his face looked a little shriveled.

"It will be the simplest thing on earth to turn you wrong side out, Professor Matthews."

It seemed to me that the professor cast a terrified glance around the room but I could not be certain, for he recovered himself instantly.

"You can't bully me," he said again.

Chet Keith's voice sharpened. "Good God, man, I'm *warning* you. The only safeguard you have is to spill the truth while you can."

The professor appealed to Sheriff Latham. "Is this man to be permitted to use his position on the witness stand to intimidate other witnesses?" he demanded.

Sheriff Latham rallied. "You'll step down," he said to Chet Keith, "and you'll keep out of this business from now on." He scowled at me. "That goes for you too, lady."

"I doubt it," murmured Chet Keith jauntily.

Nevertheless he did return to his former seat behind me, and I thought his debonair attitude was more bluff than anything else. Apparently Sheila Kelly thought so too, for she sagged back in her chair, her face deathly white.

"She's fainted!" whispered Maurine Smith.

She was mistaken. Sheila Kelly had not fainted. She was pulling herself painfully to her feet. Her eyes had a dazed look. She put out her hand as if she were feeling her, way through a fog, but there was nothing vague or indecisive about the voice which came through her bloodless lips.

"You thought I was dead," she said. "You all hated me and you thought I was out of the way. But I found the way back. Damn you, I found the way back!"

"Gloria!" cried Dora Canby, holding out her trembling arms, but the girl in the center of the room was staring at Judy Oliver.

"You double-crossing little sneak!" she said and drew back her hand.

She intended to strike the other girl in the face. Nobody there had any doubt as to her intention. It was Jeff Wayne who, his face ghastly white, jerked Judy backward out of the way while Chet Keith cleared the room with one bound and caught Sheila Kelly's lifted arm.

"Sheila!" he cried. "For God's sake!"

He shook her violently, so violently she moaned and looked up into his face piteously. "What is it?" she gasped.

Judy Oliver was clinging to Jeff Wayne and sobbing. "She would have killed me!" she wailed.

"You shouldn't flirt with Gloria's sweetheart behind her back, Judy," said Dora Canby fretfully.

Sheila Kelly was trembling from head to foot. "What is it?" she asked again.

"You were about to attack that young woman," said the sheriff in a shaken voice.

"You tried to strike Judy, you—you . . ." Jeff Wayne's voice trailed off as if he did not trust himself to go on.

It was Allan Atwood who fairly flung himself upon the sheriff's attention. "She used her *right* hand!" he exclaimed. "Did you notice, it was her right hand she drew back!"

As a matter of fact it was Sheila Kelly's right arm to which Chet Keith was still holding. He dropped it instantly, but to no avail. Everybody there had seen her draw back that right hand. It was indelibly stamped upon all our minds.

"She didn't know what she was doing," I stammered, my heart in my boots.

The girl's eyes widened in her drawn face until they seemed to drown it. "I killed him," she said. "I must have killed him!"

"Sure you did," said Sheriff Latham.

10

THE JURY'S VERDICT was no surprise. Even before Sheila Kelly's outburst the conclusion was foreordained. After her confession it was inevitable. It was found that Thomas Canby came to his death as the result of a wound in the throat from half of a pair of scissors wielded by Sheila Kelly, and it was recommended that both she and Professor Matthews be held in custody, subject to the action of the local grand jury.

"Though," said the sheriff reluctantly, "I ain't as sure as I was that the professor had anything to do with it."

The inquest had been adjourned. The prisoners had been returned under guard to their rooms, Sheila Kelly in a condition of utter despair, or so it seemed to me, the professor looking rather thoughtful. The rest of us were gathered in the lounge, waiting for the dining room to be opened for lunch, though none of us, I think, had much appetite for food. Certainly I hadn't. I couldn't rid myself of that girl's tragic face.

"How can you be so dense?" I asked the sheriff indignantly. "It is perfectly evident to anybody with a grain of perception that the girl is a victim."

He grinned at me indulgently. "I don't know about perception, but it is mighty evident to me that this trance business is a stall first to last. In the first place there ain't no such thing as hypnotism. In the second place the gal's been making her living for six months or more putting on that sort of act. Why shouldn't she be good at it by now?"

Chet Keith, who had been standing at the window, staring moodily out at the thin watery clouds which lay like a fog over the landscape, turned around and scowled at the sheriff.

"Do you actually believe that she was putting on an act there at the inquest?" he asked incredulously.

Sheriff Latham nodded. "Yep, she was putting on an act all right. I reckon she figures, as Mr. Brewster said, that Mrs. Canby will get her a smart lawyer. I reckon the Kelly girl has heard of insanity pleas."

"So she incriminated herself just to put on a smart act," said Chet Keith in a tired voice.

"Incriminate herself? You mean the confession? That was sort of forced out of her."

"I mean the way she used her right hand," snapped Chet Keith.

The sheriff smiled smugly. "I reckon it's like Mrs. Trotter pointed out, the girl's ambi—ambi—"

"Dextrous, for heaven's sake," I put in crossly.

"I reckon," the sheriff went on with complete imperturbability, "she was so busy putting on a good act, she forgot she was supposed to use her left hand. I reckon that's how come she went to pieces there at the last and spit out the truth."

"You and your reckons!" said Chet Keith explosively.

"Nobody so blind as he who will not see," I marked in my most acid manner and stalked into the dining room.

To my annoyance Fannie Parrish was sitting at my table with Ella.

"Isn't it terrible!" Fannie asked me as I pulled my chair out and settled grumpily into it. "I mean, such a young girl to be a murderess and all that!"

I ignored her but I was not to be permitted to ignore Ella.

"I think even you must admit now, Adelaide, that something very strange is going on here," she said severely, "something you can't pooh-pooh in your usual fashion."

I sighed. "No, nobody can pooh-pooh murder."

"The girl was in some sort of trance," said Ella.

"Yes."

Fannie Parrish gave us a baffled glance. "But Professor Matthews admitted that he was a fraud. He—he said none of his messages from the spirit world were authentic!"

Ella shrugged her shoulders impatiently. "I tell you I have attended every séance, and when the Gloria personality crowded Little Blue Eyes off the scene nobody was so astonished as Professor Matthews, astonished and, if you ask me, petrified with fear."

"He was anything except petrified this morning at the inquest," I protested.

Ella frowned. "Just the same," she said stubbornly, "he isn't responsible for what Sheila Kelly does when she is possessed by— by Gloria Canby's malignant spirit."

Fannie Parrish's eyes rounded to horrified exclamation points. "Goodness, Mrs. Trotter, do you really think that—that dead girl comes back and takes possession of Sheila Kelly?"

"Dora Canby thinks so," said Ella, "and so does Jeff Wayne. Have you noticed how he looks at Sheila Kelly?"

"He hates her and he's afraid of her," said Fannie, who never missed anything. "But aren't we all?" she asked with a shudder.

"If only they'd get that blasted bridge fixed!" groaned Ella. "Before something else happens!"

I stared at her. "Don't be so jittery, Ella!" I said angrily. "Why should anything else happen?"

"Thomas Canby wasn't the only one Gloria Canby hated," said Ella solemnly.

"The girl's dead," I said.

Ella merely raised her eyebrows. "Did you know she was having an affair with Hogan Brewster when Lila Atwood came on the scene?" she asked.

"No," I said in a nettled voice, "and I'm not interested in gossip of that nature."

"Everybody's interested in gossip," remarked Ella dryly. "The more they deny it, the more they're interested as a rule, and you're no exception, Adelaide."

I shrugged my shoulders, so, looking very smug, Ella went right on. "She was engaged to Jeff Wayne. She intended to marry him, but that didn't keep her from playing around."

"I heard Lila Atwood and her husband having a terrible quarrel yesterday afternoon," volunteered Fannie. "At least *he* was quarreling. She never answers him back, have you noticed?"

Ella frowned. "They've never got along, so Judy says. Right from the first they've been at daggers' points, or he has. Everything she does rubs him the wrong way."

"That's what they were quarreling about," announced Fannie eagerly. "He said she had made her bargain with his uncle Thomas and kept it, in spite of hell, but she couldn't keep him from hating both of them."

None of us had heard Lila Atwood come up behind us. We all started at her luscious voice. She was smiling, and I thought again what a beautiful woman she was, with more poise than anyone I had ever seen.

"You mustn't take everything my husband says seriously, Mrs. Parrish," she murmured. "Allan is frightfully impetuous, poor dear."

We had no way of knowing how much of our conversation she had overheard, and I had the pleasure of seeing Fannie Parrish shrink practically to the vanishing point under Lila Atwood's level dark eyes. I should have been content to let well enough alone, but it has never been my nature to overlook a challenge and I had no intention of allowing Lila Atwood to reduce me to speechlessness.

"So your husband never forgave his uncle for arranging your marriage," I said, "but then, I dare say you never forgave Thomas Canby either."

Our eyes clashed but I stood my ground, and to my perturbation Lila Atwood's lovely mouth quivered. "I hated Uncle Thomas, if that is what you are determined to find out," she said, "but not, as you seem to imagine, because he arranged my marriage to Allan."

She hesitated and I was forced to prompt her. "No?"

She gave me a rebuking glance. "I can take what is coming to me, Miss Adams. I was brought up that way, you know, not to buck my fences and above all not to whine over a skinned elbow. Thomas Canby and I did make a bargain. It was perfectly straightforward and I never held it against him. What I have held against him . . ."

She paused again, and for the second time I prompted her. "Yes?"

"He shortchanged me," she said, her lips curling.

"Shortchanged you?"

She made a singularly helpless gesture with her shoulders. "He led me to believe that Allan understood the transaction."

She glanced across the room where Allan Atwood was sitting at the same table with Hogan Brewster and Patrick Oliver. Brewster smiled at her and beckoned, but young Atwood merely scowled.

"Your husband didn't understand until afterward that your marriage was a dollar-and-cents proposition between you and his uncle?" I asked.

It seemed to occur to her at last that I had no right to be delving into her private affairs. Lila Atwood was perfectly capable of keeping her own counsel. I suppose it was only because of what my foster son Stephen calls my goading powers that she had been betrayed into saying so much.

"If you don't mind, Miss Adams," she remarked with her serene smile, "I'll keep the rest of my family skeletons to myself."

She would have moved away, but Ella halted her.

"It was Gloria Canby who told Allan, wasn't it, right after you were married?" she demanded.

Lila Atwood turned perfectly white. "Yes," she said, "Gloria told him. The house was full of wedding guests. I was still wearing my wedding veil. Gloria thought it was funny. She laughed and laughed."

"It wasn't funny to you?" I asked.

She looked at me. "No," she said, "it wasn't funny to me."

And then she turned and walked away. Hogan Brewster jumped up to pull out a chair for her. Her husband did not move. He did not even look up when she leaned toward him and spoke in that gentle tone which she seemed to reserve for him.

"Is your headache better, dear?" she asked. "Did you take an aspirin?"

"For God's sake," cried Allan Atwood in a surly voice, "can't you let me alone?"

Fannie Parrish nodded. "That's what he said over and over yesterday," she explained. "'Can't you let me alone? That's all I have ever asked of you, just let me alone.' It's rather pathetic, isn't it?"

"Yes," I said curtly but I have an idea we were not referring to the same thing.

Judy Oliver did not appear in the dining room for luncheon, and Mrs. Parrish explained that Judy was lunching with her, aunt in Mrs. Canby's sitting room. Chet Keith also did not put in an appearance. When I returned to the lounge he was still staring out the window, his brows gathered in a dark frown.

Ella nudged me. "I told you he was in love with the Kelly girl."

"He's been flirting with Maurine Smith ever since he got here," protested Fannie.

I scowled. "It must be wonderful to be so omniscient."

"Er—yes," admitted Fannie dubiously. "At any rate she says he's simply fascinating, and I know he's spent hours hanging over her switchboard. That reminds me," she said, trotting over to Captain French, who was staring gloomily out at the weather. "About the bridge, Captain. What is the latest report?"

I doubt if there was any interval of ten minutes duration during this period when Captain French was not confronted with that question. No wonder he looked jaded.

"I understand the highway commission hopes to have the bridge back in place and open for service by tomorrow morning," he said.

Fannie gave a little squeal of dismay. "Not before morning! Oh dear, do you mean we'll have to go through another horrible night cooped up in this place in fear of our lives?"

"I assure you," said Captain French as he had been assuring panic-stricken guests for the past twelve hours, "there is no danger; the officers have the situation well in hand."

As I found out from Chet Keith, it was not only the sheriff and his two deputies who had taken over the task of guarding the prisoners. Jeff Wayne had announced that it was not sufficient to have somebody stationed in the hall outside Sheila Kelly's room. He pointed out, which was true enough, that the room had windows as well as doors, so he had delegated to himself the responsibility of doing sentry duty under Sheila Kelly's windows.

"You can see for yourself if you care to look out," muttered Chet Keith with a grimace. "He's pacing up and down in the drizzle like the quixotic young fool he is."

"It has begun to drizzle, hasn't it?" I said. "That makes it just too lovely."

"Doesn't it? Of all the dismal holes!"

He shivered and I glanced at him sharply. He looked almost as jittery as Ella, which I am positive was new in his experience.

"Why quixotic?" I asked sharply.

His thoughts were far away, for he started, then grinned ruefully.

"Young Wayne, you mean? Of course you know what ails him?" I shook my head and he laughed bitterly. "He's scared to death that Judy Oliver will be the next victim."

I stared at him in astonishment. "The next victim!"

"Gloria Canby hated Judy," he said.

I could scarcely believe my ears. "I didn't expect you to endorse this hand-from-the-grave stuff," I said sternly.

"I'm only telling you what young Wayne happens to believe," he said shortly. "He's in love with the Oliver girl."

"That's why he avoids her," I remarked with what I intended for irony.

"Naturally," snapped Chet Keith. "He's afraid. Haven't you noticed how he glares at Sheila?"

He stammered slightly over the name and gave me a thoroughly miserable look. "What in the devil is going on here, Miss Adams?" he asked in a stifled voice.

"Have you tried—I believe you called it turning the professor wrong side out yet?" I countered.

His blue eyes sharpened. "You believe she killed Canby at the professor's suggestion?"

"I don't know what to believe," I confessed unhappily.

I was not alone in that predicament, as I discovered when I circulated about among my fellow guests. The parlor doors were again closed and locked with Thomas Canby's body inside. The lounge was neither comfortable nor cheerful that gloomy afternoon, with the rain whispering against the windows and everything damp to the touch. Nevertheless no one showed any disposition to go off by himself. Everybody hovered disconsolately in small groups in the lobby, talking in low tones or staring blankly at the floor. As I made it my business to find out, it was the consensus of opinion that Sheila Kelly had killed Thomas Canby. There, however, all agreement ended.

Quite a few, noticeably the men, believed with the sheriff that the girl was a designing adventuress. They were convinced that she was making a desperate play at Dora Canby's fortune. They did not put any faith in the theory that she was or ever had been in a hypnotic trance. They pointed out that the professor was an obvious quack. They said the girl was a clever actress, and why not? Hadn't she been on the stage for years? The fact that she had previously been arrested in a raided night club told against her.

"Just a bad egg," they remarked with that concerted masculine piety which always annoys me.

"She was acquitted," I said angrily.

"So that reporter says," I was reminded, "but he's obviously determined to get her out of it by hook or crook. I suppose he's counting on a slice of the Canby millions."

Others were just as positive that Sheila Kelly was guilty of the fatal blow, but they were by no means disposed to absolve the professor of complicity. It was their opinion that Sheila Kelly had not been putting on an act when she went into the alleged trance. They said the girl could not have been faking during that remarkable demonstration at the séance. They argued that it might be a deep-laid plot against the Canby fortune, but if so the professor was the manipulator and Sheila Kelly only his tool. To this I found myself subscribing.

The third group, which included Ella, though she declined to enter into the general discussion, insisted that Sheila Kelly killed Thomas Canby, but declared that the professor had nothing to do with it. They said she was actuated by Gloria Canby's malignant and revengeful spirit. They talked with bated breath of other supernatural occurrences of which they had heard, occurrences where the dead returned to contact the living, usually with hair-raising results.

"I never listened to such balderdash!" I protested indignantly. "Did you ever see a ghost? Or you? Or you? Of course not! You *heard* about someone who did."

A large elderly woman sitting in a wheel chair undertook to set me right. "Many phenomena of this nature have been vouched for by unimpeachable witnesses, Miss Adams."

I sniffed. "Seeing's believing," I snapped.

Ella regarded me in a most unfriendly manner. "I wouldn't tempt fate too far if I were you, Adelaide," she said. "After all, your room adjoins that girl's."

"I'm not afraid that Gloria Canby's phantom will come through the door and cut my throat, Ella, if that is what you mean."

Ella shrugged her shoulders. "I notice you haven't retired to your room as usual for your afternoon nap."

As a matter of fact I had had no intention of doing so, for several reasons, but Ella has always been able to taunt me into action.

"I'm going shortly," I announced in my loftiest manner and then rather spoiled my own effect by adding, "Anyway, the door between my room and Sheila Kelly's is bolted."

"As if bolts and bars mean anything to the undead!" exclaimed Fannie Parrish dramatically. "I wouldn't be alone in that room for—for . . ." She paused, unable to think of anything emphatic enough, and finished with a defiant flourish. "I wouldn't be alone anywhere in this awful place. I intend to spend the night right here on this settee."

The woman in the wheel chair glanced uneasily over her shoulder. "I don't think any of us look forward to being alone as long as that girl is here."

I lost my temper. "Why should she bother you or me?" I asked. "Granting that she did kill Canby. We've done her no harm and she stands to gain nothing from us. I think you are all a little out of your mind about this thing."

Ella frowned. "Dora Canby's canary hadn't done any harm either," she said, "and heaven knows, there was nothing to gain by strangling it, but it was strangled."

Fannie Parrish lowered her voice to a whisper. "Gloria Canby was a thoroughly vicious person," she said. "Did you know she drowned Jeff Wayne's pet pup? Held its head under water till it died. It had been a present from his mother, her last present just before she died. He was awfully attached to it—the dog, I mean."

I gave my shoulders a little shake. "The girl is dead," I said.

I meant my voice to ring with conviction, but it must not have quite come off, for Fannie Parrish went right on.

"It's all the professor's fault," she said, "though I don't believe he intended anything like this. He did, however, tear the veil aside."

"What veil aside from what, for heaven's sake?" I demanded impatiently.

"It's just as you said," pursued Fannie, knitting her brows. "The professor has been weakening Sheila Kelly's resistance to mental suggestion for months, so she was ripe for that other to take possession."

"Tommyrot!" I protested and turned away.

I did not know that Ella had followed me until she put her hand on my arm as I reached the foot of the stairs. I was more nervous than I realized, for I started violently and then turned very red.

"What do you mean, creeping up on a person like that?" I demanded angrily.

Ella for once in her life failed to take umbrage. "Don't go off to your room alone, Adelaide," she said so earnestly that I was touched. "I tell you it isn't safe."

"Nonsense!"

"Fannie Parrish is right. The professor has been tampering with forces he can't control and he's let loose a devil in this place."

"Preposterous!"

"I don't like to think of you upstairs next door to that unfortunate girl."

Ella and I are fond of each other in our way, but we do not make a habit of displaying our affection and we were both embarrassed by Ella's very evident concern. I patted her arm clumsily, not being any more adept than she at tender gestures.

"Aren't you forgetting that there is a deputy on guard in the hall, to say nothing of young Jeff Wayne outside under the window?" I asked. "I'll be all right."

My voice was a little gruff and Ella sighed. "Do, for heaven's sake, Adelaide, keep that door locked."

I looked at her sharply and wondered again if it was possible that Ella had recognized the voices in my room the night before.

"Don't be silly," I said. "Of course I'll keep the door locked."

It took me a long time to climb the stairs, longer than I can lay to my arthritic knee. I had the queerest feeling that something was tugging back upon me. I told myself it was all Ella's fault. I had forgotten until she reminded me that the door which opened into Sheila Kelly's room from mine was not locked, but bolted on her side. I had never felt in the least drawn to Butch. Nevertheless he was an extremely welcome sight, tilted back in his straight chair against Sheila Kelly's door.

He cocked an eyebrow at me when he recognized me. "You'd think there was smallpox on this floor, the way people are staying away from it," he said.

I had an idea that he himself was none too comfortable at his post. At any rate he was disposed to be conversational, but I cut him short for the simple reason that I much preferred staying there in the hall talking with him to entering my own room and I have never believed in indulging my weaknesses. I thought Butch stared after me wistfully as I grasped my doorknob and firmly turned it.

I still insist, in spite of Ella's jeers, that it was the presence of the alley cat, not Sheila Kelly, which made me shriek. "Many people have a horror of cats," I have repeatedly told her.

"I never heard of your being one of them before," retorted Ella.

Unfortunately this was true. I have never felt the aversion which is said to overcome certain persons at the glimpse of a cat. Nevertheless when I walked into that dingy, ill-lighted room on the second floor of Mount Lebeau that afternoon and saw that gaunt, green-eyed alley cat rearing its hackles and spitting at me from the windowsill, it did give me a turn.

"What is it?" shouted the deputy on the other side of the door. "What's wrong, Miss Adams?"

I swallowed hard.

Sheila Kelly was standing in the center of the floor, staring at me, her knuckles pressed against her quivering lips, the door into her room open behind her.

"Nothing," I said after a long pause. "Nothing at all. I—I merely stumped my toe on the rug."

I heard the deputy mutter something which sounded suspiciously like "Damned fool hysterical women!" Then he shuffled heavily back down the hall to his chair.

"God bless you," whispered Sheila Kelly and, sinking into a chair, covered her face with her shaking hands.

11

I SHOULD, OF COURSE, have put the alley cat out. There were several things I should have done when I discovered Sheila Kelly in my room, such as informing the deputy, if not the sheriff, of her presence. However, I had taken my stand and there was nothing to do except live up to it, or so I thought at the time, though had I foreseen . . . But it is too late now to wonder whether I could have changed the dreadful sequence of events if I had not lied to Butch Newby, if instead I had thrown my door open for his inspection.

I did lie—that remains unalterable—and I put neither Sheila Kelly nor the cat out. Once I had recovered from the initial shock I felt equally sorry for both of them. It was, as I have said, a very gaunt, miserable-looking specimen of alley cat. Its ribs showed through its mangy gray coat. It was depressingly dirty and wet and one of its paws had been injured, so that it limped slightly. Like all strays, it was embarrassingly grateful for the smallest attention.

"Here, puss, here, puss," I murmured, as much to give myself as Sheila Kelly a breathing space.

An invitation was all that Mr. Tom required. I suppose it had been a long time, if ever, since he had had a kind word. Rubbing against my ankles, he purred loudly.

"There's nothing wrong with his motor at any rate," I said and sat down rather limply in a chair.

The cat promptly jumped into my lap and, still purring loudly, stretched luxuriously before cuddling down with every appearance of having settled in for the winter.

Sheila Kelly looked at me, her lips quivering. "I've got to talk to you, I've got to talk to somebody," she whispered.

She was at the breaking point, I realized that at once. I suppose that is really why I lied to Butch. The girl looked so desperate and forlorn, as if, like the cat, she hadn't a friend in the world.

"But maybe you're afraid of me," she said. "Maybe you're scared to be alone with me."

I cannot describe the horror with which she managed to invest these words. I realized that the hand with which I was stroking the cat was trembling visibly. I tried to hide it, but she saw and shivered.

"I did it," she said. "I killed a man! Cut his throat! Oh, God!"

By my sharp revulsion of feeling I knew that, like the others, I had gradually arrived at the decision that Sheila Kelly was guilty, in spite of how I had felt about it the night before. Only, face to face with her, it did not seem possible. "She is no killer," I remember saying to myself quite fiercely. I leaned a little forward and the cat squirmed, then accommodated himself to my new posture after a reproachful glance up into my eyes.

"The professor is back of it," I said. "He must be!"

She caught her breath. "If only I could believe it!"

I made my voice as stern as possible. "The dead do not return. Remember what Chet Keith told you. The dead cannot come back to torture the living."

The girl had more pluck than I imagined. "Neither can you hypnotize a person into committing murder against his will," she reminded me in a low voice. "Don't you see? That is what is driving me crazy! Even if he—he wanted to, the professor couldn't make me cut Thomas Canby's throat in a trance. It's something—something else that—that gets into me, Miss Adams, something horrible!"

The wind was rising, and behind me something creaked. "I don't believe in ghosts," I stated sharply. Nevertheless I could not keep from glancing over my shoulder, and Sheila Kelly saw and smiled bitterly.

"Isn't there a place in the Bible that puts a curse upon you for tampering with the unknown?" she asked.

"I dare say you are referring to the incident of the Witch of Endor," I stammered.

"That's what the professor and I have done," she said with a shudder. "I let him tamper with my mind to put over a cheap racket and now—and now . . ." She drew her hand confusedly across her forehead. "And now my mind doesn't belong to me any more. We let down the bars and she—and she comes in and takes possession whenever she likes. Whenever she likes!" she repeated wildly, her voice mounting to a wail which made the cat in my lap stir uncomfortably, the hair about its neck bristling.

"Such things aren't possible!" I protested a little frantically. "You *have* permitted the professor to tamper with your mind. You *have* allowed him to break down your resistance to mental suggestion, *his* suggestion. But whatever it is that has taken possession of your mind, it is not supernatural. You've got, as Chet Keith told you, to hang onto that for dear life."

"But I killed Thomas Canby," she whispered. "You were all there and you know I killed him, and this morning—this morning I would have attacked Judy Oliver if Chet hadn't snapped me out of it."

"There is a great difference between slapping a girl's face and killing a man," I said slowly, "and about last night, the room was dark. All any of us can swear to is that you called Thomas Canby a number of hard names before the lights went out."

Again she drew a long breath. "There were no bloodstains on the handkerchief, Miss Adams, I swear it," she whispered.

It was heartbreaking to see how eagerly she leaped at even the frailest hope. It seemed to me that I could not bear it if I were unable to find some means of reassuring the poor distraught young thing.

"I'll put it to you like this," I said, feeling my way as I went. "You said yourself that Professor Matthews was a quack, but a harmless one. At least before he met Dora Canby he was engaged in a questionable game, but not a criminal one."

She winced. "Yes."

"However, he had not then come up against the temptation of several million dollars."

She made a wry face. "Until we met Dora Canby there was no money in the racket at all; none, I mean, except what we earned for a third-rate vaudeville act."

"Just so," I murmured. Curiously enough, putting it into words had the effect of clarifying my own thoughts. I went on with a great deal more confidence.

"The professor would not be the first small-time crook who lost his head when he saw the chance to put his hands on big money."

"You mean you think he—he . . ." She shook her head. "It's scientifically true, Miss Adams, that you can't use hypnosis to make a subject commit murder against his will," she repeated in a despairing voice.

"There's no proof you committed murder!" I cried sharply. "So far as the evidence goes, anybody in that room, including myself, with access to the light cord could have taken advantage of the darkness and your tirade against Thomas Canby to kill him."

She stared at me. "You think the professor framed me?" she whispered.

"There was nothing to prevent his staging these Gloria manifestations to put you on the spot, while he did the actual murder himself."

"Oh!" she gasped, her eyes beginning to glow.

"You've been maneuvered very cleverly into a position where you have not only confessed to murder but believe it," I said. "Yet it seems to me there is no real evidence that you have ever done anything except carry on like Gloria Canby."

She drew a long breath, like a sob. "The professor has been praying in his room this afternoon," she whispered. "I heard him through the bathroom wall, praying for guidance—just that, over and over for guidance."

It is nothing short of miraculous how one can delude oneself if pushed to it. "The man's suffering from a guilty conscience!" I exclaimed. "He killed Canby and, being a coward, the professor is afraid for his immortal soul."

She shuddered "I know, because I have been praying too."

She got shakily to her feet and gave me a wan smile. "You must know how much you have helped me," she said unsteadily.

I pressed her hand. "You've got to hold onto yourself. You haven't been convicted of this crime yet and"—I took a weak refuge in the old adage—"murder will out."

She clung to my fingers. "God bless you," she said again and walked into her room with a firmer step than I would have believed possible ten minutes before. I brushed my hand across my eyes, and the cat, which had tumbled to the floor when I rose to my feet, mewed softly. He followed close at my heels and I walked over to the window and looked out. The drizzle had thickened to a slow cold rain and the wind was beginning to whine about the eaves of the house, but young Jeff Wayne was still on guard below, hunched into a heavy black raincoat which he must have borrowed from someone, for it was several sizes too big for him.

I glanced at my watch. It was too early to dress for dinner. It was too early to go back downstairs, unless I wanted Ella to know how I hated to stay alone in that room. My head felt thick. After all, I had had very little sleep the night before, and the day had been nerve-racking, to say the least, nor am I so young as I might be. I did not believe I could close my eyes; nevertheless I thought it a good idea to lie down for a few minutes and make an attempt to relax. I was surprised at how good the bed felt, for the inn's mattresses will never take a prize.

I remember the cat hopping up beside me and turning around several times before curling up in a tight gray ball against my back. I remember telling myself that I should have to make him get down. After all, one doesn't share one's bed with a mangy alley cat, although it was oddly comforting to have him there with his loud purr, cozy and warm behind me. I remember telling myself with some chagrin that anything was better than being alone in that dark dreary room with the rain washing against the windows and the wind lamenting outside like a lost soul.

I don't remember anything else until I awoke, sitting bolt upright in bed, every muscle in my body taut with terror. I did not know what had aroused me, I did not know why I was literally speechless with fright. I simply sat there, the very blood in my body congealing with horror, staring straight before me at the dim gray oblongs which were the windows in a room that had grown pitch dark with the rain and the approach of night.

Then, near me, a door closed stealthily.

I still contend that I cleared the quite considerable space between me and the light switch at a single leap, although Ella persists in saying that is impossible for a woman of my age and build. The fact remains that scarcely a minute elapsed from the time I heard somebody close my door until I flicked on the lights with a shaking hand. The resultant illumination blinded me for a moment. Then my eyes adjusted themselves and I saw that horrible thing on the foot of the bed.

It was not quite dead, although it had been completely eviscerated. As I stared at it, my vocal cord paralyzed with horror, the gaunt green eyes fastened on me in dumb agony and the mangy gray tail lashed feebly while one long thin leg twitched in agony. It even made a frenzied effort, before it collapsed in its death spasms, to crawl toward me. It was then I screamed and went on screaming.

By rights the deputy Butch should have been the first to reach me, but as I discovered afterward he waited to prop his chair, under Sheila Kelly's door. So it was Ella, of all people, who came to my rescue, bouncing into the room as if she had been shot out of a gun and proceeding to shake me violently before she snatched up the water pitcher off my bedside table and drenched me. I was still spluttering when Chet Keith collided with Butch Newby and Sheriff Latham on the threshold of my room. Back of them I saw Fannie Parrish, her wiry iron-gray hair standing on end with fright, clinging to Captain Bill French, who was furiously biting his mustache.

"Good Lord, Miss Adams, I thought you'd been murdered!" exclaimed Chet Keith, suppressing a grin as he observed the trickle of water meandering down my face from the false curls on my forehead, which had taken the full force of Ella's deluge.

"We all expected you to have your throat cut," contributed Fannie Parrish with a nervous giggle.

"What's the big idea?" demanded the sheriff. "Scaring us out of our wits!"

This time I could not be mistaken about Butch's remark. "Damned hysterical women!"

It is necessary to explain that in their, preoccupation with me nobody as yet had discovered that grisly object upon the foot of my bed. I suppose I should have been flattered at their concern, especially Ella's, who looked far more shaken than I did and who still clutched the water pitcher and was inclined to brandish it.

"Do put that thing down," I said crossly. "Aren't you satisfied with nearly drowning me?"

To my consternation Ella burst into tears. "I twitted you into coming off up here by yourself and if anything had happened to you, Adelaide, I should never have forgiven myself."

"There, there," I murmured, patting her arm and feeling very foolish. "I'm sorry to disappoint everybody but I'm all right."

To my relief Ella promptly reverted to form. "Then what in heaven's name do you mean, Adelaide Adams, by scaring the day-lights out of me?"

I took a long breath and pointed, rather melodramatically I am afraid, toward the bed. I think it was Chet Keith who first brushed by me and stood looking down at that gruesome corpse, his face as white as paper. Then everybody crowded into the room to stare at the mangled alley cat. That is why, later, I could not swear to who was there and who wasn't and when. I recall Lila Atwood and how expressionless she was except for her sickened eyes, and Judy Oliver, clutching her brother's arm but gazing at Jeff Wayne, who had run in from outside and looked very cold and wet and tired, and Allan Atwood hovering for a moment on the threshold before he gave way to Coroner Timmons, and Patrick Oliver, great circles under his ingenuous blue eyes, saying his aunt Dora had sent him upstairs to find out what had happened. Even the woman in the wheel chair refused to be left alone in the lobby and managed to hobble in, supported by Miss Maurine Smith on one side and on the other by the colored porter Jake, whose black face was chalky with fear and who refused even to glance at my bed.

Everybody kept asking me questions. How had it happened and what was the cat doing in my room and why didn't I know what had taken place? I think I must have explained separately and collectively a dozen or more times that I was as much in the dark as anyone. You would have thought I had deliberately planned the episode to reduce Fannie Parrish and certain other guests of the inn to a more complete state of gibbering panic, if that were possible.

"I don't know where the cat came from," I repeated wearily. "It was just here when I came to my room and it was cold and wet and"— at this point my tone bristled in spite of myself—"I let it stay."

"Of all the silly things to do!" protested Ella, eying me sharply.

"It seemed a good idea at the time," I said weakly.

Hogan Brewster, who had taken Allan Atwood's place in the doorway, grinned at me. "I don't suppose you could have taken to walking in your sleep, could you, Miss Adams?"

"I didn't butcher the poor animal, Mr. Brewster, if that is what you mean," I said with a shudder.

He continued to favor me with his sardonic smile. "It's a little uncanny, isn't it, that you were shut in here alone with the beast when it happened. I mean there was a guard outside in the hall and Jeff here was doing sentry duty under the window, or were you?"

Young Wayne colored angrily. "Yes."

The deputy sounded slightly nettled. "I was sitting down the hall. I had my back this way, but I don't see how nobody could have come out of this room without my hearing them."

My eyes met Chet Keith's and I knew that he had remembered about unlocking the door into Sheila Kelly's room the night before.

Sheriff Latham scratched his head and looked at me very hard. "You say just after you woke up you heard a door close, Miss Adams?"

I nodded and again Chet Keith's eyes met mine.

"The door into the hall?" persisted the sheriff.

"What other door could it have been?" I demanded tartly. "Or do you think somebody is hiding in my bathroom?"

That created a diversion. The sheriff and Butch promptly strode across the room and inspected the bath. They looked both uneasy and crestfallen when they returned.

"It couldn't have been the door into the adjoining room," said Chet Keith, wearing his blandest expression. "It is locked."

He seized the knob and shook it vigorously to sustain his contention.

"Moreover, the key is on this side," he announced.

I think I must have blinked, but Chet Keith regarded me without batting an eye. There was a key in the lock on my side of the door, but it had not been there when I detoured the sheriff and his henchman into the bathroom.

"As if locks and bars mean anything to that girl!" cried Fannie Parrish, staring intently at the dividing wall between my room and Sheila Kelly's. "As I've said before," she repeated emphatically, "none of us is safe! Not one! So long as Gloria Canby's unhappy Spirit continues to roam this house!"

Sheriff Latham had a bewildered look. "I don't take no stock in this supernatural business," he said doggedly. "If that gal killed the cat, she come out of a door just like anybody else."

He fixed a piercing glance upon Butch, who colored darkly.

"I ain't saying nobody didn't come out Miss Adams' door," he said in a heckled voice. "I told you I had my back turned and I may have caught a wink or two of sleep."

"It wouldn't be the first time he's slept on duty," I put in with a sniff.

"Just the same," continued the deputy, looking baited but very certain of his ground, "one thing I can swear to: the Kelly dame never came out her door."

"When the man's asleep, you could blow a trumpet back of his ear, without waking him," said Ella with indignation.

"Oh yeah?" retorted Butch. "Maybe so, but I've had my chair tilted back against the Kelly girl's door for over an hour, and if you think she could move that chair with my two hundred pounds in it without waking me, lady, then there is such a thing as hypnotism and hants."

"You'd think," interposed Fannie Parrish, "that all this commotion next door would have aroused her."

The sheriff scowled. "We'll just see what she has to say for herself."

"The door's bolted on her side," I put in hurriedly.

Hogan Brewster frowned. "How do you know, Miss Adams?"

He had a talent for disconcerting me. "I happened to hear her shoot the bolt," I said, conscious of the sheriff's stare.

"The partitions between these rooms aren't soundproof," interposed Ellen with suspicious quickness. "From my bathroom I can hear Adelaide every time she washes her hands."

The sheriff again transfixed Butch with a glance. "You've got the key to the Kelly girl's room. around by the hall and open this door between. I want to see her face when she discovers the cat."

Butch saluted smartly and strode out. I remember holding my breath. I had a horror of meeting Sheila Kelly's eyes, of watching her come into that room before all our staring eyes to be confronted with that limp, bloodstained thing on my bed. I noticed that Chet Keith's hands were clenched. I have an idea that he, too, was holding his breath. However, although it was merely postponing the inevitable, Sheriff Latham was not destined at that time to have his promised inter view with Sheila Kelly. Butch suddenly reappeared in the doorway. He looked as if he had taken a punch in the jaw.

"Something's wrong," he said hoarsely.

"What the hell!" exclaimed the sheriff, taking a step toward him.

The deputy actually cowered. "The professor's door is standing wide open," he croaked.

We must have all stared at him incredulously, for he went on insistently. "The key's still in my pocket," he said, "but his door's wide open and—and . . ." He swallowed. "There's a little stream of blood creeping down the hall."

Again there was a period of confusion during which I cannot be positive of anybody's movements, not even my own. I have a dim recollection of everybody crowding out into the hall, just as formerly everybody had crowded into my room. I remember Ella holding onto my arm convulsively and gulping as she stared over my shoulder at that prostrate figure beyond the open door down the corridor. I distinctly remember Fannie Parrish's teeth chattering in my very ear and Judy Oliver beginning to sob loudly while Jeff Wayne took her hand and cradled it against his cheek and begged her not to be frightened because he would protect her with his life. I remember Chet Keith muttering over and over, "God! Good God! But I warned him." And I shall never forget Sheriff Latham, after a moment's hesitation, going into that room and kneeling down to murmur, "He's dead! Dead as a doornail!"

As if he needed to tell us that after we had one glimpse of Professor Thaddeus Matthews' contorted and livid face, grinning above the gold handle of the scissors which protruded from the wet red gash in his throat.

12

"YOU HAVE REFUSED from the first to put any credence in there being something supernatural about this business, Sheriff," Chet Keith kept hammering in. "From the beginning you have persisted in taking a commonsense attitude toward the situation, in which you are quite right, according to your lights, but you can't eat your cake and have it too."

It was some time later and we were all herded again into the front parlor downstairs, all of us, that is, who had attended the séance the night before. The folding doors into the rear room were closed, but Thomas Canby's dead body no longer rested there alone. Another of the hard red sofas had acquired an occupant.

"The girl killed him," said Sheriff Latham, although his voice had lost its belligerence.

The man actually seemed dwarfed in size, and while Coroner Timmons was once more putting up a pretense of conducting the investigation, the sheriff's muscular hands were not now operating the strings, or if so, very feebly.

"You can't have it both ways," insisted Chet Keith. "You don't believe that Sheila Kelly is possessed of a ghost which is able to pass through locked doors and solid walls at will, do you?"

"No," growled Sheriff Latham in an unhappy voice.

"But by the evidence of your own man she never left her room. Or are you going to turn around and say now that there is such a thing as hypnotism and she hypnotized your deputy Butch into removing both him self and his chair from her door without either his knowledge or consent?"

"Nope," said the sheriff doggedly, "she never got past Butch."

"Then she didn't kill the professor!" exclaimed Chet Keith. He did not look at me but he was perfectly conscious of what I was thinking, I feel sure. "And if she didn't kill the professor she didn't kill Canby!"

The girl, sitting between the two deputies, did not lift her head. She had not looked up since they brought her into the room, quite a while after the discovery of the professor's dead body. I had dreaded seeing her. I had wondered how on earth I could meet her eyes, knowing what I knew. It was all very well for Chet Keith to bulldoze the sheriff, but he could not deceive me. The door into her room had not been locked on my side when I went to sleep.

"Or don't you believe that the two crimes are connected?" demanded Chet Keith.

The sheriff wriggled his burly shoulders. "They're connected," he admitted miserably, "though danged if I know how."

"It's plain enough," said Chet Keith quickly. "The professor knew something. If you want it in words of one syllable, he knew who murdered Thomas Canby and he paid for his knowledge with his life."

"Might be," muttered the sheriff.

Chet Keith's face was pretty white. "As a matter of fact," he said without any signs of happiness, "I signed the professor's death warrant when I warned him in the presence of everybody in this room that I was going to get his secret out of him."

"You've been entirely too buttinsky in this whole affair," said Sheriff Latham with a scowl.

It was his last spurt of rebellion against allowing matters to slide out of his hands, and Chet Keith knew it.

"You're over your head, Sheriff," he said, not unkindly. "You have been all along."

The sheriff was a bigger man than I had thought. He was big enough to acknowledge his limitations.

"All right," he said in a muffled voice, "this thing has got me beat. If you can do better with it, help yourself."

Chet Keith needed no second invitation. There was a set to his jaw which indicated that he had determined to take over the situation and a glint in his eyes which said it would be unfortunate for anybody who tried to sidetrack him.

"Sheila Kelly could not have killed the professor," he repeated. "She could not have got out of her room. When Butch wasn't propped up against her door, his chair was wedged under it."

"That's right," said Butch in a dogged voice.

Still Sheila Kelly did not raise her eyes.

"What about the amber hairpin which the professor was clutching in his hand?" asked Allan Atwood with a sullen frown.

I caught my breath. I had not known till then that the dead man had held an amber-colored hairpin in his hand when discovered.

"Yeah," put in Patrick Oliver resentfully, "what about it, Keith? Sheila Kelly's the only woman at the inn with long blonde hair."

The sheriff took up the point with eagerness. "You wear hairpins like this, Miss Kelly?" he asked and held out another of those cheap celluloid pins which I had seen before.

She stared at it and I saw the cords in her throat work, as if she were trying to speak, but no sound came.

"Certainly she wears them," interposed Chet Keith smoothly. "She has a couple in her hair now."

Everybody leaned forward, the better to see, and there they were, neatly pinning that pale coil of golden hair on the nape of her neck.

"Let's see one," snapped Sheriff Latham.

She put up her hand with a dazed gesture and removed a hairpin. It was a mate to the one which the sheriff had laid on the table beside him.

"Might be its twin," muttered the deputy Butch.

"What of it?" I demanded tremulously. "You can buy a card of them in any dime store for ten cents."

Coroner Timmons frowned. "But it was clutched in the dead man's hand."

"On the contrary," said Chet Keith quickly. "If you remember, I called it especially to your attention, sir. The pin was not clutched in the professor's hand. It was merely resting between his fingers on the floor and they were perfectly relaxed."

"What's the difference?" demanded the sheriff. "He had it, didn't he, and it's our only clue."

Chet Keith continued to address the coroner. "You're a doctor," he said. "You know that at the moment of violent death the extremities of the victim undergo what is called a cadaveric spasm. This causes the fingers to close tightly upon whatever is held in the hand, so tightly it is almost impossible to loosen them. It is a condition which nobody can simulate."

Coroner Timmons nodded reluctantly, and the sheriff gave Chet Keith an impatient scowl. "What of it?" he asked again.

"The pin was placed in the professor's hand after death."

"Why should the girl put one of her hairpins in his hand after death?" scoffed Sheriff Latham.

"She didn't," said Chet Keith. "The pin was put there by the murderer to incriminate Sheila Kelly."

His eyes traveled slowly over the circle of faces about him.

"Somebody in this group killed Canby and framed Sheila Kelly for the murder," he said, "but the professor knew the truth and he was weakening. If he had lived, sooner or later he'd have told everything, so one of you killed him."

I think we all gasped and it seemed to me for a moment that everybody there looked both guilty and apprehensive, a reaction which even the innocent are apt to show to such an accusation.

"Aren't you covering a lot of territory?" demanded Allan Atwood savagely. "You and your cadaveric spasms! How do you happen to know so much about that sort of thing?"

Chet Keith's mouth tightened. "I've been a reporter, a police reporter, if I must be exact. I've watched the best detectives in the business work. There's not much about crime I don't know."

"Oh yeah?" muttered Patrick Oliver.

Chet Keith turned upon him so suddenly the boy involuntarily drew back. "You're due for a little explaining, Oliver," said Keith.

"Oh yeah?" muttered the boy again, but I saw how white he had become and his sister saw, too, for she moved closer to him.

"You admitted at the inquest this morning that it was you who brought the professor into your aunt's life," said Chet Keith sternly. "I believe you expressed it that you put up a job on your aunt Dora."

Patrick Oliver was trembling. "It was—was just a joke," he stammered.

"You and your eternal horseplay!" exclaimed Jeff Wayne bitterly.

"I'd never have thought of it," said Patrick, directing a glare at Sheila Kelly's averted face, "if it hadn't been that she looks like—she reminded me of Gloria."

He mopped his brow with a shaking hand.

"You saw the professor's act and you saw a way to put over a hoax on your aunt," said Chet Keith, looking very grim, "so you called the professor and made an appointment to talk business with him."

Patrick Oliver had a hunted look. "There wasn't any harm to it," he mumbled. "I swear I didn't mean any harm. I thought it would—would make Aunt Dora feel better to have a message from Gloria. That's all it was supposed to be, just harmless messages, saying Gloria was happy and Aunt Dora wasn't to worry."

"So that's all it was to be, according to your story," murmured Chet Keith. "Just an innocent prank to comfort your aunt Dora."

The boy looked at him helplessly, then he glared at Sheila Kelly.

"She threw us a curve. Me and the professor too," he said thickly. "That pretending to be Gloria wasn't in the act. She thought it up herself to get her hooks into Aunt Dora's money."

"Your bargain with Professor Matthews did not include the Gloria manifestations?" inquired Chet Keith with a skeptical grimace.

"No!"

"They were a surprise to you and also to the professor?"

"Yes."

"But you did give the professor the data for the Gloria messages?"

"For the Little Blue Eyes messages, yes," said the boy sullenly. "I had to make sure the old codger could deliver the goods."

"Just so," assented Chet Keith and glanced at Sheila Kelly. "You don't remember afterward what has happened when you're in a trance?"

She shivered. "Not unless I'm told to remember."

The girl was all to pieces. Chet Keith realized that as well as I. That is the reason, I am confident, that he avoided questioning her, as much as possible. He was afraid that at any minute she might blurt out the truth about the door between her room and mine.

I fixed stern eyes upon young Oliver. "I suppose you realize that you and you alone had the opportunity to frame this business?" I inquired coldly.

"I didn't! I didn't! Everything I told the girl to say was harmless. The professor knows. He heard every word."

"Unfortunately, or perhaps fortunately for you, the Professor's knowledge died with him," said Chet Keith gravely.

"You can't even prove I ever made a deal with him."

"No," said Chet Keith, "I couldn't have proved it. That was a leap in the dark, but it worked. You admitted that you and the professor used Sheila Kelly to play a hoax upon your aunt."

"I never put her up to pretending to be Gloria!" insisted the boy. "The first time she did it I was scared to death and I've been scared ever since."

"Nevertheless last night when Sheila Kelly wanted to back out of the séance you insisted that she had to go on."

The boy's shoulders sagged. "There wasn't anything else to do," he stammered. "Uncle Thomas was here. To have run out at that stage was as good as admitting it was all a fake. I thought the only thing to do was to bluff it out. You've got to believe me. I never dreamed it would end in murder!"

His voice rose to a scream and Judy put her arm about him.

"You haven't any right to torment him like this," she protested with a sob. "Patrick didn't mean any harm. He was—was just trying to—to help me."

"Keep still, Judy!" cried the, boy. "For God's sake, keep out of this."

I think I have never seen a more wretched face than Judy Oliver's or a more determined one as she went on in an unsteady voice. "It was on my account Pat got mixed up with the professor and that girl."

I saw Jeff Wayne make a startled movement, but she did not look at him. She kept her eyes fixed upon Chet Keith and something in them brought a lump to my throat.

"You see," she said, "I have been in love with Jeff for—for a long time and—and I imagined he was in love with me, but he used to be engaged to Gloria and Aunt Dora has the idea that Gloria could not be happy in her grave if Jeff married someone else."

"You couldn't, could you, darling?" murmured Dora Canby to Sheila Kelly.

There was a painful silence and then Chet Keith said softly, "So your brother decided to help you out, Miss Oliver?"

Judy's small tortured face quivered. "Jeff's job depended upon Uncle Thomas and so did my future. I was mistaken, but until— until last night I thought that was why Jeff did not ask me to marry him. I believed it was because—because Uncle Thomas would have cut us off without a penny if we married. It was quite hopeless, or so I thought, unless Aunt Dora could be convinced that Gloria did not want Jeff to stay single on her account."

Chet Keith's voice was very gentle. "You planned to have Sheila Kelly give your aunt a message, supposedly from her daughter, that it was all right for Jeff to marry?"

The girl's haggard face twitched. "Yes."

She threw one miserable glance at Dora Canby, who shook her head and said reproachfully, "Gloria will never give Jeff up to you, Judy, will you, darling?" she asked Sheila Kelly, who shivered and looked with despair at Chet Keith.

He again turned to Patrick Oliver. "So that's the job you put up on your aunt?"

The boy made a harried gesture. "There was nothing criminal in it," he said feverishly. "Judy's a good scout and she's never had a break. I thought if Little Blue Eyes told Aunt Dora that Gloria wanted Jeff to go ahead and marry, all Judy's troubles would be over."

"You framed up with the professor to deceive your aunt just to give your sister a break?"

"Yes!"

"But you also had Little Blue Eyes suggest to Mrs. Canby that her daughter would rest easier in her grave if your debts were paid?"

Patrick Oliver turned perfectly white. "I don't know what you're talking about."

"It's true, isn't it, Mrs. Canby, that during one of the séances Little Blue Eyes suggested to you that it would make her happier if you'd do her cousin Patrick a small favor?"

Before Dora Canby could answer the boy interrupted, "All right, all right," he said. "I did try to do myself a good turn as well, but there's nothing criminal in that either. God knows Aunt Dora will never miss the money."

"No," said Chet Keith, "but you were very unwise to have Captain French here at the inn cash the check for you. It made it very easy for me to trace and just as easy for Thomas Canby."

"Uncle Thomas!" faltered Patrick. "He knew about it?"

"You know he knew about it, Oliver."

"No! No!"

"I found out from Captain French this afternoon about the check. According to the captain, your uncle found out about it last night. That's why you killed him."

"No, no!"

"You are an opportunist, Oliver. You happened accidentally to attend a small-town picture show. You saw a fake spiritualist act. The girl reminded you of your dead cousin Gloria Canby. Right away you cooked up a scheme to cash in on that resemblance. It may be that in the beginning you intended only to pull a few strings on your sister's behalf. But it was too good a chance to reap a bit of benefit for yourself. And then Thomas Canby came and he found out that you had finagled his wife out of a whopping big check on the strength of these false séances.

"It didn't take him long to figure out who was responsible for the whole business. He meant to expose both you and the professor last night and you would have been out of the Canby fortune from then on. So Thomas Canby had to die. That's why you were determined that Sheila Kelly should go through with the séance. You had laid your plans very cleverly. You knew what was going to happen because you had primed her to put on the tirade against your uncle. All you had to do then was jerk the light cord out and cut his throat to be safe, or so you fancied."

"I didn't! I didn't!" wailed the boy.

Judy stepped in front of him, her eyes blazing.

"You can't hang this on my brother," she said. "He couldn't have killed Uncle Thomas. I was holding Patrick's arm when the lights went out. I never turned him loose until they came on again."

"We have only your unsubstantiated word for that," said Chet Keith.

"It's true."

Jeff Wayne drew a long breath. "I had hold of Patrick's other arm," he said. "He didn't kill Mr. Canby."

Patrick's frantic face smoothed out. "How's that for the perfect alibi, Mr. Sherlock Holmes?" he demanded with a slight revival of his natural exuberance.

Chet Keith shrugged his shoulders. "There is nothing to prevent the three of you from having been in on the deal," he said. "After all, by your own admission it was a plot to make it possible for Jeff Wayne to marry Judy Oliver without endangering their chances at the Canby fortune."

"Jeff wasn't in on it!" cried Judy quickly. "He knew nothing about it."

"But you knew?"

She hung her head. "Yes."

"Your brother told you before he took your aunt to the show in Carrolton?"

She hesitated and Patrick Oliver interrupted. "Judy didn't know then," he said. "She'd never have stood for it. It wasn't until—until after the professor and the girl moved up here to the inn that Judy caught on."

Judy's lips trembled. "I'm younger than Patrick," she said in a low voice, "but he—he has never had any forethought. I mean, it is just like him to get into a thing like this without seeing that it might lead to—to something dreadful."

"So you found out for yourself that Patrick and the professor had made a deal?"

"Yes."

"How did you find it out?"

She flushed painfully. "At one of the séances Little Blue Eyes said that it made Gloria unhappy for Jeff to waste his life away, grieving for her. At another she said Gloria was worried about Pat because he was in debt."

"Those messages struck you as slightly too apropos?"

"Yes."

"You taxed your brother with being responsible for them?"

Again she hesitated and, making a wry face, Patrick Oliver for the second time answered for her. "She did better than that," he said. "She followed me one night."

"Followed you?"

"The professor and I had to get together to keep the show going," said Patrick Oliver defiantly. "After all, he needed information, didn't he, to put on the act."

"So you were in the habit of meeting the professor on the sly to lay the groundwork for the séances?"

"Sure."

"Where?"

"Oh, anywhere away from the inn."

"Anywhere?"

"Down the road to town, wherever I happened to overtake him."

Judy drew a long breath. "The professor pretended that a séance was a great mental and physical strain for both him and the girl," she said. "Every night after it was over they used to take a walk."

"Yes?"

"I noticed that Patrick usually disappeared at the same time."

"Yes?"

"It was easy to trail him." She smiled painfully. "I've always had to keep an eye on him."

"You trailed him and found the three of them together?"

She shivered. "It was horrible. I came right up to them. Patrick was furious and the professor nearly had a fit, but Sheila Kelly looked through me as if I were so much air. At the time I was certain she did not know I was there."

Sheila Kelly gave her a haggard glance. "I never knew either of you was there."

"I begged Pat to tell Aunt Dora the truth and send the professor away," said Judy in a trembling voice. "I warned them that if they went on with it I'd tell her myself."

She paused abruptly and her eyes widened with terror.

"But you didn't?" asked Chet Keith.

"No," said Judy, her lips trembling, "I didn't. You see, it was that night, while I was standing there, that—that Gloria suddenly began to speak with—with that girl's lips."

"It's true," said Patrick, swallowing hard. "Until that moment everything had been according to form, then all at once *she*"—he glanced with horror at Sheila Kelly—"she began to laugh, just the way Gloria used to laugh." He shuddered. "She said she had found the—the way back. She said we'd never stop her until she'd accomplished her purpose."

Chet Keith ignored the boy to stare soberly at his sister. "So you let Sheila Kelly seal your lips?"

She was trembling. "It wasn't she. It was—was—"

She broke off and stared, her eyes dilated with horror, at the girl sitting with bowed head at the coroner's table.

"Surely," I exclaimed, "you don't believe your cousin Gloria actually takes possession of Sheila Kelly at times?"

"What else can I believe?" cried Judy in a stifled voice. "How else can she know the things she does know?"

Chet Keith moved a step nearer and she shrank back.

"What did Sheila Kelly say that night in your cousin Gloria's voice which frightened you so terribly, Miss Oliver?"

"I—I— Just the usual thing, the things she has been saying all along," stammered the girl. "That she hated me, that she hated all of us."

He regarded her with narrowed eyes. "You are sure that is all she threatened you with?"

"Certainly it was all," interrupted Patrick Oliver.

Chet Keith looked from brother to sister and again his voice sharpened. "The professor knew more than it was safe to know," he said. "The professor paid for his knowledge with his life. Bear that in mind."

I thought Patrick Oliver was weakening. I saw him wet his lips with his tongue, but after a second horrified glance at Sheila Kelly his sister seemed to make a terrific effort to recover herself.

"We've told you all we know," she said. "Patrick did bring that girl here. He did put over a hoax on Aunt Dora, but he—he had nothing to do with killing Uncle Thomas. She— Gloria did it! She came back from her grave to—to revenge herself."

"To revenge herself?" I repeated with a frown.

She pressed her shaking hand against her lips. "Yes."

Hogan Brewster, with a flippant smile, interposed. "Canby was planning to have his daughter put away in an institution, you know. That is why she killed herself."

Apparently he had come to the aid of Judy with his explanation, but it was at Lila Atwood he looked and I saw her whiten and lean closer to her husband, who promptly moved farther away.

"Where did this interview take place, Miss Oliver?" demanded Chet Keith. "I mean this first manifestation of Gloria Canby's alleged spirit?"

"I told you," muttered Patrick Oliver. "It was down the road."

"Can you be more explicit, Miss Oliver?" persisted Chet Keith.

Her lips trembled. "It was—was opposite the entrance to that old abandoned cemetery down the road," she said faintly.

"Cemetery?"

"There is some sort of shack there. It used to be a chapel, I think. The cemetery is enclosed with an iron fence, but I—I could see the—the tombstones through the pickets."

"Yes?"

"Don't you see?" she cried hysterically. "She was just standing there in a daze, and then suddenly she wasn't there at all. It was Gloria! Sneering at us as she always did! Taunting us! Gloria risen from the grave!"

"People don't rise from their graves," said Chet Keith sternly, "not even outside abandoned cemeteries."

But Judy had whirled upon Sheila Kelly. "You wouldn't stay dead. You had to come back to torture us. You should have been buried with a stake in your heart to pin you down forever, you vampire! Why didn't we think of that? Oh, God, why didn't we think of that?"

13

CHET KEITH GAVE Judy's fit of hysterics as his reason for postponing the investigation for a couple of hours. "Moreover, I think we'd all be the better for a little food," he said after Judy, sobbing wildly, had been carried off to her room by her brother, pursued by Dora Canby, leaning upon Lila Atwood's arm.

In my opinion Chet Keith seized the opportunity to adjourn the inquest because he saw, as I did, the effect which Judy's outburst had upon Sheila Kelly. Only the fact that Chet Keith acted before the girl had time to betray herself had prevented her from again blurting out an admission of guilt; I was certain of it and so, I felt positive, was he. His glance followed her as she left the room, walking after the deputy Butch with slow, faltering steps, her eyes fixed with despair.

"She believes that stuff about Gloria Canby," he said to me, being careful to lower his voice.

"Yes, and you were right about Jeff Wayne," I acknowledged. "He believes it too."

Young Wayne had not followed Judy out of the room. He had not gone near her or offered to help her. He kept his arms folded on his chest and I saw the muscles strain through his coat sleeve, but he let them take Judy away without a word and his glance also followed Sheila Kelly, with implacable hatred.

"You wouldn't think it possible," sighed Chet Keith, "that people could be taken in by such hooey in this day and age."

"Day and age indeed!" I protested. "The belief in ghouls and witchcraft goes back to the beginnings of the race. If you think we have outgrown them, what about those hex murders only a year or so ago in Pennsylvania?"

He gave me a startled glance. "Good heavens, you aren't weakening on me, are you?"

"I don't believe in vampires or that rot," I said dubiously.

He shook his head. "I counted on your common sense, Miss Adams. I sort of felt that you were a Rock of Gibraltar holding up my hands, to scramble a few metaphors."

I looked him straight in the eye. "That cat was mutilated in my room and there was no key in the lock on my side at the time."

He took a long breath. "No," he admitted, "the key wasn't there before I arrived. You aren't suffering an attack of conscience, are you, Miss Adelaide? You won't at this stage, for Pete's sake, feel called upon to tell the sheriff about it?"

He was getting around me again, and we both knew it.

"If I had told about the door earlier, the professor might still be alive," I said with a shiver, "to say nothing of the alley cat."

He frowned. "Of course you realize what part the cat played?"

"I'm afraid I don't realize anything except that I have let my sympathies betray me into acting remarkably like a maudlin idiot."

"The cat was killed to furnish a diversion. In other words to draw off the guard from the professor's door long enough to permit the murderer to get at him."

"Granted," I sighed, "but that doesn't prove it wasn't Sheila Kelly who left my room just before I discovered the body of the cat."

"The girl is innocent," he told me angrily. "The whole thing is a frame-up."

I paid no attention to his interruption. "The deputy admits he had his back turned to my door," I said, "and that upstairs corridor is dimly lighted. It was also practically deserted at the time. After she killed the cat there are a dozen empty rooms into which the girl could have dodged and hid herself until my screams drew the deputy away from the professor's door."

He was pretty white. "I don't doubt that you have described the murderer's actions accurately. He did hide somewhere on the second floor until the excitement in your room gave him his chance to do in the professor. I admit all that and still I say Sheila Kelly is innocent."

"Just saying it doesn't make it so. You're in love with her."

He colored. "Don't be silly!" he protested, then added lamely, "All right, maybe I am, maybe that's what's been the matter with me for a year and I didn't know it. But that's not why I am certain she didn't kill Thomas Canby or the professor."

"No?"

"You're a highly intelligent woman," he said. "You ought to be able to recognize a frame-up as well as I do."

I glanced at him sharply, but his face was perfectly bland.

"There is a limit to the amount of flattery which I can absorb," I cautioned him.

His grin was wry. "I'm not flattering you, or only a little. If Sheila Kelly is saved from this devilish business it's up to you and me."

"Fiddlesticks!" I protested. "Quite likely, as that sheik Hogan Brewster pointed out, a good defense lawyer aided by Dora Canby's fortune will get the girl off."

He gave me a look which made me catch my breath. "I'm not afraid that Sheila Kelly will go to the electric chair or even to the penitentiary. You are too clever a woman, Miss Adams, not to guess what it is I fear for Sheila in her present state."

My voice trembled a little. "You're afraid she—she will—"

To save my life I could not go on, but he nodded.

"That's what makes this affair so diabolical," he groaned. "The girl is desperate. She believes she cut Thomas Canby's throat, also the professor's. She even believes she has been mutilating cats and canary birds for the fiendish fun of it. Neither Judy Oliver nor Jeff Wayne is so afraid of Sheila Kelly as she is of herself."

There was a lump in my throat. "Yes."

"Don't you realize that nothing would suit the murderer better than for Sheila Kelly to kill herself?" he continued quietly.

"How horrible!"

"It would be taken as an admission of guilt, closing the case forever."

I felt a little sick. "You think he is trying to drive her to—to suicide?"

"And so far," he reminded me bleakly, "he or she has had everything his own way."

"She?" I echoed faintly.

"Everybody at the séance last night had an opportunity to kill Canby, and every member of his family, including his wife, had a motive. They all hated him, to say nothing of the money."

"I know," I said in a husky voice.

"One of them did it, but Sheila Kelly will pay the price unless you and I interfere."

"Interfere?"

He grinned ruefully. "All I'm asking you, Miss Adams, is to play a passive role for a while about the door from your room to hers."

My mouth felt dry. "Do you realize that I'll never feel comfortable again about my responsibility for the professor's death?" I demanded. "Don't you know that it will haunt me for the rest of my life that I didn't call the deputy and tell him that Sheila Kelly was in my room when I went upstairs this afternoon?" I shuddered. "If I don't tell the sheriff about that door, somebody else may be murdered. Had you thought of that, young man?"

His face was very sober. "I've thought of nothing else since this afternoon," he said. "The door is locked now, Miss Adams, and the key is on your side. I told you there was one point in Sheila Kelly's favor which you haven't considered. It is possible, as you demonstrated, for the murderer to have hidden in one of the empty rooms on the second floor after he killed the cat. It is possible for him to have taken advantage of the excitement in your room to kill the professor. But the sheriff and I checked up on Sheila Kelly immediately after the professor's body was discovered and found her in her room with the key turned in the lock on your side."

I stared at him and he made an impatient gesture.

"She may have got out to kill Matthews, but if so how did she get back into a locked room? "Locked with the key outside, you understand?"

"I have only your word for that," I reminded him.

He winced. "I deceived the sheriff about that key in the first place, so I might be deceiving you now, only I'm not. I give you my word of honor, Miss Adams, for whatever it may be worth, that the key was exactly as I left it. I did not touch it and both the sheriff and I can swear that he had to unlock the door when he went into Sheila Kelly's room."

"She was there?" I asked.

His face darkened. "Sitting in a daze, staring straight before her. I had to shake her to arouse her."

I stared at him. "In a hypnotic daze?"

"Yes."

"But the professor is dead!"

He gave me a very odd look. "Yes, the professor is dead."

Not until that moment did I look the implications of the second crime full in the face. I had been determined to believe in Sheila Kelly's innocence. I had persuaded myself that she was Professor Matthews' victim. Now all my theories crumbled to dust. The professor himself had been killed and Sheila Kelly had been found immediately afterward, apparently in a hypnotic trance.

My spine had a crawling sensation. "Is it possible he was not—not responsible for the Gloria manifestations, just as he said? Is it possible that—that Gloria Canby does come back from the grave to—to—"

"Good Lord!" interrupted Chet Keith. "Hang onto your common sense! It's our only hope."

I drew a long breath. "All right," I said. "There is nothing supernatural about this business." My throat felt as dry as dust. "If Gloria Canby had returned from the grave she wouldn't have cut the professor's throat to silence him. She had nothing to lose, no matter what he told."

"Of course not," he snapped.

I swallowed painfully. "So it's human, whatever it is."

"You can bet on it," he said in a grim voice. "The girl has been framed. So far the murderer has taken every trick, everything except that key which I slipped into the lock in your room."

I nodded. "No," I said, "he didn't figure on that."

He gave me a pleading glance. "I can count on you to keep still about the door?" he asked.

I hesitated and he immediately clapped me upon the shoulder.

"Attagirl!" he exclaimed and walked swiftly away, leaving me, as I realized at once, hopelessly committed, however dubious I may have felt. It has always been my nature when in a quandary to take steps. I did so now, but the sheriff, whom I first approached, was disposed to fob me off in no uncertain manner.

"Listen, lady, I ain't in no humor to argue with you," he said in a goaded voice and added with exasperation, "I never seen so many bossy females in one place, tending to everybody else's business."

I drew myself up to my full height. "If you are referring to my friends, Mrs. Trotter and Mrs. Parrish, let me inform you—"

However, the sheriff, making a weary gesture, had moved away, muttering something about, "Just as soon have fleas in my pants," by which I judged, not without satisfaction, that I had got somewhat upon his nerves.

At any rate, having done my duty and offered Sheriff Latham the benefit of my co-operation, I no longer felt bound to consider him and so I marched off up the stairs. Practically everybody else was at dinner. Once more I found the second floor deserted, except for Butch, who stared at me with a sour expression.

"Back again, eh?" he murmured.

I frowned. "This afternoon when I lay down to take a nap I left my door unlocked," I said. "It was my impression that, with a guard right outside in the hall, it was safer. Not to lock my door, I mean. We both know now how mistaken I was."

"Listen," he said in an injured voice, "I'm just a man, just a common ordinary man. Can I help it if *that girl*"—he gestured toward Sheila Kelly's room—"can go through locked doors like—like a—"

"Hant?" I suggested.

He regarded me sullenly and then glanced over his shoulder. "There is something up here," he whispered, "something that ain't natural."

"You seem to have changed your mind about ghosts and the like," I said with a sniff.

He leaned nearer. "I saw it," he whispered hoarsely. "Right down there at the end of the hall."

"Saw what?" I asked, turning quickly because it seemed to me I felt a movement behind me in the shadows toward which he pointed.

"A bat," he said. "A big black bat."

"Ridiculous."

"But when I got there it was gone. Gone up in smoke."

"Fiddlesticks!" I protested. "You probably stood here and gawked, scared to move, till the thing flew away, provided it was a bat and you actually saw it."

"I saw it all right," he insisted, "and it was a bat."

I left him muttering to himself and staring uneasily first over one shoulder and then the other. It was very quiet in my room. The cat was gone and I had been provided with a fresh counterpane. Nevertheless I had to set my teeth before I could force myself to close the door behind me. I went over to the window and stood for some minutes, staring out. It was only seven o'clock, but with the fog and the low-hanging clouds it was impossible to see a foot beyond the blackness of the windowpane. Realizing that I was merely temporizing with the difficult task before me, I crossed the room and slowly turned the key in Sheila Kelly's door.

"Who is it?" she faltered.

"I want to talk to you," I said.

I heard the bolt slide back, but she did not open the door. I had to do that myself. She looked at me with eyes in which I read complete despair. She did not stir or speak.

"Come in here where we can't be overheard," I said.

She shivered. "It isn't safe," she whispered. "Don't you realize it isn't any safer to let me loose than a— than a mad dog?"

"Nonsense," I said weakly.

Her hands were twisting together. "Tell me one thing," she said. "Was this door locked on your side when the professor was murdered?"

I suppose my eyes gave me away, for she uttered a stricken cry. "It's true then! I did kill that cat! I killed the professor! Oh, God!"

I realized that Chet Keith had been right. Nobody was as terrified of Sheila Kelly as she was of herself. She was shaking from head to foot.

"You mustn't let go like this," I said as sternly as possible.

She stared at me as if she did not see me. "They took away my manicure scissors and my nail file," she whispered. "They took everything out of my room with which I might—might injure somebody. The fools, as if I want to do away with anyone except myself!"

So Chet Keith had been right about that, too, I thought, not far from hysteria myself. If Sheila Kelly committed suicide, the case would be closed, as he said. They would write her off as guilty and that would be an end of it. I remember suddenly feeling entirely unequal to the emergency, which is unlike me.

"I have no doubt," I said, "that it would please the murderer to have you remove yourself from the scene."

She caught her breath. "The murderer! I am the murderer!"

"I don't believe it," I declared, wishing I could be certain.

She shook her head. "You said the professor framed me. You said he hypnotized me into talking and acting like Gloria Canby. You said he did it to put me on the spot, but the professor is dead and—and—" Her voice faltered.

"And what?" I prompted her.

"Just now, just a while ago," she whispered, "I came to there in my room. I was sitting in my chair and I was—was as limp as a rag, the way I always am after a trance."

"Yes?"

"I don't know what I had been doing. I don't know how long I'd been out."

"Yes?" I said again, my lips feeling stiff.

"Don't you see?" she cried. "I was in a trance, but the professor is dead!"

I remember holding on tightly to the sides of my chair. "You were hypnotized," I stammered, "but the professor couldn't have done it?"

"It was that other?" she wailed.

"Impossible!"

"Just as it has been that other all this week!" she cried. "I told you it wasn't the professor. I told you. I'm cursed! Don't you understand, cursed! That fiend has got hold of me. She takes possession of me whenever she likes!"

"Impossible!" I said again.

"She made me steal the scissors. She made me steal your book."

"My book?"

She shivered. "It was hidden in my laundry bag. I found it this afternoon. I don't know when I took it or why. Think of that! I don't know when I took the scissors, either, or what I did with them. The book was gone when I waked up from the trance a while ago."

"Gone?"

"And the window had been opened."

"You had opened it!" I exclaimed.

"I must have," she said. "It was bolted on the inside, but the ledge was all wet and there was a cord tied to the bolt. The cord was wet too."

"You think you let the book down from the window by the cord?"

"I don't know," she whispered. "That's what makes it so horrible. I don't know anything I do when she—she takes possession of me."

I shrugged my shoulder to throw off the weight which seemed to have settled upon me. "If, as you suppose, there is anything supernatural in these visitations," I said sternly, "why should Gloria Canby's ghost go to all the trouble of having you lower a book out a window upon a string, of all things?"

"I don't know," she said again.

"For that matter, if Gloria Canby's evil spirit in possession of your body killed her father, why did the room have to be dark? A lot she'd cared who saw her if everything they tell of her is true."

She caught her breath. "You think—you still think—"

"That you've been framed," I declared firmly. "Granting, which isn't possible, that you really are possessed of an evil spirit at times, why are all these physical adjuncts necessary, such as my book and Dora Canby's scissors? It seems the height of the ridiculous to me for an avenging ghost to bother about such trappings."

She was no fool, however distraught she might be.

"Either I was in a trance when I took those things or I did it deliberately," she said. "Is that what you believe? That I have been faking all along? That I wasn't in a trance tonight or any other night?"

"No," I said, "I have maintained from the first that the trances are genuine."

"But the professor is dead!" she cried, coming back to the same heartbreaking point. "And still I—I— The trances go on."

I laid my hand on her arm. "You told Chet Keith that before this week it never happened. Going off like that unexpectedly, out of office hours, he expressed it."

She glanced at me quickly. "Yes."

"Where were you the first time it occurred?"

"Where was I?"

"The first time you came to yourself and found that you had been in a trance which you did not expect."

Her face changed. "It's hard to remember," she faltered. "It's all so—so confused. My mind, I mean."

I stared at her sharply. Was she making a fool of me, I asked myself. I had to admit that it was possible. I had assumed from the first that she had not been hypnotized into killing Thomas Canby because it was contrary to her moral code, but what did I really know about Sheila Kelly's moral code? I had only my obstinate conviction of her innocence to sustain my belief that she was incapable of murder, and the girl was an actress. She might very well be winding me about her bloodstained fingers, I told myself with a shudder.

I don't mind confessing that I suffered a very bad moment before she went on. "I remember going for a walk," she said slowly.

"Yes?"

I was watching her closely and it seemed to me that she was making an honest effort to struggle through the murk of her thoughts.

"I remember seeing—seeing tombstones."

"Tombstones!"

"A lot of tombstones, covered with gray moss. Then I—I— Everything is blank."

"Think," I urged. "Try to think what happened."

Her face was deathly white. "I can't! I can't!"

I stared at her helplessly. "Suppose," I said, "you met somebody on that walk, somebody who wanted to gain control of your mind for reasons of his own."

She looked at me, her eyes widening.

"Suppose that person," I went on, "attempted to hypnotize you and succeeded. Suppose he or she told you to forget everything that happened. Suppose you were told even to forget meeting such a person."

She was deathly white. "If I was told in a trance to forget something, I would," she whispered.

"You may have talked to this person a dozen times but, if he commanded you not to remember, you wouldn't?"

"No."

"It is possible he met you down the road more than once." I glanced at her sharply. "Isn't it?"

She shivered. "I—I have taken a walk every afternoon this week."

"It is possible he rehearsed you over and over in your part, the part of Gloria Canby. You wouldn't remember if he ordered you not to?"

By this time my imagination was in full stride. "The professor weakened your resistance to mental suggestion," I deducted triumphantly. "I suppose if the truth was known he reduced it to nothing. Somebody has taken advantage of that fact."

Again hope flared up in her eyes. "You think someone, not the professor, has been hypnotizing me without my knowledge?"

"It's the only sane explanation if we exclude the supernatural which is preposterous."

She was trembling. "Somebody has been—been—"

"Framing you for murder," I repeated doggedly.

"If only I could believe you!" she cried with a sob.

"It's as devilish a plot as ever existed," I declared fiercely, "because you have not only been hypnotized into incriminating yourself, you have even been forced to believe in your own guilt."

Her cheeks blazed. "You almost make me dare to hope."

I regarded her shrewdly. "Are you the type to go around shedding hairpins all over the place where you have committed a crime?"

She shook her head. "I never shed hairpins."

"Exactly," I said, "and you didn't kill Thomas Canby or anyone else."

Tears began to slide down her cheeks. "God bless you," she whispered.

I cleared my throat. "We'll have no more of that talk about—about doing away with yourself?"

"No," she said with a deep sigh, "only if, as you say, somebody in this place has been hypnotizing me, Miss Adams, without my knowledge, who is it?"

For a moment we stared at each other and I could feel the wind going out of my sails.

"I am sure I can't imagine," I admitted feebly.

She shuddered and turned so white I made a very rash promise.

"But I'll find out," I said.

14

It was almost an hour later, after certain research explorations of my own, before I succeeded in separating Chet Keith from the telephone to which he had glued himself. Not until then did I understand how, cut off as we were, he managed to acquire the inside information which he did acquire about certain people at the inn. Thomas Canby's murder had brought a flock of reporters to the scene, although they could get no nearer than Carrolton. On the other hand, Chet Keith was right in the middle of the excitement. In return for first-hand stories of the crime he had his fellow newspapermen running down a dozen trails for him, not without protests, as I gathered, listening to the tail end of one conversation.

"Sure, the great reading public isn't interested in Thomas Canby's servants, but I am, see?" he informed the rebellious party at the other end of the line. "And you'll admit that I am in a position to dictate terms. If you want exclusive dope on what's going on up here, you have to play ball with me, Soaper. Otherwise you get nothing, and how will your managing editor like that, my fine-feathered friend?"

Apparently Soaper saw the light, for Chet Keith grinned.

"All right, all right," he said, "maybe it is highway robbery and grand larceny and a few other things, but, as you have pointed out, you can't help yourself. So get busy. I want that stuff I asked for at once or sooner than that."

He replaced the receiver on the hook and looked at me wearily. "Well, Miss Adelaide?"

The lines on his face deepened as he listened to my new theory of the case. "You think someone, unbeknownst to Sheila Kelly, has been hypnotizing her and forcing her to incriminate herself!" he exclaimed with a grimace. "Imagine springing such an idea upon Sheriff Latham."

"You might as well wave the proverbial red flag in the bull's face," I admitted.

"Even to me it sounds incredible," he said ruefully, "but, as you remarked, it is the only sane explanation if we exclude the supernatural."

"Providing the sheriff hasn't been right all along," I faltered, "and Sheila Kelly *is* the murderer and faking all this trance business."

"Neither of us believes that," he protested quickly.

"No," I said, "though it may be just my natural disinclination to string along with the authorities."

He paid no attention. "Patrick Oliver and the professor put up a job on Dora Canby, a shady job, but not murder. Agreed so far?"

"Yes," I said crossly, wondering if he was trying to clear his thoughts or mine.

"Then somebody saw a chance to get rid of Canby and hang the crime upon Sheila Kelly?"

"Yes," I said again.

"So he decided to work a little hypnotism of his own," he murmured doubtfully.

"He may not have known if it would be successful," I said, "but I dare say he thought there was no harm in experimenting, and I imagine in her condition it was easy enough to establish a domination over the girl's mind." I shivered. "Probably—probably even an amateur hypnotist could have done it without much trouble."

He stared at me. "Amateur?"

"He needn't have been adept, or she needn't. We can't lose sight of the fact that it may have been a woman."

"It could have been anybody who was present at the séance last night and who was at the inn when the Gloria manifestations began."

"Exactly," I said, not very happily, "and that includes every member of the Canby family. It even includes Jeff Wayne. He arrived here a week ago with Lila Atwood and her husband."

He gave me a startled look and I frowned. "Did you think any of them could be excluded?"

"Dora Canby hated her husband. She blamed him for the death of their daughter, whom she adored. The motive is there but . . ." He shook his head. "If what we suspect is true, the murderer has two qualifications, ingenuity and a brilliant mind."

"From what I have read upon the subject," I said, "it doesn't take brains, so much as will power and a natural gift for it, to be a successful mesmerist."

"Even so, Dora Canby strikes me as the most spineless person I ever met."

"Because she shrinks from strangers?"

"Because she's too timid to call her soul her own, much less to establish a diabolical control over another person's soul."

I sniffed. "Has it occurred to you that, in spite of considerable pressure brought to bear by her husband, an extremely ruthless and domineering man, Dora Canby has gone right on living precisely the life she prefers to live?"

"I suppose in a way she has."

"Doesn't it denote marked will power, the way she was able to close her eyes consistently to her daughter's real character, the way she still seems able to do so? It's been my observation that meek people often manage in an unobtrusive way to be as stubborn as mules."

He scowled. "When I think back it rather leaps to the eye that Dora Canby has never missed a chance to drive home the theory that Sheila is the reincarnation of her dead daughter and consequently the murderer."

"Precisely," I said and gave him a quizzical glance. "Are you familiar with the experiments which Duke University is conducting into mental telepathy and thought transference?"

I could see that he was startled by my apparent irrelevance. "Only superficially," he said. "I once listened to the radio program devoted to the subject. Once was enough."

He was referring to the program sponsored by the manufacturers of a nationally known article. It is supposed to be a test of little-known mental powers. They are called ESP tests, I believe, which stand for "extra-sensory perception" or something. At any rate you are requested to concentrate while certain senders in the studio perform certain mysterious rites. The night I listened they tossed coins, and the great invisible audience was asked to make an effort to catch the mental vibrations and write down upon a score card by means of pure telepathy whether the senders turned up heads or tails. I have always, no matter what Ella Trotter says, been open to conviction, so I concentrated and was prepared to write down my impressions, the trouble being that I received no impressions.

"According to the announcers," I informed Chet Keith, "they have had remarkable results from astounding numbers of people, but I take it that, like myself, you drew a blank."

He grinned. "Yet you aren't precisely a weak-minded woman."

I went on with some severity. "Quoting from Doctor Rhine's book, science is being compelled to recognize *New Frontiers of the Mind*, as he titled it. That is, it appears to be true that thought can be transferred without speech and at considerable distance."

He was watching me narrowly. "After the radio anything seems possible," he admitted.

I nodded. "The theory is the same. Certain individuals seem to have natural receptive gifts; that is, they operate like radio reception sets. Others function better as senders. There does not seem much rhyme or reason to it. At least so far science has not been able to lay down positive laws as to what types of minds will react favorably to the tests. It seems to be just one of those talents you are born with, talents, so the inventors of the principle claim, which you may possess to the fullest extent without realizing it, unless it is called to your attention." I was staring at him very hard. "No doubt many people have had it called to their attention by the radio program which you mentioned."

He flushed. "What in heaven's name are you leading up to?"

I could no longer master my excitement. "There was a piece of information which I wanted," I said, "so I set Fannie Parrish to work upon it. As a result I have been supplied, if not inundated, with information."

"Will you please come to the point!"

"Several weeks ago in the Canby drawing room in New York a large group took the ESP tests."

His lips tightened. "Go on."

"As I understand it, the whole Canby family was present with the exception of Thomas Canby who, it seems, professed the greatest scorn for that sort of thing. Mrs. Canby, on the other hand, since her daughter's death has been unwholesomely interested in anything which savors of the occult. That, of course, is why it occurred to Patrick Oliver at once that she would prove an easy victim for the professor."

"Occult?" he repeated. "It is my understanding that the sponsors of these experiments do not claim any superhuman quality for them. Don't they insist upon putting telepathy on a scientific basis, as an extraordinary but not other-worldly quality of the human brain?"

"Of course," I said impatiently, "though I don't suppose Dora Canby ever accepted that explanation."

"You said the party in the Canby house took the ESP tests," he repeated in a chastened voice.

"According to Fannie Parrish's report, Judy Oliver proved uncannily accurate at receiving thought waves."

"Judy Oliver!" he exclaimed.

"So accurate somebody proposed testing her farther."

"The hell they did!"

"She went out of the room and closed the door while everybody, one by one, performed some small act, such as sharpening a pencil or lowering a shade or straightening a picture, concentrating at the same time upon getting their actions over to Judy out in the hall."

"Well?"

I deliberately waited a moment, to sharpen his suspense. "Like yourself, Lila Atwood and Patrick Oliver drew a blank."

"Go on!" he cried when I made another provoking pause.

"They had shown no talent as receivers earlier in the evening. They showed none as senders at this time."

"Are you trying to tantalize me to death?" he demanded. "Who, if anybody, did show a telepathic talent for transferring thoughts?"

I suspect my voice betrayed some smugness over my discovery. "You'll be surprised to know that two people out of the group succeeded almost perfectly in getting their actions across to Judy by the telepathic route. They succeeded so well, I understand, that she was sent out of the room a dozen times or more and the experiment repeated and, so my informant tells me, in ninety per cent of the cases she was able to return and repeat in detail the exact actions of these two people during her absence."

I think I must have been quite pale at this point, for he stared at me and caught his breath. "All right," he said, "two people in the Canby family have the gift of getting their thoughts across to a receptive subject such as—such as Sheila Kelly undoubtedly is. Now will you stop being tantalizing long enough to give me their names?"

"They were," I said gravely, "Dora Canby and her least favored nephew, Allan Atwood."

"Allan Atwood!"

"And Dora Canby," I added firmly.

"You've narrowed it down to those two!"

"I've simply shown you, I hope to your satisfaction, that at least two other people here at the inn possessed the necessary mental equipment to run Professor Matthews a close race when it came to making mental suggestions to Sheila Kelly."

We stared at each other, and his face was quite ghastly. I think in the beginning he attached little if any importance to my theory. He had clutched at it, to be sure, as a drowning man might clutch at a straw, but without conviction. Now, however, his attitude suffered a drastic change.

"Somebody has got hold of the girl's mind," he whispered, "somebody who stops at nothing!"

"It's the only sane explanation," I repeated stubbornly.

"But do you realize what it means?" he demanded, his fists clenching. "She's been forced to incriminate herself. She's been brought to the very brink of despair and there's no telling what else she'll be forced to do."

I nodded, feeling sure that my face was as white as his. "I don't believe she can stand much more," I said. "That is why I promised her to find out who's back of this devilish business."

"Until we do," he cried in a strangled voice, "she's at his mercy!"

"Or *her* mercy," I felt constrained to point out.

15

IT WAS ELLA who reminded me that I had not had a bite of dinner and the dining room was due to close in a few minutes. I protested that I was not hungry. I even went so far as to say that I didn't know how anybody in that house had the heart to sit down to a meal after everything that had happened. I might as well have talked to the wind.

"Of course you're hungry," said Ella, propelling me bodily across the lounge. "You've got to keep your strength up, Adelaide. There's another session with the coroner in half an hour."

"I realize that as well as you do," I said shortly.

Ella shrugged her shoulders. "Even if you and Chet Keith have had your heads together for the last hour, I doubt if you can pull it off."

"Pull what off? Our heads?" I demanded.

"You know very well," said Ella, wrinkling her brows, "that you and that newspaper chap are determined to get Sheila Kelly out of this thing."

I tried to read her face, but Ella can be inscrutable if she likes.

"Mr. Keith is interested, like myself, solely in seeing that justice is served," I remarked in my most dignified tones.

"Oh yeah?" retorted Ella with her deplorable tendency to pick up current slang.

I could not think of a suitably crushing retort, so I contented myself with compressing my lips and studying the menu. To my relief Ella seemed satisfied to let it go at that. Because of the lateness of the hour we had the dining room practically to ourselves. Only

Allan Atwood was at the Canby table, picking listlessly at the food before him, absorbed, as was evident at a glance, in thoughts of his own, painful thoughts to judge by the darkness of his expression.

I was not aware that I was watching him until Ella caught me at it. "He's maladjusted and awkward and self-conscious," she said, "thanks to Thomas Canby and his daughter Gloria. I understand they made Allan's life miserable for years, but do you think a fellow who can't walk across the floor without barking his shin against a chair could jerk a light cord out and cut a man's throat in the dark and get back to his place in less than a minute without mishap?"

"I have not accused Allan Atwood of murder," I protested, although I fancy I looked guilty.

"It's perfectly apparent," remarked Ella in scathing accents, "that you and that reporter are willing to pin the guilt on anybody if it will clear Sheila Kelly."

"Don't be absurd!" I protested. "I told you we want only to see justice done."

"You even tried to make out that poor little Judy Oliver was an accomplice," said Ella indignantly. "As if Patrick isn't the most transparent person in the world!"

"He did bring the professor here."

"And look how quickly he admitted it when pressed," Ella pointed out.

"I don't believe Patrick is a murderer," I admitted.

"I should hope not!" cried Ella. "Nor Judy either! Have you any conception how much courage it required for her to confess in front of Jeff Wayne that she is in love with him, after the pains he has taken to deny that he cares for her?"

"He cares for her all right," I muttered.

"Certainly he does," snapped Ella, "but he'll never admit it so long as Sheila Kelly is at large."

At this point I lost my temper. "While we are on the subject," I said, "I might remind you, Mrs. Trotter, that your own attitude is not in the strictest sense impartial."

"What do you mean by that crack?" demanded Ella with more asperity than elegance.

"You are perfectly willing to shove the guilt off upon Sheila Kelly, aren't you? Anything, in fact, so long as it does not involve your pets in the Canby family."

I should have known Ella better than to arouse her antagonism. I suffered a qualm the minute I did it, but it was too late.

"I do like Judy Oliver and that young scamp Patrick," said Ella. "I like Allan, too, if he *is* a hobbledehoy. I even have a sneaking admiration for Lila Atwood, although she lets Hogan Brewster hang around for no good reason. So what, Adelaide?"

There was a challenge in her eyes which made me definitely uneasy. "So nothing," I grumbled, "except I claim the same privilege. I like the Kelly girl. At least I feel desperately sorry for her and I do not believe she is a killer."

Ella gave me a very odd look. "Has it occurred to you, Adelaide, that those two might be pulling the wool over your eyes?"

"What two?"

"Chet Keith and Sheila Kelly," she explained. "They knew each other before. I thought the first time I saw them there was something between them. I think so still. Isn't it a trifle peculiar that he happened on the scene at this precise time?"

"What, if anything, are you driving at?"

"Big metropolitan newspapers don't usually send their ace men to obscure places like this *before* a murder breaks."

"I was given to understand," I announced with hauteur, "that his city editor received a tip, something to do with Thomas Canby, who, I infer, did not have to get himself murdered to be news."

Ella leaned a little forward. "Suppose Sheila Kelly sent that tip, Adelaide, if such a tip was ever sent. Suppose the whole thing is a frame-up between her and Chet Keith to secure the Canby fortune. Suppose"—there was a note in her voice which made me sit up very straight—"suppose they are just using you, Adelaide, to put the scheme over."

It was feasible, I could not deny it. Certainly without my co-operation Chet Keith would never have been able to handle the coroner and the sheriff as they had been handled.

"How do you know they aren't taking advantage of your being a sentimental goose?" demanded Ella.

"The idea!" I gasped indignantly. "I've been called an old battle-ax. I don't deny the allegation, but I vigorously rebel at being referred to as either sentimental or a goose."

"Bushwa!" exclaimed Ella, whatever that may mean. "You've always been a sucker for the underdog, Adelaide. That girl has only to roll her eyes at you and look abused to have you leap into the fray like a flea-bitten old war horse."

"The idea!" I said again, very feebly, with a paralyzing conviction that Ella had hit the nail on the head, my head.

"It might be different if everybody was on her side," continued Ella sarcastically, "but you know perfectly well, Adelaide, that you are fundamentally unable to resist an opportunity to be contrary."

"I have a mind of my own, if that's being contrary," I said tartly.

Ella was not impressed. "Use it then," she snapped and added with a frown, "For all you know, Adelaide, that girl brought Chet Keith down here to help her murder Canby."

"Nonsense!"

"Naturally they had to get rid of the professor afterward."

"Why naturally?" I demanded, feeling slightly dizzy.

"He knew enough hypnotism to tumble to the Gloria manifestations."

"Tumble to them?"

"At first they scared him silly, just as they did me," she was honest enough to admit. "Then he began to put two and two together and he got an answer that satisfied him."

"You think so

"He wasn't frightened this morning. He looked like a cat that had located a bird's nest."

"I concede the point."

"He had figured it all out," said Ella. "I'm convinced of it."

"Consequently he had to die," I remarked with what I intended for irony.

"It was that or cut him in on part of the Canby fortune," said Ella, "so Sheila Kelly or Chet Keith—I give you your choice—killed him."

I drew a long breath. "I have just recalled that Chet Keith could not have killed the professor, Ella. It cannot possibly have been done except during the time the deputy Butch was in my room."

"Nobody disputes that."

I felt a great deal better. "I can take a solemn oath that Butch and Chet Keith entered my room at the same moment and, while I cannot swear to who all came in and out during the confusion of the next few minutes, I do know that Chet Keith never left the room again until we all streamed out together into the hall after Butch gave the alarm about the professor."

"Then," said Ella with so much conviction my heart sank, "the girl killed him."

"It was brought out at the investigation this afternoon that she could not have got out of her room," I faltered.

Ella gave me a long look. "Chet Keith brought it out," she snapped, "just as all along he has been confusing the issue where Sheila Kelly is concerned."

My guilty knowledge was not the most comforting companion and I realized that my voice was by no means so confident as I could have wished. However, I attempted to carry the battle into Ella's own camp.

"I thought you believed the girl was actuated by Gloria Canby's dead hand," I stammered.

I was disconcerted to have Ella bestow upon me a pitying glance. "You are hard put to it, Adelaide, if you have to take refuge in that argument," she said.

"I take it you have abandoned the idea?"

Ella sniffed. "An idea at which, until this moment, you have seen fit to scoff, if not sneer, Adelaide."

"I never have believed that the dead can return," I said stiffly. "I—I don't believe so yet."

Ella nodded her head. "It's been too pointed," she said, "or too theatrical if you like, the way dead cats have been found lying around, and amber-colored hair pins such as Gloria Canby used to wear." She frowned. "I can't quite see a phantom taking care to leave such obvious clues to itself, can you, Adelaide?"

"I can't see a phantom at all," I confessed ruefully.

"The build-up has been too elaborate," complained Ella, "precisely as if somebody with a rather lurid taste in fiction had set out to lay the horror on with a trowel. The bats, for instance, and that

horrible laugh which Sheila Kelly gets off in the person of Gloria
Canby, and the way she has changed her hairdress and her make-
up this past week to increase her resemblance to the dead girl."

I shifted uneasily in my chair. "Are you now trying to make out
that Sheila Kelly has deliberately cultivated her resemblance to
Gloria Canby?"

"A police reporter and a former fan dancer in a night club might
be expected to go in for lurid effects, mightn't they, Adelaide?"

"I have no idea," I said tartly.

Nevertheless, as Ella had pointed out, the build-up *had* been
elaborate. Whoever had framed Sheila Kelly had taken the greatest pains with details. I did not doubt, although she could not remember it, that she had been told to dress her hair differently and
there *had* been something extremely theatrical both in her gestures and her choice of words when she was impersonating Gloria
Canby, exactly as if she had been rehearsed by somebody with a
strong leaning toward the melodramatic.

"I wouldn't worry so," Ella continued with a sigh, "if I weren't
obliquely responsible for your being here, albeit against my will."

I felt decidedly nettled, an effect which Ella and I often have
upon each other. "I can look after myself," I said haughtily. "I always have."

"So thought the professor," Ella reminded me. "He thought, no
doubt, that he had stumbled upon a little private mint, but look at
the shape he's in now."

"Are you trying to frighten me, Ella?"

"No, I'm merely warning you, the way Chet Keith warned or
threatened Professor Matthews this morning, that it isn't condu-
cive to longevity to share secrets with a murderer."

Now had I had nothing on my conscience, I should unquestion-
ably have demanded what secret Ella suspected me of harboring
and I dare say she read volumes into the fact that I did nothing of
the kind. The truth is I did not dare have it out with Ella. It is very
unlike me to let a challenge slide, but that is what I did, dropping
my napkin petulantly upon the table and getting to my feet with

the bald announcement that I had gone through the motion of dining and I hoped she was satisfied.

"No," snapped Ella, "I'm not satisfied, but knowing you, I realize I have done all I could."

I did not for one minute believe that she was referring to the
fact that, like Allan Atwood, I had merely toyed with my food;
nevertheless I again evaded the issue by pretending to think so.

"You can lead a horse to water, Ella, but not even you can make
him drink," I said, realizing from Ella's expression that I had succeeded merely in being trite.

When we came into the lounge we found Fannie Parrish once
more besieging Captain French about the latest report from the
bridge. "The highway department insists that everything will be in
good order by morning," he said in a tired voice.

"Goodness knows, I hope so," murmured Miss Maurine Smith.
"They've nearly run me ragged today with telephone calls. The
press, you know," she confided to me. "I think every newspaper in
the country has either sent a correspondent to Carrolton or called
up. I don't know what I should have done," she smiled coyly, "if
Mr. Keith hadn't told me to refer all the reporters to him. Naturally, being in the newspaper game himself, he is the one to give
out information, don't you think?"

"Oh, naturally," I said dryly and could not resist a triumphant
glance at Ella. "I understand that Mr. Canby has always been what's
called big news."

Ella merely tossed her head. It lacked only a few minutes of
nine, the hour which had been set for resuming the interrupted
hearing in the parlor. Everybody involved was more or less standing around waiting for the signal to file into the room, including
Sheriff Latham, who was over by the window conversing with Coroner Timmons, neither of them looking very well pleased with themselves. There was no sign of Chet Keith. I wondered where he had
disappeared to. I even went to the door and glanced out. The rain
had stopped but the wind was still high and the sky overcast with
scudding black clouds.

"Looking for your alter ego, Miss Adams?" inquired Hogan Brewster with his usual flippant smile. He was just behind me, quite close to Lila Atwood, and as I turned with a frown I met her eyes.

"Hogan loves innuendo, Miss Adams," she said lightly. "I think he was trying to imply that you have a crush on the fascinating Mr. Keith."

"So you find him fascinating also, do you, Lila?" asked Hogan Brewster, grinning at Allan Atwood. "But then, Lila always has had a weakness for dashing, debonair gents, eh, Allan?"

I thought for a moment that Allan was going to strike the other man, and although I have never considered myself a bloodthirsty person I recall wishing he would. It seemed to me that no self-respecting husband under the circumstances could ignore that particular insult. It was so painfully apparent that, while Hogan Brewster was both dashing and debonair, Allan Atwood was neither. I even thought that Lila Atwood stared at her husband eagerly, but if so he disappointed us both.

"I have never bothered a lot about my wife's taste in men, Brewster," he said and turned away, managing, as he went, to trip over the umbrella which Fannie Parrish had brought downstairs with her with the statement that if there were any more murders she for one intended to walk to town.

Hogan Brewster grinned at me. "'Sfunny how old Allan always puts his foot in it every time he opens his mouth."

I glanced at Lila Atwood. She was trying to smile, but her lips were not steady.

"Everybody can't have your well-known facility, darling," she murmured, and this time she made no effort to move away from the carefully manicured hand which he placed upon her arm.

I do not as a rule have any patience with the married flirt, male or female, but I remember thinking to myself that if ever a man asked for such treatment it was Allan Atwood. I had supposed all along, Lila being such an exceptionally beautiful woman, that poor fumbling Allan Atwood was hopelessly in love with her. Now for the first time I wondered if everybody was mistaken in assuming that this was the typical triangle of the unattractive husband and the too attractive other man. Thomas Canby had arranged his nephew's marriage, that much was certain, but it did not absolutely follow that Allan Atwood had lost his heart to his wife. From all appearances the reverse was true. He acted as if he hated her. He had said as much, according to Fannie Parrish. With a queer feeling I realized that if actions meant anything Lila Atwood was far more in love with her husband than he gave any signs of being with her.

"All set for the next encounter, Miss Adams?" murmured a voice behind me.

I turned sharply. "Where have you been?" I demanded.

Chet Keith grinned. "Oh, here, there and yonder," he said airily.

Sheriff Latham at that moment looked around with a frown. "Nine o'clock," he announced, referring to a huge gold watch attached by a braided leather fob to his belt.

Everybody began moving toward the parlor door which Mart Butler was unlocking. I realized I had only a moment but I intended to make the best of it. Ella had succeeded in thoroughly unsettling me. I suppose the glance I fixed upon Chet Keith must have been severe; at any rate he made a squirming movement with his shoulders.

"That tip to your city editor," I said, "was it Sheila Kelly who sent it?"

I took him by complete surprise. "How on earth did you—"

He paused, bit his lip and stared at me.

"So it was from her?" I asked with a sinking feeling in my heart.

He grinned wryly. "Pretty neat about setting traps, aren't you?" he inquired. "All right, it was from her. Otherwise, I don't suppose I'd have utilized my week's vacation to run it down."

"Week's vacation?"

"Yes, Miss Adams, I'm here on my own time, not the paper's."

My heart must have been as low as my shoelaces by this time. "What sort of tip was it?"

"Anonymous, that's why the city editor tossed it into the wastebasket."

"Oh, he did, did he?" I muttered and frowned. "And the tip was anonymous?"

"Yes, but it was from Sheila. I might not have recognized her writing if she hadn't mentioned a spiritualist angle. When she did, it was the giveaway. You see," he flushed, "I tried to look her up three months ago and discovered that she had gone on the road with a fake psychic, namely Professor Thaddeus Matthews."

"So you recognized her writing, just like that."

He met my eyes without a tremor. "Just like that."

"Why should she have tipped off the editor of a Chicago paper that something was up down here?" I asked sharply.

He shrugged his shoulders. "I got the idea that the poor kid was frightened. I flattered myself that in spite of the poor opinion which she has of me in affairs of the heart she had some faith in my ability as a friend in need. Perhaps I am more quixotic than I believed possible until I met Sheila Kelly."

"You thought she sent that tip in deliberately, knowing it would fall into your hands?"

"I guess you were right in the first place," he said with a wry grin. "I fell for the girl over a year ago and I've never got over it. I just thought I had. Amusing in a hard-boiled egg like me, eh what?"

I did not find it in the least amusing. Ella had been partly right at any rate, I told myself with consternation. Sheila Kelly *was* responsible for Chet Keith's presence at the inn, and he and I together were responsible for hoodwinking the sheriff and otherwise playing hide-and-seek with the law. I had a sudden ghastly vision of Professor Matthews' bloodless face, stamped with a hideous grimace above the horrible red gash in his throat.

"How do you know," I asked in a shaking voice, "that she isn't making a fool of both of us?"

Had he tried to put me off, I think I should have blurted out the truth then and there, the moment I could have reached Sheriff Latham, but Chet Keith paid me the supreme tribute of dropping his guard for an instant during which we exchanged a distracted glance.

"Good Lord," he groaned, "don't you suppose that thought has me going around in circles half the time?"

"Maybe the sheriff is right," I said again. "Perhaps she *is* just a clever actress, making a play at several million dollars."

"Sure," admitted Chet Keith miserably, looking like a wretched small boy. Then he squared his shoulders with an effort. "I'm pinning my faith on two things, Miss Adams. If she intended to kill Canby why did she want me here? And if she killed the professor how did she get back into her room with the key on the outside?"

"She might have wanted you here," I said slowly, "to do exactly what you have done—manipulate the officers of the law, as well as the press, to suit her purpose."

"She couldn't have counted on the bridge going out."

"No," I admitted, "but you were relieved when it did go out, and I'll have to remind you again that there is only your word for the key being on the outside of her door after the professor's murder."

He stared at me, his face white. "Are you implying that Sheila and I are in cahoots on this thing?" he inquired, his lips curling.

"I still refuse to believe that the trances are faked," I said slowly, "but there's only your own testimony to prove that you drew a blank on the ESP tests."

"Good God, you can't believe that I am Conspirator Number One!" he protested. "With Sheila in the role of my victim!"

"People have done worse things for a million dollars, and maybe she isn't a victim at all," I suggested miserably. "Maybe I have jumped to conclusions in thinking so. After all, I have no reason, except her own protestations, to believe that murder is contrary to her moral code."

He looked genuinely aghast. "You think we plotted this together and I hypnotized her into committing the crimes!"

"Or maybe you just hypnotized her, so she could put on a good act, while you committed the crimes yourself."

He wiped his forehead. "You don't believe any such thing," he stammered, again reminding me of a small boy, a desperate one.

"It's possible, isn't it?" I demanded.

"Anything is possible in this damnable business," he admitted with a groan. "Nevertheless I am no hypnotist, Miss Adams, and I'd stake my life that Sheila is incapable of murder. Somebody has framed her by means of mental suggestion, just as you figured out, but I don't dare face Sheriff Latham with that theory, any more

than I dare let him know that the door between your room and
Sheila's was unlocked this afternoon; not, at least, until I have
smoked the murderer out."

He drew a long breath. "Give me an hour, just another hour,"
he pleaded.

I hesitated, although as a rule I am not an indecisive person,
and at that moment Butch came down the hall with Sheila Kelly in
custody. She looked worse than ever, paler and more dejected if
possible, but as she passed she glanced up at me and tried to smile.
I suppose Ella is right, though I have always flattered myself otherwise, and I am a sentimental old goose. At least that is my only
excuse for acceding to Chet Keith's request.

16

WE WERE ALL SEATED and Marty Butler had closed the parlor doors before I realized that our number had been augmented since our last sitting with the coroner. For a moment I did not recognize the muscular young man in the neat blue serge suit with the carefully plastered-down brown hair and guarded expression. I had seen him only once before and then he had been wearing his chauffeur's uniform, in which he looked trimmer, especially across the shoulders. It was not, in fact, until Chet Keith called him to the witness stand that I was certain of the man's identity.

"You acted as chauffeur to the late Thomas Canby?" the coroner asked, referring to the notes with which Chet Keith had supplied him.

"Yes."

"Your name is Jay Stuart?"

"Yes."

He had a hoarse, unpleasant voice and apparently he was determined to be as laconic as possible. He kept glancing at Chet Keith with unconcealed antagonism. Later I found out where the newspaperman had been when I missed him from the lounge. He was spying upon Mr. Jay Stuart, much to the latter's discomfiture.

"How long have you been in Mr. Canby's employ?" was the coroner's next question.

"Three months or so."

"What was your occupation before that?"

"No, but the gun does, which you were wearing the first time I saw you, and Canby was the last man in the world to get panicky without cause."

"He had nerve all right," admitted the chauffeur with the first flicker of animation which he had displayed.

"And yet all at once, three months ago, he decides for no special reason to hire a bodyguard."

"Looks like it."

Chet Keith leaned closer to the other man. "What was Canby afraid of, Stuart?"

The chauffeur's face closed up as if he had pulled a screen over it. "How should I know?" he demanded. "He didn't pay me to pry into his secrets."

"No?"

"No!"

"You don't know why Thomas Canby suddenly decided that his life was in danger? In enough danger to justify his hiring a professional bodyguard?"

"I told you I didn't draw a salary for prying into his business."

Chet Keith's eyes narrowed. "You won't be drawing a salary from Canby much longer."

"I was hired to the first of the month."

"No doubt you have cause to believe that it pays to keep your mouth shut."

"I don't know what you're getting at," said the man sulkily.

"I think," murmured Chet Keith, "that since Thomas Canby's death you have acquired a new employer."

The man turned a little yellow. "Oh yes?" he muttered.

"Somebody who is making it worth your while to keep Canby's secrets."

"You can't be arrested for thinking," muttered the chauffeur, although I thought he looked uneasy.

Evidently Chet Keith thought so too, for he pressed his advantage.

"You know what Canby was afraid of, Stuart. You know of whom he stood in terror of his life and why. If you've struck a bargain to keep your knowledge to yourself, let me warn you that you can't get away with it."

"Says you!"

"Says I!" retorted Chet Keith and, leaning over suddenly, he snatched a wallet out of the man's breast pocket.

It was a very fat wallet. Jay Stuart made a spring at it, but Chet Keith was too quick for him. He dumped the contents on the table before him. The wallet was stuffed with crisp new greenbacks.

"In this state," said Chet Keith, "an accessory after the fact is equally guilty. You don't want to hang, do you, Stuart?"

The man was positively livid. "You ain't got nothing on me."

"Nothing except that you were broke this morning. I heard you say so. You said you lost all your money in a crap game night before last. You said you had one dollar to run you to payday. Then, a while ago, I observed you with interest, out behind the inn, counting off greenbacks like a millionaire."

"You damned snoop!" snarled the chauffeur. "I found that money. If you don't believe me, try to prove I didn't."

"That's your story, is it?"

"Yes."

Chet Keith smiled unpleasantly. "The professor thought it would pay *him* to keep his mouth shut. Now he's dead. I warned him and I am warning you, it isn't healthy to put your trust in murderers."

The man wet his lips as if they were parched. His eyes flickered furtively about the room, and suddenly I knew he was frightened. I think Chet Keith knew it too.

"Come clean, Stuart," he said softly.

"I told you the truth," muttered the man. "I wasn't hired to pry into the boss's affairs, and I didn't. If I prefer to keep what I suspected to myself, that's my business."

"So you did suspect something?" asked Chet Keith.

The chauffeur scowled. "I ain't deaf and I ain't blind. Sure I suspected something. I suspected a lot. Just the same, the business Canby had me on didn't have nothing to do with his being killed."

"You think not?"

"Didn't I tell you? The girl bumped Canby off, but he didn't hire me because of her."

"No?"

"She didn't come into the picture till about two months after he took me on."

"Exactly," said Chet Keith with a triumphant glance at Sheriff Latham, who merely shook his head and looked baffled.

"The boss was expecting somebody to try to get him, but he didn't think he had anything to fear from a quack professor and that girl," said the chauffeur scornfully. "That's why he didn't have me at the séance last night."

I leaned forward quickly. "What were you doing while we were all in here at the séance?"

He scowled at me. "Searching the mountain," he said. "Not that it's any of your business."

"Searching the mountain!" I repeated incredulously.

"The boss wanted to make sure nobody was hiding out up here."

Even Chet Keith looked baffled at this. "Thomas Canby suspected that somebody was concealed on the mountain?"

"Yep."

"He believed the danger to himself lay outside, not inside the inn?" demanded Chet Keith in a disconcerted voice.

"Looks like it, doesn't it?" snarled Jay Stuart.

"And did you find traces of somebody's having been concealed on Mount Lebeau?"

The chauffeur hesitated and again his eyes flickered uneasily about the room. "Nope," he said.

An interruption came from an unexpected quarter "The man's lying," said Jeff Wayne.

Everybody stared at him, and there was a dogged, unhappy look upon his face as he went on. "I heard him report to Mr. Canby just before the séance started last night. He said he hadn't finished searching the mountain, but he had discovered a hut down the road. He said it was supposed to be unoccupied, but the floor was littered

with cigarette butts and there were car tracks back of the hut, coming and going and overlapping, as well as oil drippings on the
ground, as if a machine had been parked from time to time behind
the trees."

Chet Keith eyed the chauffeur with a scowl. "So somebody *had*
been hiding on the mountain."

"First I've heard of it," said Jay Stuart with what I can describe
only as a leer.

The man's insolence provoked me into an outburst. "Sheriff
Latham, aren't there ways to make a witness speak when he is deliberately impeding justice in a murder case?" I demanded. "This
man has plainly accepted a bribe to withhold evidence. That is a
penitentiary offense."

The sheriff grinned. "I might let Butch here take him out and
work him over," he suggested with what I regarded as extremely
misplaced humor.

Butch scratched his ear and looked embarrassed, and Jay Stuart
shot him a contemptuous glance. "I've been manhandled by ex-
perts," he said out of the corner of his mouth. "You've got nothing
on me. I found that thousand dollars. Understand? I found it and
try to get anything else out of me."

Chet Keith's face was scarlet, and so, I feel sure, was mine. I
had heard of seeing red, but I had supposed the expression was a
figure of speech until I stared at Jay Stuart's mean, tight face.

"You know what Thomas Canby was afraid of!" I cried.

I am afraid I flourished my clenched fist under his nose. At any
rate he flinched, but his lips only buttoned up the tighter. I remember realizing that we had reached an impasse and being perfectly furious about it. I glared at Patrick Oliver.

"It's all your fault," I said bitterly. "But for you and your sister
none of this would have happened."

Jeff Wayne moved closer to Judy and gave me an irate look. To
this day Chet Keith persists in saying that young Wayne would
never have come to the front as he proceeded to do if I had not
goaded him into it.

"At the same time Mr. Canby hired this man," he volunteered with a miserable but defiant glance at Allan Atwood, "he employed a private detective."

"A private detective!" exclaimed Chet Keith.

Young Wayne flushed. "I am supposed to be fifth vice-president in charge of personnel," he said. "I—I make out the pay roll. That is how I know."

I stared at him. "What on earth did Thomas Canby want with a private detective?"

Jeff Wayne's face was ashen. "He was investigating Gloria's death," he said in a voice scarcely louder than a whisper.

"Her suicide, you mean?" I asked sharply.

"If it was suicide," he whispered.

There was an electric silence in which I think we all caught our breath, and when I looked at Chet Keith his eyes were like gimlets.

"Are you suggesting that Gloria Canby did not commit suicide?" he asked.

"Of course she committed suicide," said Allan Atwood, but his face belied him.

"So," murmured Chet Keith, "Gloria Canby was supposed to have opened her wrists with a razor blade because her father was going to have her put away in an institution, only Thomas Canby didn't believe it."

"You see," said Jeff Wayne, hesitating painfully over his words, "there was a note."

"A note?"

"A note from her father, enclosing a doctor's certificate, saying she wasn't crazy and couldn't be put away."

"Gloria never read the note," expostulated Dora Canby. "They found it beside her unopened."

Jeff Wayne drew his hand across his brow. "That's why Thomas Canby employed the detective. The note was found by Gloria's body unopened. Only it—it had been opened, opened and resealed."

"Good God!" breathed Chet Keith.

"Thomas Canby believed that Gloria did read the note!" I deduced excitedly. "He believed she was murdered and the murderer resealed the note to provide a motive for suicide!"

"It isn't true," whispered Dora Canby. "You heard Gloria last night. Her father drove her to her death. She said so, didn't you, darling?"

Allan Atwood glared at young Wayne. "Everybody knows that."

"Then there was the razor blade," said Jeff Wayne, looking unhappy.

"What about the razor blade?" demanded Chet Keith.

"Nobody in the house used that brand. They never knew where she got it. The detective has been unable to find any record of Gloria's ever having had that kind of blade."

I was too intoxicated with my own mental gymnastics to keep still. "That's why Thomas Canby hired a bodyguard!" I announced triumphantly. "He was determined to trap his daughter's murderer, but he knew he was dealing with a killer, a killer who had already killed once and who, as Canby knew, would not hesitate to kill again to save himself."

"It's preposterous!" protested Allan Atwood, again glaring at young Wayne. "Gloria killed herself. Jeff knows it, Uncle Thomas knew it."

Young Wayne returned his scowl with one equally violent. "I warned you, Allan," he said rebelliously. "It's all very well for you to insist that we shouldn't wash our dirty linen in public. The truth is the truth, and when it narrows down to blaming Judy for this mess, I refuse to keep what I know to myself. Thomas Canby did believe that Gloria was murdered. He told me so and I think he told you too."

"Thomas Canby discovered that his daughter was murdered!" cried Chet Keith and turned with blazing eyes upon the sheriff. "He was about to expose the murderer, so Canby had to die, and Sheila Kelly was framed for the crime."

"We ain't got no reason to think that Canby knew who murdered his daughter, if she was murdered," protested Sheriff Latham cynically.

Chet Keith looked slightly dashed. "Canby did know who killed his daughter, didn't he, Wayne?"

Young Wayne shook his head. "Whatever suspicions he had he kept to himself, but it's my belief that, although he refused to give up the idea, he was unable to make out a case against anybody."

"There you are," murmured the sheriff with maddening complacence.

Once more I was provoked into snatching up the gauntlet. "Thomas Canby was a ruthless individualist," I said. "If he started a line of action, he never abandoned it, short of success. Knowing this, the slayer was bound to realize that he would always be in danger while Canby was alive to pursue his investigations."

"Exactly," snapped Chet Keith, again bearding the sheriff. "There is your motive. As soon as Canby arrived at the inn last night he sent for you. His daughter's murderer did not know how much Canby had found out. He probably believed that Canby had finally secured the evidence for which he had been looking or, as Miss Adams says, the killer may simply have realized that he would never be safe while Canby was alive. At any rate he took advantage of Sheila Kelly's manifestation at the séance to dispose of Canby for ever."

"How did he know that Uncle Thomas had phoned for the sheriff?" objected Allan Atwood. "You're forgetting that the man Uncle Thomas suspected wasn't here at the inn. He was hidden out on the mountain."

Chet Keith frowned. "Where is this hide-out you're supposed to have discovered, Stuart?"

The chauffeur hesitated, and the sheriff, abruptly abandoning his humorous attitude, leaned forward and laid his hand heavily upon the man's shoulder.

"This here is serious," he said, "a lot more serious than I realized at first. Talk, fellow, or by God you're going to jail and you'll stay there till you rot if you don't talk."

Chet Keith nodded. "A thousand dollars is a thousand dollars in any man's language, Stuart, but it isn't worth hanging for."

The chauffeur's lean furtive face twitched. He reminded me of a ferret run to earth without the courage to bare his teeth and defend himself.

"The hut's been cleaned up now," he muttered, his eyes darting frantically about the room, as if he were looking for covert. "I ain't got nothing but my word to prove the cigarette butts were ever there, or the car tracks either."

"Your word's sufficient for me," said Chet Keith.

Just then Dora Canby, who had been sitting listlessly in her chair, taking no interest in the proceedings, looked up and cried out in a startled voice, "Gloria!"

Everybody turned. Sheila Kelly was getting slowly to her feet. There was that blurred look which I had noticed on her face before. Her hands were wavering in front of her as if she were feeling her way through a fog.

"God!" whispered Chet Keith.

He took a quick step toward her, but she did not see him. She was staring across the room.

"Ask Lila where the razor blade came from," she said in that mocking, perverse voice which always sounded so strange upon her lips. "Ask her why she put me out of the way."

I have never seen anything more tragic than Lila Atwood's eyes. She seemed to be frozen in her tracks.

"Or ask Allan," Sheila Kelly went on. "He knows."

I do not believe that anybody who saw Allan Atwood's ravished face at that moment failed to realize that he did indeed possess some guilty knowledge.

"Allan!" cried his wife and put out her hand to him, but he drew away with a shudder.

And then the lights went out. I heard Sheriff Latham's muffled curses. I heard Butch cry out and somewhere quite near me Chet Keith kept calling Sheila Kelly's name in an anguished voice. I was conscious of a great deal of confusion, of people moving about, of other people pleading with somebody to turn on the lights. Above all I was conscious of that terrible gurgling groan, followed by a coughing gasp which made my blood run cold.

"Lights! For God's sake turn on the lights!" shouted Sheriff Latham.

And then Fannie Parrish gripped my shoulder convulsively.

"Look!" she screamed. "Oh, look!"

We all saw it, that weird ghostly emanation which floated in the air above our heads.

"Gloria! Gloria darling!" wailed Dora Canby.

It had a face, a malicious yellow face like Sheila Kelly's and yet unlike hers. The eyes were indescribably evil, the mouth twisted into a perverted and shocking smile. It seemed to be jeering at us as it hung there, suspended in mid-air. And then it vanished and Chet Keith found the light switch and pressed it. We were all blinded after the darkness. I remember rubbing my eyes to clear them and being afraid to remove my hand. I think I knew what I should see in that chair in front of the coroner's table.

"He's dead," whispered Sheriff Latham, his face as gray as a piece of blotting paper.

The chauffeur *was* dead, slumped down in his seat, the handle of a large butcher knife protruding from the breast pocket of his neat blue suit.

17

I HAVE NEVER DENIED that I lost my head for a few minutes after the discovery of Jay Stuart's dead body, nor was I the only one. I do not believe anybody could give a coherent account of what happened there in the parlor for the next quarter of an hour. Fannie Parrish had hysterics, I do remember that, and I think from the expression on Sheriff Latham's face he wished he might follow suit.

"I saw it! We all saw it!" shrieked Fannie over and over.

She was referring to the apparition which had floated above our heads. She glanced at me reproachfully.

"You said it wasn't possible for the dead to come back," she said. "But you can't deny the evidence of your own eyes."

Dora Canby was weeping. "Gloria! Gloria!" she kept saying in a desolate voice.

They would not let her go to Sheila Kelly. They would not allow Chet Keith near the girl either. Upon Sheriff Latham's orders Butch had taken the prisoner upstairs to her room and locked her in with instructions not to take his eyes off her door for a moment.

"Though I'm beginning to realize that you're right, ma'am," the sheriff said with a sigh to Fannie Parrish. "Locks and bolts don't mean nothing to what we're up against here."

The sheriff's skepticism had suffered a sad blow. He was a thoroughly materialistic man and, like Fannie, he was constitutionally unable to distrust the evidence of his own senses. He had seen Gloria Canby's spirit rising from Sheila Kelly's body. The sheriff no longer bothered about how she had been able to kill the professor while she was, as he believed, incarcerated in a locked room.

"I never took no stock in spooks," he said, wiping his brow, "but I ain't too old to learn."

Chet Keith, looking tired and shaken, tried to protest. "It was a trick. There is no such thing as ghosts or apparitions."

He might as well have saved his breath.

"You talked me into letting you run this business," growled Sheriff Latham, "and what have we got to show for it? Another corpse!"

"The girl's being framed!" exclaimed the newspaperman in a despairing voice. "Your men searched her. They searched her room. They took away everything of a lethal nature. If she killed Stuart, where did she get the butcher knife?"

The sheriff shook his head. "Locked doors don't mean nothing to her. She's in traffic with the Devil and the Devil looks after his own." He crossed himself and glared about the room. "Clear out, all of you. The investigation is over. We've got the murderer, though we may have to burn her for a witch to be rid of her."

"I tell you the girl isn't guilty," groaned Chet Keith.

Nobody, least of all Sheriff Latham and Coroner Timmons, paid any attention to him. Judy Oliver was assisting her aunt to her feet. They walked out, followed by Jeff Wayne and Patrick. Lila Atwood started to go with them, but Dora Canby turned on her.

"You killed Gloria," she said, "because of Hogan Brewster. I never want to see you again. Come, Allan."

I saw the look which Lila gave her husband. He hesitated, then he turned and walked out of the room behind his aunt. With a short laugh Hogan Brewster took Lila's arm.

"Lean on me, old dear," he said.

I saw her stumble and then her shoulders lifted. "Thanks," she said and they went out together.

Ella Trotter sighed. "I suppose that settles it. She'll surely divorce Allan now and marry Brewster."

"Do you believe she killed Gloria Canby?" I asked.

Ella shrugged her shoulders. "Allan Atwood believes it. No wonder he shrinks from her. He thinks she killed Gloria on account of Brewster!"

It explained a great deal which had puzzled me about Allan Atwood's attitude toward his wife. He thought she was in love with Brewster, who, according to Ella, had been having an affair with Gloria. It did not, however, explain one thing.

"She *isn't* in love with Hogan Brewster," I protested. "I'd almost be willing to swear that she's in love with her husband."

Ella shook her head. "I dare say she's stuck to Allan for fear he'd betray her to the police if she left him."

"That's possible," I muttered, but it did not satisfy me.

We were all gathered in the lounge again with the exception of the Canby family. Lila Atwood was there, sitting a little apart on one of the hard settees, talking to Hogan Brewster. She must have known that everybody present was discussing the charge which had been made against her, but she held her head high and I heard her laugh at one of Brewster's sallies.

"She's going to brazen it out," remarked Ella. "After all, I don't suppose she'll ever be arrested. With Thomas Canby dead, there is nobody to press the case, and even he doesn't seem to have been able to prove that she killed his daughter."

I frowned. "Doesn't it seem a little queer that even Gloria Canby's ghost appears to have been confused on the issue?"

"What issue?" demanded Ella, knitting her brows.

"At the séance last night she blamed her father for her suicide. Tonight she accused Lila Atwood of murdering her."

Ella sniffed. "Are you still trying to give Sheila Kelly a clean bill of health, Adelaide?"

"I have said from the first that the dead don't come back," I explained wearily.

Ella shrugged her shoulders. "The kindest thing you can say for Sheila Kelly is that she's possessed of something," she pointed out.

"But not of a ghost," I insisted, looking about for Chet Keith.

He appeared to have vanished. At least he was not in the lounge. Fannie Parrish said she had seen him a little while before putting on a slicker, as if he intended to go out.

"If you ask me," she said, which nobody had, "we'd better all start walking to town before we get our throats cut."

"I imagine he's gone to look for that hut which the chauffeur discovered," I said to Ella.

"What good will that do?" she retorted. "Whoever was hiding out on the mountain had nothing to do with the murders."

"Then why was the chauffeur killed just as he was on the point of revealing the whereabouts of the hut?" I demanded with, I believe, some acumen.

"Gloria Canby never needed rhyme or reason for inflicting pain," said Fannie with a shudder.

"Tommyrot!" I cried.

Ella looked at me as if she would like to shake me.

"You've been saying 'Tommyrot!' ever since you got here, and weird and horrible things have gone right on happening in front of your eyes. Isn't it about time you climbed down off your high horse, Adelaide?"

Now, had Ella been less sarcastic or had I been less contrary, as she says, I might have confided in her at that moment and spared myself one of the most dreadful experiences of my life. Or if Chet Keith had not wandered off in search of the abandoned shack which Jay Stuart had found, I should certainly have taken Chet into my confidence. As it was, I took nobody, not even Miss Maurine Smith, from whom I elicited my information, such as it was.

"Yes, Miss Adams," she admitted, regarding me with puzzled eyes, "we have such articles on sale. It's inconvenient for people to go to town from here, so we keep a lot of stuff on hand."

She glanced apologetically at the cigar case at the side of the desk which was indeed cluttered up with a variety of ill-assorted objects, such as gumdrops and shaving cream and chocolate bon-bons in boxes and small bottles of perfumery, not to mention several toy automobiles, a couple of jumping jacks and a yo-yo top.

My heart skipped a beat. "You have them on sale!" I exclaimed. "The point is, have you sold one?"

She shook her head. "I haven't. I am not on duty all the time, you know. Shall I ask Captain French and let you know?"

"Please do," I said and drew a long breath. "I'll be in my room."

Her eyes opened very wide. "Oh, but, Miss Adams, I thought we all decided we'd be safer if everybody stayed down here in the lounge together."

"I'll be in my room," I repeated firmly and stalked over to Sheriff Latham, who had just finished telephoning to town with regard to the latest report from the bridge.

"They say we can get across by six in the morning," he muttered, scowling at nobody in particular.

"Seven hours!" breathed Fannie Parrish. "If we survive that long!"

At first Sheriff Latham was disposed to shelve both me and my complaint without ado. "I got other things on my mind, lady," he said irritably, "without worrying about petty larceny."

"It may be petty larceny to you," I announced with all the dignity at my command, "but it's my property and I insist that you do something."

"Getting all worked up over a trifle like a book at this stage," he grumbled.

"The book was stolen after I arrived at the inn," I pointed out. "That means somebody in this house took it. By seven o'clock in the morning everybody will be scattered to the four winds. If you hope to recover my property, it's got to be done tonight."

"Listen, lady," grumbled the sheriff, "I'll buy you a book. I'll buy you any book you want. I ain't got time to bother with chasing down a thief right now."

"I don't want you to buy me a book," I snapped. "I want you to take steps to recover the book I've lost. And I warn you that I am not without influence in this state. I am also a major taxpayer. I should hate to have to write you up in the papers as being criminally negligent in your duty."

I do not believe it was my threat to take action which finally
moved Sheriff Latham. I am inclined to think, with my foster son
Stephen Lansing, that the sheriff yielded because he was tired of
being harassed to death by me and Fannie Parrish, who was after
him every minute to do something or other. At any rate he did yield.

"All right, all right," he said wearily, "what is it you want, lady?"

He stared at me, when I had explained. "I'm to search their
rooms?" he asked.

"Or have your deputy do it after you've sent them up to me."

He rubbed his ear. "'Tain't likely they got the book where it
can be found in their possession," he protested.

"You'll never know till you look," I pointed out acidly.

He shook his head. "I'd feel better if you'd stay off that second
floor."

"I'm not afraid, Sheriff Latham," I assured him, though my
voice carried less conviction than I intended. "Anyway," I added,
"your man is on guard right outside my door."

He shook his head again. "That didn't save the professor."

There was no answer to that, so I attempted none. "I wish you'd
let me know the results as soon as you search each room," I said.

"It's all a piece of foolishness," he muttered.

Nevertheless he lumbered off to issue orders to Mart Butler,
and I turned toward the stair.

"Where are you going, Adelaide?" demanded Ella.

I was for the second time tempted to take her into my confidence. Unfortunately Ella elected to press the question.

"Not to your room, I hope," she said with so much emphasis I
bristled.

"And why not, I pray?"

I suppose all our nerves were the worse for wear by this time.
At any rate Ella and I glared at each other like a couple of hostile
mastiffs.

"I've kept silent," said Ella, "because I'm fond of you, Adelaide,
and, after all, I don't know that you have been aiding and abetting
that girl."

"What on earth are you talking about?" I cried with heat, although I am positive my face gave me away.

"I can't prove that she and Chet Keith were in your room last night," said Ella, "but I did hear voices."

"Nonsense!"

"And they didn't come from the hall."

"Rubbish!"

"I hate to go to the sheriff behind your back, Adelaide."

I lost my temper completely. "You can go to the devil if you like!" I snorted and marched off up the stairs.

I have always prided myself upon being a levelheaded woman, but there is no denying that my courage descended in exact proportion to my ascent toward that upper floor at Mount Lebeau Inn where Butch was again propped up in his chair against Sheila Kelly's door. He had lost a great deal of sleep and his eyes were bloodshot, yet he seemed very wide awake. He kept glancing here, there and everywhere while I explained about the visitors which I expected shortly.

"It'll be nice having folks about," he said. "I've seen a lot of spots I'd rather be in alone than this."

I heartily agreed with him. The second floor was not a cheerful place under the best of conditions.

"I never saw a house so full of creaks," muttered the deputy, again glancing over his shoulder. "You need eyes in the back of your head."

I knew what he meant. The wind had risen and the ancient walls of the inn popped and squeaked, exactly as if somebody or something was creeping up on you from the rear.

"I keep thinking I hear that door open," said the deputy, looking toward Professor Matthews' room.

I shivered. I didn't need to close my eyes to see the professor's livid face as I had last beheld it.

"Don't be silly," I said irritably. "The door's locked, isn't it?"

"Yep," admitted Butch with a gloomy nod, "it's locked and the key's in my pocket, as if that meant anything to *her*." He gestured toward Sheila Kelly's room and I sighed.

"There's no such thing as ghosts," I said firmly.

"That's what I thought yesterday," muttered Butch, turning suddenly to stare down the shadowy corridor beyond us.

It took me quite a while to unlock my door. My fingers seemed to be all thumbs. Once inside I had even more trouble closing the door behind me. I felt the greatest reluctance to being alone in that room. I felt reluctant to be there at all. My first glance was for the door between me and Sheila Kelly. The key was in the lock, just as I had left it when I went downstairs. After I had pulled down the shades and turned on every light in the place, including the one in the bath, I went over to the door and listened.

There was not a sound from the adjoining room. I had expected more of that forlorn weeping which had distressed me before. I found its absence no less distressing. I could not forget how the girl had looked when they took her out of the parlor downstairs, dazed, mute, completely desperate. I kept remembering what Chet Keith had said he feared for Sheila Kelly. I knew that they had searched her again to make sure she had no lethal weapons upon her such as the butcher knife which had been plunged into Jay Stuart's breast and which the sheriff said came from the kitchen at the inn.

"There are other ways to do away with oneself," I remember thinking with a shudder.

Then someone knocked at my door. "The sheriff says you wished to see me, Miss Adams," murmured Jeff Wayne.

I have wondered since why he and the others submitted so tamely to my request, even when reinforced by the sheriff's orders. At the time I was too busy trying to put a proper face on my actions to worry about anything else.

"I want to ask you some questions, Mr. Wayne," I said. "Will you take a chair?"

He gave me a resentful glance, but he accepted the seat to which I motioned him and waited with obvious impatience for me to sit down across from him. Now that I had him there, I realized that I had only the vaguest idea what I wanted to ask him. I was obsessed with one thought, to kill enough time to permit the sheriff to make his search.

"You are in love with Judy Oliver, aren't you, Mr. Wayne?" I asked.

He colored darkly and I think he flirted with the notion of telling me that it was none of my business, which of course it wasn't, but I continued to stare straight into his haggard eyes, and he suddenly shrugged his shoulders, which I chose to take as assent.

"Was Gloria Canby in love with you?" I demanded.

"She intended to marry me," he said harshly.

"That wasn't my question."

Again I thought he meant to defy my right to interrogate him, and again under my unwavering glance he thought better of it.

"If she was capable of being in love with anybody, it was with Hogan Brewster," he said with a scowl.

"But she was engaged to you?"

"To spite Judy!" he cried. "She couldn't bear for Judy to have anything she wanted!"

I looked at him very hard. "Was Gloria Canby murdered?"

"I don't know. She may have been. God knows we all had reason enough to kill her."

"You too?"

His hands clenched but he said nothing.

"You could have killed her, couldn't you," I prodded him, "the time she attacked Judy with the can opener?"

His face worked. "Yes."

"That's why you have never told Judy that you love her, isn't it? You were afraid of Gloria Canby. You're still afraid of her."

"Yes," he said in a whisper.

I put my hand over his. "The dead cannot return to torture the living, Mr. Wayne."

"You never knew her!" he burst out. "There was nothing she wouldn't do! When she died I thought Judy was safe, but she isn't! She'll never be safe as long as *that girl*"—he threw a haggard glance at Sheila Kelly's door—"is at large."

The telephone rang. It was an old-fashioned instrument on the wall. I watched Jeff Wayne's drawn face as I crossed the room. I could see him distinctly in the mirror over the dresser. A nerve was jumping in his temple.

"Nothing doing," said Sheriff Latham gruffly when I picked up the receiver.

"You didn't overlook anything?" I asked.

"No," he growled and hung up in my ear.

So nothing incriminating had been found in Jeff Wayne's room. I wondered how I was going to get rid of him, but he solved the problem for me by rising to his feet.

"Have you quite finished with prying into my affairs, Miss Adams?" he inquired in a resentful voice.

In spite of his obvious animosity toward myself I felt sorry for him. "Why don't you go downstairs and take Judy into your arms and ask her to marry you?" I suggested.

"And have Gloria get her as she got the others?" he asked and walked out.

Lila Atwood also stared at me curiously when I let her and her husband in. "The sheriff said you wanted to speak to us, Miss Adams," she murmured.

Allan Atwood said nothing at all. He avoided meeting his wife's gaze. He pulled out a chair for her, but he was careful not to touch her. I saw her flinch when he moved away from her, but she faced me with perfectly level eyes.

Again I was at a loss how to proceed. "You young people got off to a very bad start, didn't you?" I asked, more or less at random.

Allan glared at me. "Suppose we did?" he inquired angrily. "What's it to you?"

I was too conscious of the weakness of my position to take umbrage at his tone. However, Lila chose to be as gracious as her husband was rude.

"Yes, Miss Adams," she said in her beautifully modulated voice, "Allan and I got off to about the worst possible start when we were married, if that is what you mean."

"It's rather a shame that Gloria Canby spoiled everything for you on your wedding day," I murmured.

Allan shot me a furious glance. "Lila didn't kill her," he said in a stifled voice.

I saw his wife draw a quick breath. "Thanks, Allan," she said and half held out her hand to him, but he looked hastily away and she flushed painfully.

"How long have you suspected your wife of killing your cousin?" I asked him outright.

"I told you she didn't kill Gloria," he muttered.

My eyes met Lila Atwood's and hers were quite tragic. We both knew, in spite of his denials, that her husband did believe her guilty of murder.

"It isn't true, Miss Adams," she said. "I did not kill Gloria."

"Do you know why I believe you?" I demanded, watching Allan closely.

She shook her head and I said, still watching her husband, "You aren't in love with Hogan Brewster."

"No," said Lila, "I am not in love with Hogan. I don't even like him."

Allan turned sharply. I caught a glimpse of the light in his eyes, then it faded, leaving his face even more drawn and haggard than before.

"Why bother to lie?" he cried. "Gloria had Hogan hooked. She would have killed him before she let him go. He knew it and so did you. That's why you—"

He paused, biting off the word, his face deathly white.

"So you do believe I killed her," she whispered.

His lips worked. "I told you I didn't believe it."

"Is that why you hate me, Allan?" she asked, turning white. "Is that why you haven't been able to stand the sight of me since Gloria's death?"

"What do you care whether I hate you or not?" he asked bitterly. "You've got Brewster. You've got what you want."

She was a proud woman and it must have cost her a great deal to say the thing she said in the face of his hostile scowl.

"Hogan Brewster is nothing to me, Allan, less than nothing. You see, I had the bad luck to—to fall in love with my own husband. Funny, isn't it, when he can't bear me?"

His hands clenched. "You can't fool me and you didn't fool Uncle Thomas," he muttered.

"What do you mean?" I asked quickly.

He drew back, regarding me with wary, defiant eyes. "I didn't mean anything."

"Did Thomas Canby believe that Lila murdered his daughter?" I persisted.

"I don't know what he believed," he replied and added with a short, mirthless laugh, "and now nobody will ever know."

I stared at him, my pulses racing. Allan Atwood had ceased to puzzle me. He did not hate his wife. He was madly in love with her.

"No," I said slowly, "Thomas Canby did not live to accuse anybody of his daughter's murder."

I was thinking of those ESP tests, of the facility which Allan had displayed at getting his thoughts across to a receptive subject. Chet Keith had said that Canby was killed to cover up the man who slew his daughter. It occurred to me that Chet was wrong. Perhaps Canby had died to prevent his accusing Allan Atwood's wife of murder.

"I can explain about the razor blade," said Lila suddenly. "It came from a package in my possession."

Her husband took a quick step toward her. "Keep still," he said.

No, I thought to myself, it was not beyond reason to believe that, no matter of what he suspected her, Allan would go to any length to protect his wife.

"It was a sample package," said Lila steadily, "though why anybody should have sent me a sample razor blade I couldn't imagine. It came through the mail the day before Gloria died. I put the parcel on my desk and forgot about it. But when they found Gloria's body I looked for the blade and it was gone. Remember, Allan, you came into the room just as I was putting the empty box and the wrappings into the fire? You insisted on looking at them before I burned them."

He colored darkly. "I don't remember anything of the kind."

I nodded. "So ever since you saw that package in your wife's possession, you have suspected her of murder."

"It never was in her possession!" he cried furiously. "I'll swear to my dying day she never had it."

"Thanks, Allan," said Lila again, with a note in her voice that brought a lump to my throat. "I didn't know you liked me well enough to lie for me."

And then the telephone rang. I stumbled slightly crossing the room. Those two were staring at each other. I am sure for the moment they had forgotten me.

"Darling!" whispered Lila. "Oh, my darling!"

The sheriff sounded both tired and disgruntled. "All right, Miss Adams," he said, "your hunch was one hundred per cent good."

I felt my knees weaken under me. "You found it?" I quavered.

"Tucked away in a pocket of Atwood's traveling bag."

"Oh dear," I whispered.

"I'll send it up by one of the boys."

"Thanks," I faltered and replaced the receiver on the hook.

The hardest thing I ever did in my life was face Lila Atwood. Her eyes were radiant. She was clinging to her husband's arm. I knew then that I had made no mistake. Those two were in love. I remember telling myself that they deserved a break. Then I recalled the girl next door and those three mutilated bodies down in the parlor and shuddered.

"That's all," I faltered. "I mean, you're free to go if you like."

But not for long, I told myself, and tried to look away from Lila's bright smile as she walked out of the room, still clinging to her husband's arm. They were in love and he had killed to protect her and there was nothing ahead of her except heartbreak, I thought, my throat aching. For I knew to what use that book of mine had been put. I knew even before Miss Maurine Smith telephoned me from the office.

"Captain French asked me to tell you, Miss Adams, that he hasn't sold a toy balloon this summer," she announced brightly, "but he bought two dozen and one is missing."

"A yellow one?" I asked in a faint voice.

"Yes, Miss Adams, a yellow one."

My hand was shaking as I hung up the receiver. I never had believed that spirits can be materialized. I still did not believe it. There had been in my missing book a clever exposé of a so-called ectoplasm. It was effected by means of a toy yellow balloon on which a face had been painted.

18

I KNEW WHY THOMAS CANBY had been killed. It was to cover up a murder nearly a year old. I also knew how Gloria Canby's spirit had been made to seem to materialize that night in the parlor. For my own conviction I needed only the fact that a toy yellow balloon had disappeared from the showcase in the lobby. It was thoroughly explained in my book on pseudo-spiritualism. I recalled the page as distinctly as if I had it before me. There was even a photograph, showing the medium inflating the balloon under cover of her voluminous robes. It had been treated with phosphorus, the features first painted on, then traced over with wet matches, so as to shed a sepulchral glow when the balloon was released. Naturally the operator always insisted on holding the séance in the dark. It was a simple matter to puncture the thing at the proper moment, leaving only a few pieces of yellow rubber which could easily be disposed of.

I even fancied I could recall, during the confusion of that hectic scene in the parlor, having heard a tiny pop such as a punctured balloon might make. Proving my contention was another question, as I realized at once. Allan Atwood had done nothing so obvious as to purchase the yellow balloon. It had been filched from the showcase in the lobby. I felt positive that by this time any scraps of yellow rubber which might have been found in the parlor had disappeared. Certainly I had no hopes of finding them at that late date upon the murderer's person.

"I've got to confer with Chet Keith," I told myself nervously.

However, when I called downstairs, Miss Maurine Smith informed me that Mr. Keith had not returned to the inn. "Do you
think he has run away?" she inquired with her usual naïveté. "Mrs.
Parrish is certain of it."

"I suppose nothing of the sort," I snapped and hung up.

If I was convinced of anything, it was that Chet Keith was not
the kind to run away. He was persuaded that Sheila Kelly was the
victim of a diabolical plot. He would never give up the fight so long
as there was a remote chance of saving that unfortunate girl. I
glanced at the door between her room and mine. What was she
doing, shut up there alone with her horror and despair? I shivered
and when somebody knocked I started so violently I barked my
elbow on the table.

However, the knock was at the corridor door. "Miss Adams?" a
voice called out.

It was Hogan Brewster, of all people, which did not improve
my temper. I had never liked him and, knowing how much embar-
rassment he had caused Lila Atwood, I liked him less than ever.
Nevertheless I opened the door, although neither my tone nor my
glance was friendly.

"Well?" I demanded.

He grinned. "The sheriff asked me to bring you this," he said
and handed me with his customary flippant smile the book which
was responsible for my ever going to Lebeau Inn in the first place.

Sheriff Latham had taken the trouble to wrap it in a newspaper
and tie a string about it, and although Hogan Brewster stared at
the bundle curiously I did not gratify his inquisitiveness by un-
wrapping it in his presence.

"Thanks for the favor," I said in grudging accents.

He grinned. "Don't mention it. The sheriff pressed me into service because he is short a deputy."

"Short a deputy?"

"One of the cast seems to have taken a vanishing powder."

"Would you mind speaking English?" I inquired coldly.

He chuckled. "Your friend, Mr. Chet Keith, has been missing
for an hour, and the sheriff has sent out a searching party."

"They think something has happened to him!"

It had not until that moment dawned upon me to feel uneasy about the reporter's prolonged absence.

Hogan Brewster shrugged his shoulders. "I think myself the fellow has beat it, for reasons best known to himself, but that Negro porter Jake, or whatever his name is, came in a while ago with a cock-and-bull story which has the sheriff all worked up."

"What sort of story?" I demanded in an agitated voice.

Hogan Brewster laughed. "You know how these ignorant Southern coons are about hants."

"Hants! What has that to do with Chet Keith?"

"Nothing, I feel sure, but it seems that Jake claims to have seen Keith go into a shack across from that old deserted cemetery down the road over an hour ago, and according to Jake nothing has come out except a huge black bat."

"A bat!" I repeated, catching my breath. "In the hut by the cemetery!"

He nodded. "The sheriff has sent a deputy to investigate."

I felt shaky and upset. I remember reaching out to steady myself against a chair and then the commotion broke out downstairs. A great many people appeared to be shouting and running around. Hogan Brewster and I stared at each other and as if by common consent turned to the door which I had left slightly ajar. Butch was standing right outside peering toward the stairs.

"What's the matter down there?" he yelled.

"They've found Chet Keith," somebody called up, I think it was Captain French, "and he's been knocked in the head."

"Good Lord!" exclaimed Butch, and I remember Hogan Brewster making some similar exclamation.

They both started for the head of the steps, and I was right behind them when I recalled that newspaper-wrapped bundle which I had placed on my bedside table when Hogan Brewster handed it to me. I still contend, no matter what Ella says, that I had no choice except to go back for it. It is true that I nearly paid for my foresight with my life. Nevertheless I went back and in spite of those dreadful ten minutes which followed I would do the same thing all

over again if the same circumstances arose. That, I suppose, is what
Ella means when she says that I cannot be trusted to mind my own
business, even if there is a murder going on at the moment.

At any rate the tumult downstairs was still proceeding in fine
style when I re-entered my room. I did not close the door behind
me. I intended to seize the book and be back in the hall within a
minute. I did not expect to be more than a few steps behind Butch,
whose hoarse voice I could hear bellowing out from the top of the
stairs. I could even distinguish his progress as far as the landing
halfway down, where he seemed to be hanging over the banisters,
carrying on a loud and in coherent conversation with Sheriff
Latham.

"Is he hurt bad?" was one of the things he shouted.

"Got a crack on the head, knocked him out," came the reply.

I remember saying, "Tut! Tut!" to myself and feeling a little
sick. Although I had not stopped to take it into account until that
minute, I seemed to have grown quite fond of Chet Keith. I distinctly recall picking up the newspaper-wrapped parcel off the table
and thrusting it under my arm. I even remember noting absent-
mindedly that the string was carelessly tied, so that a bit of the
book cover showed. I was in the act of turning to the door when it
happened, that grating sound which was the bolt sliding back
between my room and Sheila Kelly's. It stopped me dead in my
tracks. I stared at the connecting door. The key was on my side.
The sight of it steadied me. I recall drawing a long breath, then I
went rigid again.

The disturbance downstairs was still going on. I could hear the
rumble of voices, but they sounded very far away. The blood left
my heart. For a minute I could not move. I could scarcely breathe.
The door to the hall was no longer open. I knew it, though to save
my life I could not bring myself to turn around and look. Somebody had stealthily closed the door behind me. Somebody was
standing at my back, breathing hard. I can't tell how I knew it was
the killer, but I did.

In my panic I must have made some small involuntary sound,
although I failed to hear it because of the frantic pounding of my

heart. Maybe I merely stiffened and so warned him that I was aware of his presence. I shall never know. I dare say he was afraid I would scream and arouse the house, which was no part of his horrible plan. At least I was given no chance to scream. He struck like a spitting cobra. One moment I was standing there, paralyzed with horror. The next moment his hands were about my neck, choking me into unconsciousness.

The wonder is that he did not kill me then and there, except of course strangulation was not part of his plan either. When I knew anything again I was lying on my bed, trussed up like a fowl for market. My wrists and ankles were securely bound with towels from the bathroom. My eyeballs felt as if they were about to burst from the pressure which he had exerted upon my windpipe. There was a washrag thrust between my teeth, so that I could only gag and mouth inarticulately as I watched Hogan Brewster turn the key between my room and Sheila Kelly's.

"Come," he said and opened the door.

She had her hands before her, feeling her way. Her eyes were dazed, her face ghastly. She lurched a little as she walked into the room.

"You are going to kill yourself," he said softly.

It was then I saw the knife in his hand, an ordinary silver table knife, but even at that distance I could see that the blade had been filed to a sharp edge.

"After I have cut Miss Adams' throat, you are going to lock the door behind me and wake up," he said. "Understand?"

His voice was perfectly expressionless, a monotone. He kept his gaze fixed upon the girl. Her eyes were wide open but they had the blurred look of somebody walking in his sleep. Nevertheless she slowly nodded her head.

"You will not remember that I was here," he said. "You will find yourself alone in a locked room with a murdered woman. You will believe you killed her. You won't be able to go on living. Understand?"

Again she nodded and I tried to throw myself off the bed, succeeding merely in wrenching my thigh almost out of its socket.

Hogan Brewster looked at me. "You would nose into things that don't concern you," he said and glanced at that newspaper-bound parcel upon the table, "you and Chet Keith. He doesn't have to die because I didn't give him time to discover anything incriminating in the hut, but you are different. The Parrish woman caught me disposing of some scraps of yellow rubber tonight. She didn't know what they meant. With you gone, she never will know."

It was maddening to lie there helpless and listen to him. Like a drowning man, I lived an eternity in a minute. All the events of the past two days whirled through my mind like a kaleidoscope with vertigo. It was Hogan Brewster who had killed Thomas Canby and the professor and Jay Stuart, and now he was preparing to kill Adelaide Adams and Sheila Kelly.

I should have known Brewster was the murderer the moment I saw the face upon the yellow balloon. It was a work of art, however gruesome, and I had been told that he boasted artistic talents. Two things had kept me from connecting him with the plot. Since he was not at the inn when the Gloria manifestations started, I had supposed he could not be responsible for them, and I had not been able to supply him with a motive. I knew now that he had the most powerful motive in the world—self-preservation.

It was Hogan Brewster who killed Gloria Canby.

He killed her to make way for his infatuation with Lila Atwood and tried to pass his crime off as suicide, but her father was not deceived. He was determined to bring his daughter's murderer to justice, and Hogan Brewster did not want to die in the electric chair. He had lied about the time of his arrival on the mountain. It was he who had been hiding out in the hut across from the cemetery.

Patrick Oliver had admitted that he was in the habit of meeting Professor Matthews down the road every night for a surreptitious conference in connection with the hoax which they were playing upon Dora Canby. Brewster had undoubtedly eavesdropped upon these conferences and that is how his own desperate plan came into being. Having waylaid Sheila Kelly near the hut, he succeeded in hypnotizing her. Too late I recalled that, when I questioned her about the first unauthorized trance, she spoke of seeing tombstones and remembering nothing else, poor child. She had been no match for Hogan Brewster. The man was a rabid egoist and a killer. He had taken complete possession of the girl's mind and he had been directing her ever since, like a puppet, toward her own destruction.

He must have read the horror in my eyes, for he laughed softly. "Strange as it seems," he said, "it isn't going to be as hard to slit your throat as it was to mutilate those cats. I rather like cats. Kindred spirits, I suppose."

There *was* something feline in his movements as he came toward me, something of the padded grace of a huge and lecherous tomcat. I had not realized before how swiftly and noiselessly he could move when he pleased. He was still smiling. I wondered how I could ever have thought that smirk was flippant.

I tried to writhe away from the hand which he put out toward me, and the girl Sheila Kelly stirred and moaned.

"Keep still," he said to her.

For a moment I thought she was going to be able to throw off the stupor which he exercised over her will. There was a flicker of intelligence in her eyes as she tried to free her gaze from his, but he made a weaving motion with his hands in front of her face.

"You are going to do as I say," he murmured. "It is useless to struggle. You will lock the door of this room behind me when I go out and you will forget I was ever here. Understand?"

I recall trying to project my mind in opposition to his. I remember frantically attempting to suggest to Sheila Kelly that she scream for help before it was too late for either of us, but I have never had any hypnotic powers and I might as well have saved myself the strain. With a heavy sigh the girl's shoulders dropped. Her face took on a dulled apathetic look, and I sank back upon the bed, cold sweat standing out on my brow.

Hogan Brewster laughed. "Wonderful thing, this mental suggestion business, Miss Adams," he said. "My only regret is that I didn't discover the knack sooner and that Lila Atwood doesn't seem receptive, at least not to my brand of mesmerism."

I glared at him. No, in spite of all he had done, Hogan Brewster had not been able to win the woman he loved away from her husband. It was then I realized that Brewster had planted my book in Allan Atwood's traveling bag.

"You fiend!" I gasped, although the sounds which emerged through the gag were unintelligible.

I saw the muscles about Hogan Brewster's handsome cruel mouth tighten and closed my eyes. I lived years before I drew my next breath, though it could have been only a matter of seconds. Downstairs I could still hear faint sounds of people rushing about and exclaiming. I knew that Hogan Brewster had taken advantage of the excitement over Chet Keith to return to my room unobserved. I knew he was counting on getting out the same way. It was the identical ruse which he had employed when he killed Professor Matthews. I had been very foolhardy to go back to my room after Butch had been decoyed from his post.

"Not," I told myself grimly, "that it does any good to recognize my indiscretion now."

I remember wondering if the authorities would know how to get in touch with my foster daughter Kathleen, so as to notify her and Stephen of my death. I remember feeling very sorry for Sheila Kelly. She was so young to die with, as she believed, multiple murders upon her soul. Then I felt the thin edge of the knife at my throat.

It had never been my intention to submit without a struggle to being murdered in my own bed. I was practically helpless, but I had been gathering my strength and as Hogan Brewster stooped over me I drew my knees up and butted him with all my might in the stomach, at the same time lashing out ineffectually with my bound fists. I did not flatter myself that I could do any material harm, but I had the satisfaction of hearing my assailant grunt as the breath was knocked out of him, and in the fracas he dropped the knife. His face was black with anger as he stooped for it and he snarled something at me, an epithet commonly bestowed on the female of the dog species.

The knife was back in his hand. I saw his arm go up and the blade flashed. It was all over, I recall thinking to myself with a sob, and then something huge and black hurtled through the air and caught the killer on the temple. It rocked him back upon his heels, and for the second time the knife flew out of his grasp. At the same moment Ella followed Fannie Parrish's umbrella into the room.

"Help! Help!" she shrieked and began to belabor Hogan Brewster with the heavy wooden handles of her knitting bag.

"Murder! Help! Help!" she continued to scream at the top of her lungs while I, to my eternal shame, fainted dead away.

19

I owed my life to Ella and I would never live it down. I realized that at once. She had arrived, as she expressed it, in the nick of time.

"Simply because I knew that with your temperament, Adelaide, nothing could have kept you away from all the excitement over Chet Keith—nothing, that is, over which you had any control," she explained, looking very smug.

"Are you trying to pretend that, when you opened my door, you expected to see a murderer in the very act of cutting my throat?" I demanded scathingly.

"Well, no," she admitted, "I wouldn't go so far as to say that."

"I should hope not," I snapped.

"Just the same," murmured Fannie Parrish, eying me reproachfully, "if Mrs. Trotter hadn't got a hunch that you were up to something and gone after you, you would have been killed, Miss Adams."

We were all together again in the lounge downstairs and I had told my story a dozen times, first to Sheriff Latham and Coroner Timmons, and finally to Chet Keith, who was lying on a settee, propped up with pillows, a bandage tied in a rakish manner about his head, his hand tightly held by Sheila Kelly, sitting beside him.

"So that is really why you came upstairs after me," I said to Ella. "You couldn't bear to think I might be into something about which you knew nothing."

Ella tossed her head. "Well, you were, weren't you?" she retorted.

Fannie Parrish looked from one to the other of us with a baffled expression. I have no doubt she had expected Ella and me to fall into each other's arms after what had happened. What Mrs. Parrish did not realize was that both Ella and I were badly shaken by the narrowness of my escape, more shaken than either of us cared to admit.

As a matter of record, when I came to after Ella's brash arrival upon the scene in my bedroom, she was feverishly dabbing cologne upon my forehead with one hand while pleading with Sheriff Latham to do something at once about my prolonged faint, as if he were not sufficiently occupied with Hogan Brewster, who was struggling in the sheriff's grasp and cursing furiously because with the other hand Ella was still jabbing him in sundry unprotected spots with the point of Fannie Parrish's umbrella.

"Ruined by two old hellcats!" he kept saying, showing no traces of his former urbanity.

It was Ella who finally remembered to remove the washrag from between my teeth after I had attracted her attention to it by a series of violent "Glugs!" It was also Ella who untied the towels that fastened my wrists and ankles and assisted me to my feet and, no matter what Fannie Parrish may think, Ella and I are fond of each other. It is just that it embarrasses us to betray it.

That is why Ella's first remark was, to say the least, unsympathetic. "It is exactly like you, Adelaide Adams, to try to get yourself killed, so I'd have it on my conscience for the rest of my life."

Her caustic tone had nothing whatever to do with the concerned manner in which she was patting my shoulder, and I know she understands perfectly that the reason I barked at her in my turn was because I had to or make a fool of myself.

"Pleasesh put thash bottle of cologne away," I said haughtily. "You know how I hate to smell like a barber shopth."

I have not found it necessary until now to explain that I wear a pivot tooth upon a removable bridge in the front of my mouth, the absence of which causes me to lisp in the most disconcerting fashion. I may be wronging Ella to insinuate that she deliberately removed the bridge along with the washrag which she took out of my mouth. On the other hand, it would be exactly like her, for, as she is well aware, nothing so handicaps me as an impediment in my speech. At any rate she was provokingly slow about remembering where she had flung the washrag, and by the time I had recovered it and my missing denture both of us felt more ourselves.

I cannot say as much for Hogan Brewster. He had killed three people and been on the point of two other cold-blooded murders, without attracting suspicion to himself, but he went utterly to pieces when the case broke against him. There is usually a streak of cowardice in such a complex and cruel personality as his. As Chet Keith said later, his sort can dish it out but they can't take it. On the other hand, Brewster laid the entire blame at my door and Ella's.

"Not content with butting the breath out of me," he said bitterly, "they had to batter me over the head with a knitting bag and puncture me from head to foot with an umbrella."

He did look considerably battered up, even before Sheriff Latham knocked him down with a blow to the chin. There was no fight left in the man when Butch picked him up by the scruff of his neck and stood him on his feet.

"All right," he said with that smile of his which was now a grimace, "I surrender. Call off your dogs, Sheriff. Hanging's no worse than being killed by inches, and for God's sake make that old hellion lay down her umbrella."

Looking a little guilty, Ella placed her weapon upon the foot of the bed, and I will swear that Hogan Brewster drew a breath of relief. He cast a wry glance at Sheila Kelly when they started to take him out of the room. She had stood there like a statue all during the melee, but I doubt if anything would have convinced Sheriff Latham or Ella of what had actually happened to the girl except the small demonstration which Hogan Brewster then proceeded to put on. It is the only score in his favor among all the black marks against him, although I have never known whether he meant to do anybody a favor or whether it was pure exhibitionism on his part. The man *was* theatrical, with a strong appetite for the lurid, just as Ella had predicted.

"Stand up. Sit down. Laugh," he directed Sheila Kelly rapidly. "Laugh like Gloria Canby, as if you didn't give a damn for man, God or the Devil."

It made the hair at the base of my skull prickle to watch her. She stood up, she sat down, she laughed. It was horrible.

Hogan Brewster smiled. "How do you like my robot, Sheriff Latham?" he inquired mockingly.

I am positive that the sheriff had never heard of a robot, but nobody could have watched Sheila Kelly's performance without realizing that her mind was in complete subjection to that fiend across the room.

"Too bad," murmured Hogan Brewster, "that there are some things which you cannot hypnotize a subject into doing, such as—murder."

I have commented before upon his swiftness and I have never blamed Sheriff Latham for what happened. It was too unexpected. Not until Hogan Brewster had jerked away from Butch and scooped up the knife did anybody realize his purpose and then it was too late. He fell at Sheila Kelly's feet, and to me the most macabre thing about the whole frightful business was that it was not he but she who screamed and clutched frantically at her throat as if it were her lifeblood streaming out, as if it were she, not Hogan Brewster, gasping in his death agony.

"It's better so," said Chet Keith when I talked to him later.

I knew he was thinking of Sheila Kelly. She had collapsed after Hogan Brewster's death. It kept Ella and me busy for an hour, looking after her, for which release I think the sheriff was grateful. However, the girl's first conscious thought was for Chet Keith. She knew nothing of that grisly scene in my room. The last thing she remembered was hearing the tumult downstairs and shooting the bolt on her side of the door with the intention of finding out, if possible, how badly the newspaperman was hurt. That was still paramount in her mind when she came to. As soon as her fit of hysterics had subsided she insisted on going downstairs and seeing for herself the extent of his injuries.

Chet Keith was disposed to make light of them. "What's a tap on the head to a he-man?" he scoffed, though he looked very pale, I thought.

I caught his eye. "Let her fuss over you all she will," I whispered. "It'll take her thoughts off herself."

He nodded. "I expect you're right."

I knew I was right. Sheila Kelly had been through a hideous experience. Her nerves were on the ragged edge. I thought it would be a long while before she recovered entirely from the degenerating influence which had played hob with her mind, but I was ready to pin my faith upon the old principle that love and time will work miracles, and you had only to watch her hovering over Chet Keith as he reclined upon the couch to know that she was in love with him. I suppose she had been all along, although she had been too proud to admit it.

"We're going to be married as soon as we can get down off this damned mountain," he said, and while she caught her breath she did not deny it.

"Yes," admitted Fannie Parrish when I questioned her, "I saw Hogan Brewster put something in the wastebasket after the chauffeur was killed. It may have been a piece of yellow rubber. In fact I'm sure it was."

I shrugged my shoulders. I knew that, until I prompted her, Fannie had no idea what she had seen nor the slightest conception of its meaning.

There was another thing which I badly wanted to know. "About those ESP tests which you took in the Canby drawing room," I asked Lila Atwood, "was Brewster present?"

She shook her head and I frowned. "But he must have heard about them?" I persisted.

Her lips curled. "Oh yes, Aunt Dora told him at great length, although he ridiculed the idea. Nevertheless"—she turned white—"I caught him several times attempting to worm his way into my thoughts."

"Without success?" I asked quickly.

"Yes," she said with a spirited tilt of her head.

However, I reminded myself, as material for Hogan Brewster to try out his embryonic hypnotic powers upon, Lila Atwood was a very different proposition from Sheila Kelly, whose resistance to mental suggestion had been reduced to zero.

"It was nauseating," Lila continued with a shudder, "feeling him squirming about, trying to get inside my mind. As if he hadn't done me harm enough when he planted the razor blade in my possession."

"Have you any proof that Hogan Brewster mailed you the razor blade?" I exclaimed.

She glanced at her husband and he colored darkly. "I recognized Brewster's writing on the wrappings," he confessed, "but when I taxed him with it he convinced me that Lila had helped him kill Gloria. He said if I turned him over to the police he'd name Lila as his accomplice."

"That's why you let him hang around?" I ventured. "You didn't dare kick him out."

"And have him take Lila to the chair with him!" cried Allan Atwood. "I couldn't, no matter what I believed about her and him, because—because I love her."

His wife's eyes were radiant. "Darling!" she whispered, and this time when she put out her hand he seized it and pressed it tightly.

My own eyes misted. I was glad those two were due for a little happiness at last. It no longer seemed strange to me that Lila Atwood should have fallen in love with her inept young husband. There is a maternal strain in every woman, even spinsters, and she was a thoroughbred if I ever saw one.

It remained for Dora Canby to present me with the most surprising reaction to that night's work. "I sent for you," she announced when her niece Judy conducted me into her room, "to ask you one question."

"Yes?" I said, feeling uncomfortable.

I am still unable to decide whether to feel sorry for Gloria Canby's mother or just plain irritated with her.

"Is it true that, when my daughter died, she was in love with Hogan Brewster?" she asked.

"Everybody says so," I replied, pursing my lips.

She sighed. "I never trusted the man. I told Allan that Brewster was a snake in the grass. I told Gloria so too, but she paid no attention." She regarded me sharply. "If Gloria was in love with Brewster, she couldn't have been in love with Jeff, could she?"

I have never known why she seemed to believe that I was familiar with all the inside details of the case unless it was because I was in at the death, so to speak, and I have always known that I had no justification for my reply except my own impression. Nevertheless it does not trouble my conscience.

"She was never the least in love with him," I said.

The light in Judy's eyes was my reward.

Dora Canby frowned. "Then I suppose it is foolish for him to stay single on Gloria's account."

"It is extremely foolish," I said firmly.

She gave Judy a petulant glance. "You want to marry him, don't you?"

The girl flushed painfully. "He doesn't care for me."

"Nonsense!" I cried. "He is desperately in love with you, child."

"You think so?" she faltered, her lips quivering.

"I know it," I snapped and this time I was not forced to tamper with the truth.

"Then," said Dora Canby in her fretful way, "they had better get married at once, don't you think?"

"The sooner the better," I said fervently, feeling touched at the passionately grateful glance which Judy bestowed upon me.

"Even Patrick is deserting me," murmured Dora Canby mournfully. "He wants to be an aviator and I have promised to buy him a plane." She frowned again, then went on quite brightly, "At least I know that my darling Gloria is at peace at last, now that Thomas is dead."

I simply stared at her. "But you must have realized, Mrs. Canby," I said in a feeble voice, "that all those—those messages from your daughter were faked."

"How absurd, Miss Adams!" she replied coldly. "Of course I realize nothing of the sort."

I opened my mouth to protest, then closed it. I felt completely uncertain of my ability to disabuse Dora Canby of any conviction upon which she had set her heart. As I have said, for all her timidity, she was as stubborn as a burro and fully as exasperating in her cerebral processes.

"Naturally," she continued, her weak mouth setting in obstinate lines, "I shall see that that girl comes to no harm."

"You mean Sheila Kelly?" I faltered.

She glanced at me with a trace of impatience. "I mean the envelope which my daughter Gloria deigned to occupy for a time," she said with so much finality I was silenced.

Judy followed me to the door and squeezed my hand. "Thank you," she whispered and added guiltily, "It was because of Lila I didn't expose the professor after I caught him and Pat in the act."

I must have looked puzzled, for she hurried on. "That girl—she threatened if I told Aunt Dora to have Lila arrested for murder."

"You also believed Lila killed your cousin?"

"Gloria said so—I mean that girl said so, and—and Lila has always been kind to me, about Jeff, you know. She even begged Uncle Thomas to give Pat a break."

"So that's why you kept still."

Her lips quivered. "I couldn't betray Lila. What if she had killed Gloria? It was no more than we'd all been tempted to do." She swallowed painfully. "You were right," she said, "but for Pat and me, none of this would have happened and I don't know how I can ever forgive myself."

I had not even seen Jeff Wayne until he glared at me over Judy's shoulder. "Don't be silly!" he protested. "Nobody who matters a darn blames you for being the most loyal person in the world!"

With another defiant glance in my direction he took Judy into his arms. As I walked away she was clinging to him with a blissful smile upon her face while he kissed her very thoroughly and murmured small endearments into her ear. Needless to say, the sight met with my full approval, in spite of the resentment which Jeff Wayne appeared to nourish in my regard. I'm afraid to him I shall always be a nosy old maid with an unholy talent for prodding him into unhappy disclosures.

When I returned to the lounge it was almost two o'clock in the morning and everybody had settled down with pillows and blankets and overcoats to pass the remainder of the night upon the leather settees and in the deep armchairs which were scattered

about. The death of Hogan Brewster had not removed the aversion
with which we were all filled for the second floor at the inn. At
least nobody showed any disposition to retire to it, not even Sheriff
Latham, who was snoring away with his feet up on a windowsill,
and least of all Butch, asleep in a straight chair by the desk, with
Miss Maurine Smith's head coyly resting upon his burly shoulder.

Sheila Kelly was sleeping too, huddled down on the couch beside Chet Keith, but he looked up at me with a faint smile. "The
bus will be here at five o'clock," he said. "The highway department
telephoned Captain French."

I glanced across the lobby to where the manager of Mount
Lebeau Inn was reclining upon one of the stiff settles, his toupee
slightly off center where it had slid over one ear. Clinging to his
arm, even in his slumber, was Fannie Parrish, silent practically
for the first time since I had met her.

I suppose I must have looked scandalized, for Chet Keith chuckled. "It's an ill wind that blows nobody's ship home," he remarked.
"They are going to be married."

"Fannie and Captain French!" I exclaimed.

"The inn is done for, I'm afraid," he explained, "but Mrs. Parrish
has quite a neat little income of her own, or so I understand."

"What about her poor dear Theo?" I inquired with a sniff.

Chet Keith chuckled again. "As she reminded us a while ago,
we all heard the message her poor dear Theo sent her. He wants
his Little Butterfly to be happy."

"Fannie Parrish knows as well as I do that those spirit messages were a fake!" I cried indignantly.

Chet Keith grinned. "People have a great facility for deluding
themselves if it is to their advantage to be deluded."

I borrowed one of Ella's wisecracks. "You're telling me," I said
and repeated for his benefit that amazing conversation which I had
had with Dora Canby.

He drew a breath of relief. "It will be a great deal simpler with
Mrs. Canby taking that attitude," he said with a wry grin, "and who
am I to quarrel with what the gods provide?"

I dare say I looked a little blank, for he went on to elucidate. "The sheriff is convinced, you are convinced, everybody here is convinced that Sheila was the victim of that devil's machinations, but it is going to be a lot easier to get her out of this business if Thomas Canby's widow refuses to prosecute."

"Hogan Brewster pointed out from the first that, with the Canby fortune behind her, Sheila Kelly would never be convicted," I reminded him.

His face darkened. "I should have known he was our man. The clue was right under our noses all along. I don't doubt that is what put the professor wise."

"What clue?" I asked in a startled voice.

"Brewster said himself that he alone knew Gloria Canby's nickname for him, yet Sheila called him by that name the night he was supposed to have arrived at the inn for the first time. She could have learned it from no one else."

I recalled the scene distinctly, there in the dining room.

"The idea even occurred to me," continued Chet Keith, "but I was obsessed with the notion that Thomas Canby's millions were the motive for the crimes and, Lord knows, Brewster had money enough of his own."

I sighed. "What put me off was having every reason to believe that he did not arrive at the inn in time to be responsible for the Gloria manifestations, which were the cornerstone of the entire plot."

He nodded. "I think he had been hiding out somewhere in this vicinity the whole week. I don't believe the telegram which he claimed to have received was ever sent. In my opinion he followed the Atwoods down here—trailed them, in fact."

I was prepared to go a step farther. "Like most murderers, he was a self-centered brute," I said. "He realized, when the others left Long Island in a hurry, that something was up and, no doubt, he believed the exodus concerned him. I don't think it improbable that, having a guilty conscience and a wholesome respect for Thomas Canby's pertinacity, Brewster even went so far as to believe that Canby had secured the evidence for which he was seeking."

"Probably," agreed Chet Keith. "At all events we know from Jay Stuart's report, which Jeff Wayne overheard, that Brewster spent a lot of time in the hut across from the cemetery before he let his presence on the mountain be known. I suspect in the beginning he hid out in order to spy on the situation. Then he met Sheila and concocted his devilish plan and, concealing his presence until after Thomas Canby's arrival, was an essential part of it."

"Of course Brewster was responsible for the rock in the road," I remarked, knitting my brows. "Though whether he uprooted it himself or forced Sheila to do so we'll never know," said Chet Keith quickly.

I shook my head. "He could not force her to commit murder, but she might have been persuaded to dig up the rock, just as he persuaded her to appropriate Dora Canby's scissors, without her realizing that the act had criminal intent."

He winced. "I know."

"She told us herself that when she came to that afternoon she had dirt on her hands as if—as if she had been digging in the ground," I faltered and then I drew a long breath. "But I prefer to believe, and I shall steadfastly maintain if asked, that he made her dig up a—a flower or something, so as to leave her with soiled hands and the conviction that she alone had been guilty of the attempt upon Canby's life."

"Oh, sure," muttered Chet Keith, his arm tightening about the girl beside him, whose face looked like an uprooted flower itself, a drooping, haggard flower with a broken stem.

"He must have killed the chauffeur to prevent his telling about the hut," I continued with a frown, "but if the cigarette butts and car tracks had been removed, as Stuart claimed, I don't understand why Brewster believed the hut would incriminate him."

Chet Keith felt gingerly of his wounded scalp. "Jay Stuart was a square-dealer, according to his somewhat sinister code. He tried to the last to earn the thousand dollars he had been paid. In other words he lied when he said the hut had been cleaned up. At least it hadn't been when I got there tonight, although Brewster went over the place with a fine-tooth comb after he knocked me out. Nevertheless, in spite of his elaborate and drastic precautions, he overlooked this."

He held out a fragment of black cloth.

"What is it?" I asked.

"A piece out of an opera cape which the sheriff uncovered awhile ago under the mattress in Brewster's room. He must have caught it on a splinter and torn off this bit without noticing. Anyway, I found it clinging to a rough spot in the door of the hut."

"What on earth did he want with an opera cape in this benighted spot and at this season?" I exclaimed.

"There was a skeleton key in the pocket," remarked Chet Keith significantly. "Although we'll never know all the truth, I don't doubt that Brewster employed the key to his advantage with nobody the wiser, worse luck. He was probably here, there and everywhere when least suspected, and the cape must have been extremely useful when he wished to get about unobserved. It is black and, you might say, all-enveloping. I am certain he was wearing it when he attacked me tonight in the hut." He gave me a rueful glance. "At least if I had had to go into court I should have been forced to testify that the thing which set upon me came out of that old deserted graveyard and resembled nothing so much as an enormous bat."

"A bat!" I exclaimed. "Brewster was the hant which the colored porter said he saw again and again on the second floor!"

"The man was an athlete," Chet Keith reminded me. "It would be no feat on his part to shinny in and out of windows in this old barn. I don't doubt he did so freely whenever it suited his purpose. There were the cats, you know."

I shuddered. Jake had declared that he saw a big black bat hovering over the body of the first disemboweled cat, but he had gone on to contend that it was a vampire, in possession of Sheila Kelly's body, so his story was disregarded.

"No wonder," I said weakly, "we were always thinking we heard something sneaking up behind us on the second floor. Even Butch saw the bat and took it for Jake's hant."

He nodded. "Brewster was plenty active all right," he said grimly, "and what he couldn't manage himself he forced Sheila to do for him, such as the amber-colored hairpins which were scattered about in all the suspicious places and the book which was abstracted from your luggage."

I frowned. "How did he know about my book? It disappeared almost as soon as I got here."

"We have to guess at a lot. Thank God, Sheila remembers none of it. However, I think there is no question that he made her meet him every afternoon at the hut. He had to rehearse her in the role of Gloria Canby, you know. He may even have slipped up to her room whenever he got the chance, damn him! One thing you can bet on. He picked her brains from start to finish about what was going on at the inn. Sheila knew about your book, didn't she?"

"I think everybody in the house knew about it," I said tartly, "thanks to Ella and Fannie Parrish."

He grinned. "And Mrs. Trotter, I hear, gave everyone emphatically to understand that with the book as authority she would be able to expose the professor as a fraud. Beyond a doubt Sheila transferred that impression to Brewster."

"And he couldn't afford to have the séances broken up before he had a chance to murder Thomas Canby," I deduced excitedly.

"Exactly, so he took the book or had Sheila take it, though Lord only knows why he waited till tonight to plant it on Atwood."

I had an inspiration. "Brewster's original plan revolved about the fake spiritualistic act and so he expected to implicate nobody except Sheila and the professor, but things were getting too hot for him there at the last. Don't you agree that he must have been badly rattled to attempt the balloon trick, with me knowing what I did? He never intended for us to learn that Gloria Canby was murdered. When that came out he lost his head. All he could think of was framing yet another suspect to stand between him and his crimes."

"And for obvious reasons he picked on Lila Atwood's husband?" murmured Chet Keith. "I'm sure you're right."

I sighed. "Nobody paid any attention to Jake's tales, because he is a superstitious darky, and there really *were* bats in the house."

"I think we can thank Brewster for that too," said Chet Keith with a wry smile. "I found traces of bats in the hut. I'd like to wager that he turned one or two loose in the inn, maybe to add to the horror atmosphere which he was building up for the Gloria manifestations, maybe to cover his disguise after Jake saw him."

"And to think Ella practically caught him red-handed, leaving the professor's room the night before he was murdered!" I ejaculated.

Chet Keith looked at me askance. "You neglected to tell me about that."

"I thought it was her imagination working overtime," I admitted sheepishly. "Her story sounded preposterous, you must admit."

He did admit it when I finished. Nevertheless he was convinced that Ella had actually observed Hogan Brewster stealing away from an interview with Professor Matthews, while the deputy slept at his post.

"The professor had divined the murderer's identity and meant to capitalize upon his information," theorized Chet Keith. "Brewster was a wealthy man. I don't suppose he minded paying the dole, not, at least, until he realized that the old quack hadn't the stuff to keep a secret."

"Sheila heard him praying for guidance this afternoon," I said unsteadily.

"He was undoubtedly on the verge of confession, so Hogan Brewster killed him, after first stealing into your room and destroying the alley cat."

I shivered. "While I slept! Heavens, I don't know how I'll ever be able to close my eyes in the dark again."

"An old battle-ax like you!" he protested with a sly grin. "I don't believe it. No woman who makes it her business to goad people into telling their blackest secrets is afraid of the dark or even of the hereafter." His voice softened and he turned very red. "Of course you know how grateful Sheila and I are, Miss Adelaide."

"To me?" I stammered, highly embarrassed. "I'm sure I don't know why, except that my heart was on the right side from the first."

He grinned at me affectionately. "Be yourself," he exclaimed and all but chucked me under the chin. "You're the swellest backer-upper I ever saw! Especially of lost causes!"

He glanced down at the girl, sleeping against his shoulder, and his expression sobered. "God knows I can't face what would have happened without you," he said in a husky voice.

"Most of the time I was staggering around in an impenetrable fog," I felt constrained to confess.

"Weren't we all?" he demanded ruefully. "But you at least staggered to some purpose."

At that moment Ella, whom I had believed fast asleep, raised her head and regarded me with a jaundiced expression. "Are you going to spend the rest of the night exchanging compliments with that young man, Adelaide?" she inquired in withering accents. "If so, please do not expect me to commiserate with you if your bronchitis prevents you from speaking above a whisper in the morning."

"I have never asked you or anybody else to commiserate with me, Ella Trotter," I said with cold dignity. "I am quite capable of coping with my own difficulties."

"Oh yeah?" drawled Ella in an insulting voice and, leaning over, she stared pointedly at the remains of Fannie Parrish's umbrella which she had laid on the floor at her feet for the express purpose, I feel sure, of annoying me.

"Just because you once stumbled inadvertently into the role of my rescuer, it does not follow that I have permanently surrendered all my rights to independent action," I said bitterly.

"That's what *you* think," murmured Ella with infuriating sweetness.

Fortunately for her state of mind, Ella could not in her wildest imaginings foresee that excruciating moment some months later when, in an attempt to trap the devil in what Olive Lambert called her split personality, I found myself helplessly bespraddling the steeple of a clubfooted financier's summer pagoda, while a fiend incarnate stood on his head in that hideous and stunted tree, in which we found the bloodsucking leeches, and shot the fringe of false curls off my forehead with a weapon commonly employed, believe it or not, in a rendition of the Suzy-Q.

Coachwhip Publications

CoachwhipBooks.com

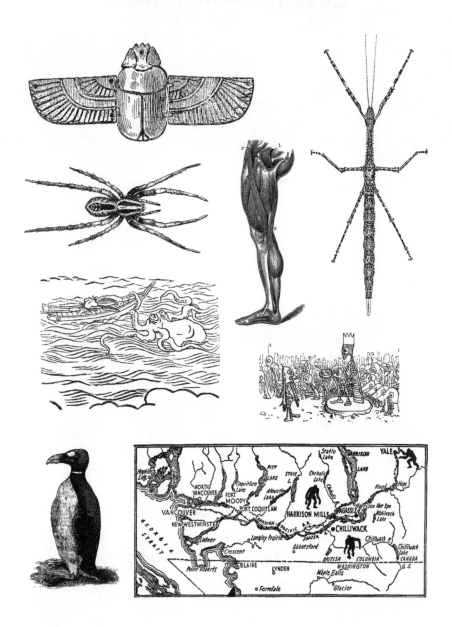

COACHWHIP PUBLICATIONS

COACHWHIPBOOKS.COM

ISBN 978-1-61646-222-2

COACHWHIP PUBLICATIONS

NOW AVAILABLE

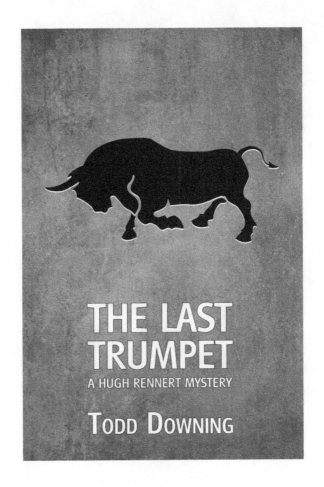

THE LAST
TRUMPET
A HUGH RENNERT MYSTERY

TODD DOWNING

ISBN 978-1-61646-152-2

COACHWHIP PUBLICATIONS

COACHWHIPBOOKS.COM

MURDER
IN BERMUDA

WILLOUGHBY SHARP

ISBN 978-1-61646-198-0

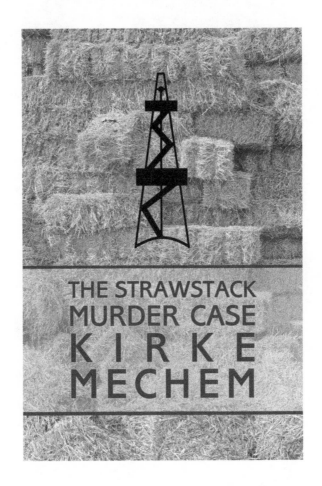

THE STRAWSTACK
MURDER CASE
KIRKE
MECHEM

ISBN 978-1-61646-179-9